A man like Wolf feels nothing. He is moved only by vengeance. The destruction he brings to the world is payment for the injustice he has suffered. He believes that only he has endured pain. To be in his mind is to be in a primal black hole of sensory disregard.

We matter to him only as objects, pieces of his community in need of rearrangement. Murder is his way of imposing order on his world. When you are the reaper, you do not fear the reaper. . . .

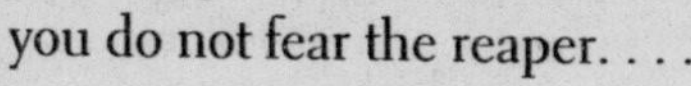

The Prettiest Feathers

John Philpin and

Patricia Sierra

BANTAM BOOKS

New York Toronto London

Sydney Auckland

THE PRETTIEST FEATHERS
A Bantam Book/May 1997

Grateful acknowledgment to reprint "Song in the Blood," copyright © 1958 by Lawrence Ferlinghetti. Reprinted by permission of City Lights Books.

ISBN 0-553-57555-4

Published simultaneously in the United States and Canada

Bantam Books are published by Bantam Books, a division of Bantam Doubleday Dell Publishing Group, Inc. Its trademark, consisting of the words "Bantam Books" and the portrayal of a rooster, is Registered in U.S. Patent and Trademark Office and in other countries. Marca Registrada. Bantam Books, 1540 Broadway, New York, New York 10036.

PRINTED IN THE UNITED STATES OF AMERICA

OPM 10 9 8 7 6 5 4 3 2 1

For Philip E. Ginsburg

The wolf howled under the leaves
And spit out the prettiest feathers
Of his meal of fowl;
Like him I consume myself.

from "The Wolf Howled"
Arthur Rimbaud

BOOK ONE

John

◆

I'm not going to tell you about any of the others—the aerobics instructor, the lawyer, the teacher, the actress, the housewife, the bartender, the grocery clerk. Not in detail. The list is too long, and it would be a waste of time.

I want to talk about her, and only her, because she is the exception. If I reveal anything about the others, it will be only to illuminate the ways in which *she* was different.

Sarah

◆

It was an unbearably hot, brilliantly sunny day in the midst of my eleventh summer. We were at the beach, my uncle Donald and I, walking barefoot through the sand.

We had been talking about nothing, everything, when—for a reason that I can no longer recall—I realized that I had no shadow. This alarmed me. I stopped and stared at the stretch of beach ahead of me and to both sides, but all I saw was the sand, without my silhouette on its surface. I turned slowly, rotating, but nowhere did I see any hint that I was there.

"I must be dead," I told my uncle. "I don't exist."

He laughed and said, "Your shadow is beneath your feet, where you can't see it. That's what happens at noon, when the sun is directly overhead. When the time is right, you will know that you are alive."

Within minutes my shadow returned, moving just ahead of me as we walked down the beach. But I felt no different than I had when it was gone; I still felt dead.

When the time is right, you will know that you are alive, he promised. And I waited for years for that time to come.

Then I saw him, the stranger, and I felt a release, an unfolding, like a flower opening in the sun. He gave me both sustenance and substance; he gave me life.

John

◆

My art is the art of murder. My instruments, people (women, primarily). And my tools are finely crafted from leather, hemp, or steel. Perhaps, without realizing it, you have seen my work. It has been displayed, unsigned, throughout the metropolitan area to the south of here.

I am an avid reader, with a taste for T. S. Eliot, e. e. cummings, Wallace Stevens, Arthur Rimbaud. But I am not a poet; merely one who appreciates the way words can be woven into pictures. I, too, can create pictures—but in my mind, not on paper. These pictures are elaborate—entire scenes, really, complete with the stage directions, dialogue, soundtrack, and choreography of my art.

One of my favorite books was written by Farley Mowat. To satisfy his curiosity about wolves, he went to live among them—eating and sleeping as they did, crawling around on all fours. By entering their world, making their behavior his, he learned more than all the science-minded fools who'd spent years watching wolves through the bars and glass walls of cages.

We have no Farley Mowats for the human predator. No one has ever come to talk with me, ask me questions, discuss poetry, listen to music, spend the night, or accompany me on my excursions.

What we have, instead, are the ladies and gentlemen of the FBI—the behavioral science experts from Quantico, Virginia—who visit only those who are already caged, administering questionnaires. The specimens they study are bored, with an agenda all their own. They aren't about to tell the "experts" *all* the truth; just enough to toy with them.

No questionnaire, ever, could capture the soul of a man like me. I am not one of those who is careless enough to be caught and caged. No word has appeared in any newspaper suggesting that my missions may be connected. Investigators in the various cities where my work has been displayed have no idea that one of America's most prolific killers has been operating in their midst for several years.

Theodore Bundy always selected his victims at random, killing them soon after—almost never developing any sort of relationship with them. How artless. Virtually anyone could succeed—at least for a while, perhaps even a long while—doing it that way. But where is the challenge, the risk, the sense of fulfillment?

Bundy bores me. He had no sense of variety, no finesse.

Hasty Hills, the town where I live, is called a bedroom community—an expensive boudoir that's every bit as pretentious as its haughty neighbor, Greenwich, Connecticut. I've lived here for five years. People leave me pretty much alone. No one comes to collect for anything charitable. No Girl Scouts selling cookies or Little Leaguers hoping to improve their wardrobes. I can recall only one unsolicited guest—an attractive young woman who came to my door some years ago, asking to use my phone. She was having car trouble, she said. To help pass the time until the tow truck arrived, I offered her a glass of wine and pleasant conversation. When the truck pulled up at the curb an hour later, I allowed her to thank me and leave. I would never foul my own nest.

I own a new car, a reliable Japanese model that I drive into the city whenever I require amusement—such as a new film, the latest album from Julian Cope, something decent to read.

It was on just such a sojourn that I discovered her. It was as if she were waiting for me.

The bookstore was a quaint and musty little place on the Lower East Side. The sign in black and gold said, Emily and Others. Brontë? Dickinson? Very clever.

It was surrounded by a Korean grocer on one side, a soul food take-out on the other, and a massage parlor above. When I parked my car—legally—and stepped out onto the sidewalk, a thin, young black man pushed himself away from the wall of the grocery store and sauntered in my direction.

"Dude can't park here," he said.

His hands were shoved deeply into the pockets of pants that threatened to drop to the pavement. He chewed the remains of a toothpick and worked on a baleful glare that just missed me—glancing off my left shoulder and bouncing out into the street somewhere. It was wasted. So was he.

I slipped my right hand into my pocket and allowed it to close over my car key. I inclined my head so that I could watch what his hands were doing and, with my left hand, slowly removed my sunglasses. I found his eyes, smiled, and asked, "Do you want to die here?"

"Say what?" the man said.

He was still moving like a loose-jointed puppet toward me.

The car key was for his left eye. The glasses, ready to shatter into both eyes, were for the bridge of his nose. If he remained standing, the palm of my right hand would drive that portion of his anatomy into his brain and drop him instantly. I continued to smile.

He stopped. Somehow a message had made it through his crack-clouded senses. His eyes were locked on mine.

"The building needs you to hold it up," I said.

He shrugged, turned, and shuffled back to the wall.

A brass bell chimed once as I entered Emily and Others. It was dimly lit, dusty, damp. Before I saw her, I knew she was there. I smelled her. It was the delicate scent of a soap only a woman would use. I knew she would be clean and out of place.

Perfume doesn't arouse me. It is cloying, fouls the air, makes it difficult to breathe. A lanolin soap seems to bring out the scent of the woman herself, the essence of her. Perhaps it was the distance between us, or the dank atmosphere of the subterranean shop, but at first there was no essence; only the smell of the soap.

Then, faintly at first, I could smell leather, the bindings of old books. The shelf to my left held Melville, Poe, Whitman, Emerson, Thoreau. Early American literature in nonalphabetical order. Shakespeare was to my right, and above him, Oscar Wilde, Thomas Hardy, Chaucer, Keats, Wordsworth.

I heard her move behind the stacks into the shadows farther off to my right.

"There are no Emilys," I said.

"There are the others," she said.

There was no laughter, not a hint of humor. I expected at least a chuckle, and I'm seldom wrong about these things.

"There are no women," I said.

"Were you looking for a woman?"

"The sign," I began, then gave it up. "No. Actually I'm looking for Henry Miller."

"I understand he had a lot of women," she said. "Including Anaïs Nin. Is she the one you want?"

It *was* humor. Dry and flat and cerebral and funny.

She moved into view in front of me, but was shrouded in the dust and the dim yellow light that filtered through the shade on the plate glass window. She was slender, of medium height, fit in an athletic sort of way—and wore a black skirt that touched her knees, a white blouse with all the buttons buttoned, and a pageboy hairdo. Late twenties, I guessed. What I could see of her face looked plain, almost austere.

"Only if she's featured in *The Time of the Assassins,*" I said.

"She's not. That's his book about Rimbaud. We have a copy. It's over here with the other New Directions paperbacks. Patchen and Ezra Pound and all of those."

She walked to my left toward the back of the store. I followed her.

"I read *Crazy Cock,*" she said. "One of those old manuscripts they just found and published. It wasn't very good. I think Miller was anti-Semitic."

As I approached, the smell of her soap was more noticeable. I had no trouble hearing the flat, toneless voice almost devoid of inflection. But even when I stood two feet away from her, bathed in the same dust and sickly light that shrouded this woman, I still had trouble actually seeing her. It wasn't that she was nondescript. It was as if she weren't totally there—elusive somehow, becoming even more vague the closer I was to her.

"My name is Sarah . . . Sarah Sinclair," she said, as she handed me the book. "It's a bit battered. The book, not the name."

Most of the time when I have been that close to a woman, I've slipped something around her neck or between her ribs. It was an odd sensation when, finally, I saw Sarah Sinclair's eyes. She had no secrets from me. I was surprised by what I read there, but even more shocked by my own feelings. I knew that I would kill her, of course—not right then, but soon—yet there was something else. I wondered if she knew what her eyes were telling me—that she had begun searching the shadows for death a long time ago. I experienced a surge of risk like no other. I was light-headed, slightly dizzy.

"This book is fine," I told her. "I'm grateful to find it. I've looked everywhere."

"You must have, to come down here."

She turned and walked toward the cash register, asking me my name as she moved.

I still couldn't see her clearly. I knew that once I left the shop and tried to picture her in my mind, I would fail.

"John," I lied. "John Wolf."

She turned and, for the first time, smiled. "No wonder you were looking for the women."

The brass bell behind me rang. It was the black slouch from the sidewalk with a friend who looked like Mike Tyson with indigestion. This is one of the reasons I hate the city now. Thugs with nothing to do but make life miserable for everyone else. I decided to handle him with a little less subtlety this time. I pulled the .38 special from its holster against my spine.

I never come into the city without my weapon, which I am licensed to carry.

I flashed a laminated card with a gold seal that looked vaguely official, though it indicated only that I was a lifetime member of the Total Fitness Health Club.

"I'm a cop," I said. "Where do you want to sleep tonight?"

The big guy started to raise his arms over his head, but the slouch reached up, rapped him on the chest, and gestured with his head toward the door. The bell rang again as they left.

I turned to explain, and to make my apologies to Sarah for the scene, half expecting her to have retreated again into her shadows. She hadn't moved. Before I could speak, she said, "You're not a cop."

Because the gun hadn't bothered her, I knew she'd been around cops. Maybe her father was a career cop with the city.

"No," I said. "It seemed necessary."

She shrugged.

I walked to the counter and paid for the book. Close to her again, I experienced the same feeling as earlier—the sense that I couldn't take her all in, grasp her, understand the quirks of her personality (something that I've been able to do, effortlessly, with any other woman). For the first time in many years, perhaps ever, I felt a degree of discomfort.

"I keep the Emilys and others back here," she said. "If you're ever interested."

I thanked her and left the store.

On the drive back I realized that I had been right. I could conjure up no image of Sarah.

Once, I selected a victim, decided on a plan, and carried it out in less than two hours. The longest I've ever been about it was nine days. This time I had no plan. All I knew for sure was that this victim, this woman, this Sarah, would require something different, something more. A slow dance toward death.

Sarah

Early on in my therapy, Dr. Street asked me what I would be if I could be anything, anything in the world.

"A virgin," I said.

I think I do pretty well with people, but only until things get physical. When I told Dr. Street that, he asked if I thought that was what went wrong between Robert and me. He's always bringing up my divorce. But to me, it's just something that I have, like my diploma or my vaccination scar. It's there, and in some ways it may be meaningful, but I hardly ever think about it.

I had never worried that my husband would leave me. To my mind, we were married, and that was that. Then one night he told me that he loved another woman: a rookie cop named Lane. She was tall, with auburn hair, and not exactly pretty. But there was something exotic about her—the shape of her eyes (almond) and the color of her skin (olive). I had seen her when I stopped by the police station the night before he told me about her. She smiled at me, and I believe I smiled back.

Robert insisted that he hadn't set out to be unfaithful; it just happened.

"It was the proximity. The body heat works on you, wears you down," he said, as if that made it all right. And as if I wouldn't know about such things.

I sometimes went to the beauty shop just to be touched—to feel someone else's fingers massaging my scalp, lifting my hair. I required so little, but he gave even less.

Robert didn't leave after he told me about Lane. Not right away. He went on like before, as if the words had never been spoken. As the days rolled into weeks, I waited and watched, wondering when he intended to finish ripping my heart from me. Eventually I realized that the act itself couldn't possibly be as agonizing as the wait, so I forced the issue. I sent a note to his girlfriend, telling her that I would appreciate it if she would stop by the following Saturday to pack his belongings and move them to her place. Without a word, Robert moved out late Friday night. When I heard the door close behind him, cells throughout my body seemed to shut down, suffocate, die.

Before Dr. Street, there had been many others: white-coated professionals intent on telling me how well I was doing—but, with each reassurance, I felt more deeply troubled. I wondered why they didn't *see*, why they didn't *know* how sick I was.

One Monday morning when I was still married, I awakened feeling thoroughly committed to my hopelessness. I felt that I had to live up to it, prove it true. By ten o'clock I was still in bed. I was supposed to be at work at nine, but couldn't decide what to wear. I was certain that whatever I chose, it would be permanent; I would wear it to my grave.

I hated my work. Hated Mondays. And I hated walking to the bus stop, getting aboard with all those strangers, standing body to body with them all the way to the building where I worked, getting off, going in, pressing for the elevator, riding to the eleventh floor, getting off, turning left, entering my office, hanging up my coat, and sitting down to do nothing of consequence, absolutely nothing, until it was time for lunch.

That's why I telephoned the personnel department. I identified myself as my sister and announced that Sarah had died, suddenly, during the night. I was surprised that the woman at the other end of the line was so shaken by this news. She mentioned that she had spoken with Sarah only a few days earlier, on Friday, in the elevator. That was untrue, and I wondered why she had said it. Then I thought that perhaps it *was* true, and I just hadn't noticed her or heard her. I was doing a lot of that in those days—tuning out.

A week later Robert opened an envelope that arrived in the mail. It held my final check (payable to me, a dead woman, making the situation even more surreal), plus a letter from the woman in Personnel. She expressed her sympathy, and repeated the story of how she had talked to Sarah only a few days before the terrible event.

Robert must have been wondering why I wasn't going to the office anymore, but he had been careful not to mention it. After the final check arrived, he was unable to discuss the matter for several days. When, at last, he did mention it, he was unable to admit just how crazy he thought my behavior was.

All he said was, "Why." But because he had said it more like a statement than a question, I didn't even try to answer. Except to myself.

Tonight I felt the opposite of crazy. Almost sane.

I settled back in the leather chair opposite Dr. Street's desk.

"I met someone," I told him.

"Oh?"

"His name is John Wolf. You should hear how he says it—drawing out the 'ooul' sound, down deep in his throat."

I was talking too fast, and with too much animation. I didn't want Dr. Street to think that I was manic again. I made a conscious effort to breathe deeply, to slow down, to sound less excited. I didn't want him to start writing a prescription for lithium.

"He came into the shop today," I said. "Looking for women."

"Hmmm?"

I giggled. "Female authors."

"Oh."

"But what he really wanted was Henry Miller. I just finished reading *Crazy Cock* last night. Isn't that amazing?"

Dr. Street lifted one eyebrow, slightly, but didn't say anything.

"I mean it," I said, leaning toward him. "There was something predestined going on today . . . something magical."

No response.

I hate it when he does that, and decided that two can play his game. I made up my mind to just sit there in silence until he said something.

But he said nothing.

Because I detest sitting in silence with Dr. Street, I was the first to give in. I started talking, rambling, making things up, hoping that something in what I was saying would please him, win his approval. But I withheld what I really wanted to discuss—because I couldn't stand the thought of Dr. Street ruining it with his questions.

I knew what he would say if I were to describe for him how I had felt when I first looked into John Wolf's eyes. It was as if I had found myself there, my destiny, but Dr. Street would have made it sound like a symptom, something to be cured. John Wolf brought out an unfamiliar side of me. I had an almost irresistible urge to touch him. And I felt so female, so thoroughly female. It was wonderful. It was terrible.

But the gun: what was he doing with a gun? I know he's not a cop. He's nothing like Robert. Cops walk with an air of arrogance, moving their shoulders oddly, as if they're made of wood. And they like to narrow their eyes when they look at you, pretending they're thinking deep thoughts when all they're really doing is sizing you up. But John Wolf moved toward me with a friendliness and a warmth that cops don't understand. I could see the acceptance in his eyes.

And then there were his hands. No cop, ever, has had hands like John Wolf's. They belong to an artist or a musician. I imagined them reaching for me; I could almost feel the heat of them on my skin. I remembered what Robert had said about Lane—how he had explained their affair: "The body heat works on you, wears you down."

These were the thoughts spinning through my mind as I left Dr. Street's office, as I walked toward my car, as I became aware of the footsteps behind me.

Pulling away from the curb, I glanced in my rearview mirror. A man in a dark-colored car, something small and foreign-looking, was following me. I turned down a side street, but so did he. My world tilted. I forgot to breathe. At the next corner, I turned left; he turned left. I speeded up; he speeded up. I circled through narrow residential streets, back to the highway. I saw a patrol car facing toward me, stopped at a red light just ahead.

The man in the foreign car moved into passing gear, slipping past me as I pulled up opposite the patrol car. I honked, rolled down my window. The officer was young, grinning at me as if he thought that I had stopped to tell him a joke.

"A man has been following me," I told him, surprised that I sounded so excited, so breathless.

"I don't blame him, lady," he said. He was smirking. The other policeman, on the passenger's side, laughed.

I sped away.

I thought about John Wolf—how efficiently he had handled the men in the bookstore. I wished that he and his gun were beside me. I wanted him there when I walked to my door. I wanted him to see me safely inside, to check each room, each closet. He isn't like other men. He makes me feel safe. Protected.

But I also sense a great risk in getting to know him. He is too attractive for comfort—a bit taller than I, and nearly as thin, but sinewy, especially through the chest and upper arms. The stitching on his tailored leather jacket was taut, suggesting that he was smaller when he bought it. I wondered if he was bulking up, lifting weights. A new convert to physical fitness.

His eyes intrigued me. At first, they were a gentle blue, but as we talked, I watched them turn gray. He wore wire-rim spectacles, which he put on after placing his sunglasses in his pocket. But the lenses looked plain, nonprescription. It crossed my mind that his glasses weren't necessary; perhaps they were a prop, a fashion accessory. Or a disguise.

His hair is thinning, although he seems to be too young for that. Forty at the very most. But the hair that remains—and there is still an ample amount—looks as soft as a whisper. His skin has a soft look, too. I don't mean that he's effeminate; not at all. It's just that there's a feeling of velvet about him. And fluidity. He seems to be without bones, beyond bones, moving with a grace that we with knees and knuckles could never duplicate.

And there was one more thing I noticed about him: he was spotless. Freshly shaved. Well manicured. Even his shoes shone with fresh polish. I found that seductive, yet off-putting, as if he weren't made for touching. But that was only a guess. I wanted to find out for sure.

John

◆

When I was a child, my mother always promised that she would tell "him," my stepfather, to leave. "Once he's gone, our lives will improve, son," she said. But he never left. He sat in front of the TV sucking down quarts of Schlitz and watching baseball when he wasn't hammering on me. But, because my sister was their kid, she could do no wrong, received no hammering.

We lived in a rural state, in a house that he had built from somebody else's sheets of leftover plywood, odd lengths of two-by-fours, and slabs of wallboard in different thicknesses. The yard was filled with lath and chunks of plaster destined for the dump. I chose some of this, a few bits of that, but never took much of any one thing because I didn't want to attract attention to myself.

After school each day, before anyone else was home, I pushed my treasures down inside the front of my jacket, careful of the nails. I walked back through the woods, crossed the brook, and hiked up the small slope on the property to the quarter-acre clearing that in another era had been an orchard.

I started my work under the first of the remaining three apple trees because it offered the greatest concealment and the ground was easy to work. I pulled out the few clumps of grass by hand, leveled the dirt, pried the rocks loose with my fingertips and, where I could, used these natural cavities to begin excavation on cellar holes for the hardware store, the post office, a general store, a garage, old New England capes and rambling Victorians, the train station, a municipal building with the police station underneath, and, at the edge of town, in a prime location, my school.

I began this work in the early spring, just after the snow was finally gone and the brook was no longer swollen with runoff. The days were longer and warmer, and I would work until my mother called me down for supper. Often, if the man I was supposed to call Father had drunk enough beer and fallen asleep in his chair before the light was gone, I would return up the hill. Most nights, though, I sat at the kitchen table and worked on math, or a paper for English class, or read a chapter in my science book.

I did the schoolwork, and I did it well, although not so well that it would attract too much attention. But while one part of my mind was calculating percentage problems for a coat marked down during a sale, another part was like a spirit that could drift up and out of my body, up through the woods, to hover in the evening air above my town. My mother called it daydreaming, and she could tell when I was doing it, but I was doing the math problems, too, and my grades were okay, so she left me alone.

I don't know when I first sensed that I could remove myself like that, but I had been doing it for a long time—since long before I began building my town. My first real memory of it is somehow connected to my pregnant mother's disappearing for three days. I lived at an uncle's house until they brought the baby girl home from the hospital.

When I returned home, I was allowed into the bedroom to say hello to my mother, who was half dead from exhaustion—and to glance down, briefly, at the shriveled pink piglet asleep at her side. I was told to call it "sister."

They called her Sarah.

One day in May of that year, I failed to hear my mother's call for supper. The work on the lower end of Main Street had been complicated by the need for a bridge. My first attempt—using twigs that had dropped from the apple tree—was a failure, so I was working with lath, supporting the span with sections of old metal wire casing. She walked up the hill behind me.

Somehow I knew that she was standing there, but it was more than just the sense of another's presence. I knew that it was my mother.

I didn't acknowledge her. I didn't allow my awareness of her to distract me until I was certain that my efforts on the bridge would be successful. Then, slowly, I turned my head and looked up at her.

She was smiling. I told her about the town, about my problems with the bridge, and about my plans for expansion. She continued smiling, nodding her head, glancing occasionally back toward the house. Then she said that I should wash up; my stepfather would be home soon. It was difficult to know if she was impressed by my handiwork. I thought perhaps she was, but then she was being pulled back toward the house, too. I wondered if she would say anything to him.

At the supper table I paid more than the usual attention to the tones of voices, facial expressions, gestures. Everything was ordinary—the same as always. My mother served. My sister played with her food. My stepfather ate.

Mother said a few things about what went on in the factory that day. He pushed his plate back, went to the refrigerator for a quart, then walked into the parlor and turned on the TV. I watched my mother, examined her face, and knew that she had said nothing to him about my town. It was a secret, the first I had ever shared with anyone, and it appeared to be safe.

My sister reached across the table, teasing, tapping on my fingers. When she was only a few months old, still in a cradle, I reached down one day and clasped her hand where it emerged from the receiving blanket. I felt as if I were off in another part of the room, watching myself do this—watching myself squeeze her fingers, wishing for her bones to break. Now, years later, as we sat at the dinner table, it was as if she knew, as if she remembered what I had done and was threatening to tell. I knew that wasn't possible, that she would have no memory for what had happened so early in her life, but then she would look up at me with a sort of smile at her mouth, and squeeze my hand.

In the beginning with the man I was supposed to call Father, and later with my sister, I believed that my mother could have stopped everything from happening. I knew there was no need for us to have him in the house, but she had done nothing to change that. At times she even seemed to prefer his company to mine.

She had said so little about the changes ahead of time—just that we would be moving in with him, and that I should call him Father. Then she had expected me to be happy that I had a little sister.

She tried to tell me what my feelings were. She was putting them together with her own feelings—confusing them, blending them. "You'll like having a man in your life," and "You'll love being a big brother."

These were not my feelings, but I kept silent, didn't complain. And in time, I was no longer certain what my feelings were, or if I had any at all. The one thing I knew for sure was that my mother could have prevented all the bad that had come into my life, but she had chosen not to.

I found the folding knife on the last day of school as I walked along the side of the road toward the bus stop. It was lying near a torn bag and some broken bottles, the roadside debris from somebody's drunk the night before. The morning sun reflected up from the fragments of green and clear glass, a sharpness of light almost cutting into my eyes, attracting my attention, begging that I see the flat brown handle resting in its bed of glitter. I picked it up and put it in my pocket, afraid to look at it, my heart racing. I kept it in my pocket all of that day through school, knowing that there was something magical about finding the knife, and realizing that if anyone knew I had it, it would be taken away from me.

It was only when I was up at my town that afternoon that I took the knife out of my pocket, ran my finger along the wooden handle, examined both sides and each end of it, then carefully, lovingly, exposed the single, four-inch blade.

The knife would be useful in my work on the town, in making things fit together the way they were supposed to, or carving out a door here, a window there. It would allow me to make things go more smoothly. And, for the first time, it provided me with a sense of power, of control—a feeling that there was nothing I couldn't do.

On the second of my mother's visits to the town, she said that she admired my work, that she thought it might be a nice place to live. "But," she wanted to know, "where are the people?"

I got up from my knees and stood gazing down at my world. "People would just mess things up," I said. "There wouldn't be any . . . order."

Eventually I placed a few cars and trucks on the main street of the town, evidence that it was inhabited, but I would do no more as far as people were concerned.

On Sundays I lost half the day because of the family's attendance at church. In the early morning I was sent to Bible class, where an intense young man read passages and talked about the paradise that would be there for all of us who accepted Jesus as our personal savior. After class I would join the family upstairs for the services.

There wasn't any one minister. The men took turns standing up at the front and talking about the right way to live a spiritual life in a world that was afflicted with sin. After one talk about sin being in every home because it was coming through the TV set, my stepfather unplugged ours and put it in the attic. But when it was in the newspaper that the intense young reader of Bible passages was going to jail for committing lewd and lascivious acts on his young charges, my stepfather disconnected the family from the church and brought the TV back down to its old place in the parlor.

I wanted to know what those two words—*lewd* and *lascivious*—meant. On the day of my mother's third visit to my town, I wanted to ask her about them. There was mystery and power attached to them, and I knew that she could explain—but there were so many things she hadn't explained, ever. And there were all those times she changed things around so that they seemed to mean something different from what they really meant.

She was distracted that day—preoccupied—so I didn't ask her about the words. Her mind seemed to be filled up with something. She didn't say much—just sat on a stump and gazed off at the mountains in the distance.

"What kind of bird is that?" she asked.

I listened to the bird's deep, throaty, owl-like phrases coming from the brush. She knew I would have an answer for her. I roamed the woods, climbed into the foothills, absorbed every sound and smell and track of an animal—then read voraciously until I knew all the vibrations of the world in the wild.

"Mourning dove," I said.

"It doesn't sound sad, exactly. Just thoughtful."

My town was in danger of becoming a city. The buildings were crowding in upon one another, growing taller, creating an architectural congestion that I wouldn't wish on rats. I knew I would have to tear some of it down, destroy it, and I feared that once I started, I wouldn't be able to stop.

A long time passed before I spoke again to my mother, and, by the time I did, she had started back down the hill through the creeping fog of late afternoon. "Some people hunt them," I said to her back.

For as long as I could see her, I watched her go. She was dressed in light colors, and the mist was gray, almost white. She drifted like a ghost, down and out of sight.

I followed her. I don't know why. Moving at an angle across the side of the hill and through a stand of birch trees, I got to the edge of the yard just as she disappeared through the back doorway. I stood in the dampening silence and waited. I don't know what for.

Her bedroom light went on. I stepped to the back of the house and stared through her window.

We are all voyeurs. Given the chance to look, we look—and, sometimes, the images we capture are held for a lifetime.

My mother stood with her back to the window and stepped out of the pale yellow dress she had worn to work that day. She turned her head from side to side, as if she were stretching the muscles in her neck. Then she moved her hands over the front of her body, caressing herself.

I was fascinated, mesmerized, and grabbed at the hardening between my legs. Even as she started to turn in my direction, I was unable to move.

Our eyes locked and her scream shattered the quiet of the late afternoon. I had to stop her. *He* would be home at any minute. I had to shut her up.

I ran into the house and down the hallway to her room. The door was locked. I pounded on it, but the door never opened.

My sister had come out into the hall and I pushed past her, rushing outdoors, into the deepening fog, and up the hill.

I was frenzied—kicking over buildings and smashing bridges with a length of limb wood. The only real sound was the apocalypse I brought down on my town, but still I could hear my mother's screams echoing inside my head.

At supper that evening I sensed the change, the absence

of the empty chatter about the day. It was the game of Nobody Talks. Even my little sister played the game well, looking down at her plate as she pushed peas into her mashed potatoes. My mother served. My stepfather ate, shoved himself away from the table—and, on his way to the living room with his quart, he stopped, turned to look at me, then motioned for me to follow.

I stood, stuck my hand down into my pocket, and wrapped it around the knife. I didn't know what would happen when I walked into the parlor behind him, but I wasn't afraid. I left my body. Drifting. Watching from above. I saw myself looking down at the threadbare carpet, my hands behind my back, like someone who was waiting.

But I could also see that my hands were moving the blade of the knife—unfolding it and locking it open.

Mother grabbed me from behind, of course, before I could bring the blade down into the flesh of his neck. But I had drawn the blood that trickled down the wall, the blood that seeped into the fabric of his overstuffed chair, the blood that pooled on the pine floor. There was another beating. He called the police. And I had my first encounter with the mental health industry.

A large woman wearing thick glasses said, "Your parents told me what happened. I'd like to hear your side of things."

I think the chair was made of real leather, and there was a hump in the middle of the seat. Each time I hoisted myself up, I slid forward again. I had to grip the arms to hold myself in place.

"This isn't comfortable," I said.

"Some things are hard to talk about," she said, nodding.

"The chair," I muttered.

"What were you going to do with that knife?" she asked.

"Kill him," I said.

"But why?"

"I couldn't very well kill *her*."

They all agreed that I should be put away somewhere.

The state had places for people like me. I was no good. I would hurt somebody someday.

They were right.

I left the subway at Houston and walked to Emily and Others. I wanted to approach the place on foot, get a feel for the neighborhood, and to avoid the unofficial parking attendant I had encountered on my first visit.

Emily and Others is in a demilitarized zone that's surrounded by Puerto Ricans, blacks, elderly Jews, and poor, white Irish. I walked the length of the street resisting the urge to cover my nose and mouth with a handkerchief against the stench of waste, and all the dust that hadn't yet settled from last night's wars.

I made the brass bell ring, then walked to the New Directions shelf and found a copy of Rimbaud's *Drunken Boat*, the Varèse translation.

"Emily isn't here," Sarah said from behind me. "She's at lunch with the others."

Today she wore a navy skirt with a white blouse that was open at her throat. There was color in her face and definite humor in her voice.

"That brings us directly to why I'm here," I said.

"Which? Emily, lunch, or the others?"

"You," I said, and smiled my most engaging smile.

"I think we better start over."

"Wouldn't you rather have lunch? We could start over with a Caesar salad and some iced tea."

"I can't," she said, looking genuinely disappointed. "There's a girl who usually covers for me, but she isn't here today. Harry, the owner, doesn't like the place to be closed."

"What about after work? We could go for coffee."

She hesitated.

"My name may be Wolf," I said, "but I'm not one."

Sarah smiled. "There's a little place down the block. I get off at five."

"Five is fine," I said. "But I'd like to choose the place, if you don't mind. I'm very particular about my coffee."

Again she hesitated, then finally shrugged. "I always thought coffee was coffee, but sure."

I bought the Rimbaud and left.

Five hours later Sarah was waiting for me outside the bookstore when I pulled to the curb. The ebony guardian of the bricks was in place, hiding behind hooded eyes. I detest complications, and that particular piece of human debris had made himself one.

"Where are we going?" Sarah asked as she got into my car.

"Uptown," I said. "There's a place I like called Fast Eddie's."

"Never heard of it."

Fast Eddie's may not be well known, but Eddie takes pride in his coffee and dessert menu. The name is derived from Eddie's having seen *The Hustler* too many times.

After settling down at the table Eddie had saved for us in a quiet corner, I recommended that Sarah try my favorite blend—half Colombian supreme, half French roast—with a piece of Eddie's cheesecake.

"But I haven't had dinner," she said.

"Who ever said we have to eat our food in a certain order?" I asked. "Rules are made to be broken."

She laughed. I looked at her hairline, forehead, eyebrows, the bridge of her nose, her eyes, her mouth—so that her face would become a picture in my mind, one I could conjure up at any time. And, of course, there was the uncorrupted scent of her soap. Finally, I had her to hold for as long as I wished.

"Who are you really?" she asked.

"I grew up on the coast of Maine, preacher's kid. Went to college in the Boston area, made a few decent business deals in the seventies, a few better ones in the gluttonous eighties, and now I can afford to indulge my passion for literature, music, and excellent coffee. What about you?"

Sarah frowned. "I wouldn't know where to start. I went to college for a while, but it was kind of a waste."

She was struggling. I didn't want that, but it did give me an opportunity to accomplish one of the purposes of the trip. I reached out and covered her hand with mine.

"We can share biographies another time," I said. "Try the coffee."

I didn't let the moment drag on, become awkward. It's always enough for me to touch a woman's hand for just an instant. I learn what I need to know, and move on.

"This is good," she said.

"Coffee isn't just coffee."

"No. I mean, I know."

How pathetically pliant she was, instantly becoming whatever she thought I wished her to be.

We talked about the bookstore, the man named Harry who owned it, the types of customers it served, the fact that she loved to read but never did at work. It was enough for a beginning.

When I drove her home I accomplished the second goal of my mission: to find out where she lives. Sarah rents the upstairs apartment in a brick duplex opposite a small park on the west side of the city.

In *The Hustler*, Piper Laurie is the foil for all the male posturing. She lives in a walk-up flat, reads serious books, but can't stay sober. She walks with a limp.

Sarah reminds me of Piper Laurie. She doesn't walk with a limp, she thinks with one. When I dropped her off, I told her that I would see her again. She thanked me, nodded, and smiled—but looked preoccupied. I half expected her to limp up the front steps.

Sarah

Everything fell into place. My car was in the shop for an oil change. I'd taken the train to work, so when John Wolf said he'd pick me up, it was perfect. I ran upstairs to the massage parlor and borrowed a blazer from Sheila, the woman who worked up there. She was reluctant to part with it—she'd just gotten it back from the cleaners—but when I explained about my date, she understood right away.

I took John's invitation as an omen. A sign. The notion of predestination appeals to me. But my feelings for him seemed to shift by the moment. I ricocheted from fear to fearsome attraction, and back again. That's why, when we left Fast Eddie's, I directed him away from the street where I lived, to one nearby. I pointed to a house that had been converted into a duplex, with a wooden stairway built onto its side—leading to an upstairs door that must have once opened onto a sun porch.

John's good breeding was evident in his manners. He insisted on seeing me to my door, but I was just as determined to say our good-byes right there, in the car. When I got out, he remained at the curb, watching me make my way up the steps. At the top, I turned and waved—and was relieved to see him pull away. If he had stayed, I would have had to invent some story about having lost my keys.

I paused before starting back down the steps. I wanted to make certain that he was truly gone. It was then that the apartment door behind me opened and an elderly woman asked what I wanted.

I turned and smiled. "Hello," I said. "I'm a Jehovah's Witness. You know—the *Watchtower* people?"

She slammed the door.

The house where I live is comfortable: a century old this year. My parents used to live here, and so did I, as a child. I left when I married Robert, and did not return until both Mother and Father were gone and the will had traveled through probate. By then my divorce was final, but incomplete. Robert kept inventing reasons to see me. One day after he had stopped by, I found his jacket on a chair. That was the beginning of his moving back in. His clothing accumulated over time, with the whole process taking less than a month. I didn't even realize it was happening until it was complete.

I gave him a room that we considered "his." It used to be the only bedroom on the first floor. By building shelves along three walls, we turned it into a place where he could keep all his guns and magazines. He had a telephone in there, too, because he never knew when he'd get a call and have to leave. Robert was (and is) a cop. Homicide.

He used to spend a lot of time in his room, reading or working on his reports. There were whole days when he wasn't in the house at all. Cops don't live like real people; sometimes they work around the clock and into the following day.

My reunion with Robert turned out to be as pointless as our marriage. Although there was nothing like love between us, I did like having him in the house. I didn't want to be in the same room with him, but a room away was fine. I felt safer with him there. He was the only continuing thread in my life, the only person who had ever seemed reluctant to be without me. But then one day I went out to run some errands. When I returned, I noticed that Robert's house key was lying on the kitchen counter. That struck me as odd because I knew that he kept it on a chain with all his other keys.

Then I went into the bathroom—his toothbrush was missing from the holder on the wall. I knew then that he had returned to Lane. I pitied her; I hated him.

Robert's parents are dead. His sister died in a car accident when they were children. Even his best friend took a bullet in the heart two days before his thirtieth birthday. I guess I shouldn't have been surprised when, one drunken night, he turned to me and said, "I'm going to walk in here sometime and find you dead."

Toward the end of our time together, I was afraid to be alone in the house with Robert. There seemed to be violence boiling beneath the carpet—bubbling from room to room, following us wherever we stepped. Sometimes when I walked toward him, to hand him his mail or a can of beer, I expected there to be an explosion, sudden and thorough. Armageddon. But there was nothing, not even shouting.

Now it is John Wolf that I fear, but in a different way.

That night, after our coffee date, I found it impossible to sleep. His face was right there in front of me, even when my eyes were closed. His hands and his lips were everywhere, reminding me of all those things about my body that I had worked so long and so hard to forget.

I hated him. I never wanted to see him again. Yet, the next day, I opened the phone book, looking for his number.

Luckily, I didn't find it.

I was safe again.

John

◆

Sarah lied.

This morning I sat at my computer and accessed city records. Helen Zane, eighty-three, owns and resides upstairs in the building where I dropped Sarah off. She rents the lower floor to a local school for storage of old records. All the taxes and fees due the city from Mrs. Zane, are paid.

Curious. Sarah doesn't want me to know where she lives. No doubt she is afraid. But she's not afraid of John Wolf. She fears something inside herself that has been awakened by his arrival in her life—some wanted, yet unwanted, excitement that disturbs the familiarity and comfort of her tedium. The details really don't matter. She can share those with her shrink in the time she has left.

Her routine is to drive to Emily and Others, then home. On Thursday, I followed her to Dr. Street's office. Fifty minutes. Then she stopped at a grocery for a few items. Then home. Friday she was back on schedule.

This voyeuristic toying with the life of another isn't essential. But it *is* enjoyable. Sarah requires every ounce of skill

I possess. I wouldn't have been ready for her earlier in my career. She's so cautious, so repressed, she seems only half alive. I want to see her fully alive before I make her fully dead.

Via the computer, I learned that if she owned or rented property, it wasn't in the name of Sarah Sinclair. I decided that she wouldn't have inconvenienced herself by having me drop her too far from where she lives. So I checked a map, examined the area within five blocks of the good Mrs. Zane, and returned to city listings.

Four blocks to the west I discovered a telephone listing for a gentleman named Robert Sinclair.

I called. Four rings, then the tape began: "Hi, I can't come to the phone right now . . ." I hung up. It was her voice.

Sarah is no longer married. She just didn't bother to change her name after the divorce. The building is owned by Sarah Farnum. All taxes and fees due the city have been paid.

Court records revealed that a Sarah Farnum and a Robert Sinclair were married and divorced. She inherited the house from her parents. From the taxes she pays, and the car she drives, it's clear that the bookstore isn't her only source of income. Mom and Dad have been good to daughter Sarah.

I don't know why I checked for birth records, but I did. On October 11, 1987, Robert and Sarah Sinclair became the proud parents of a baby girl. Is the daughter why Sarah doesn't want to bring a man home?

Bank files are more difficult to access, but far from impossible. Sarah receives a quarterly check from a moderate-size trust account. She isn't wealthy, but she isn't poor.

Even though I was able to obtain his date of birth from the marriage license, Robert Sinclair proved to be more elusive than Sarah. It's as if he doesn't want anyone to know who, or where, he is. But I need to know everything about this man. He is connected to Sarah, therefore he is relevant.

Another reason why I must know the who, what, why,

when, and where of Robert Sinclair has to do with survival. I need to protect myself. City records show seven different firearm registrations in his name. Perhaps he was the cop in Sarah's life.

I intend to learn every detail of her wretched little life, even the peripheral ones like discarded husbands. Only by knowing her will I be able to refine my technique enough to elevate it from mere workmanship to craftsmanship. I want this one to be a masterpiece. My defining work.

Once, years ago, I walked through the business district of a city with a young woman who had picked me up in a bar. I had been sipping an early evening beer when she approached me and said, "You seem preoccupied."

She was a nursing student whose home was a farm in Vermont. She was flawed, as so many of the early ones were—speaking with self-assurance about things she didn't understand.

The bar was a college hangout, a place for pairing off. "Want to talk about what's bothering you?" she asked.

"Nothing bothers me," I said.

"Then what are you thinking about?"

"Taking a walk," I said.

"Where?"

"Downtown."

"Okay," she said, and swallowed down half her drink.

As we walked, we exchanged the usual pleasantries—what she did, what I was doing. It was all very mechanical.

"You seem so cold," she said.

I shrugged.

"Don't you like people? Don't you like meeting new people?"

"I can take it or leave it." I stopped walking. "Come here," I said.

"Why?"

"Because we all love the sea."

"What?"

"Because I want to kiss you."

"Why?"

"Would you rather I stand under your balcony and recite poetry?" I asked.

"I don't have a balcony."

"And I don't have any poetry. But maybe I could climb a tree and sit outside your fourth-floor window and read from the phone book."

"How do you know I live on the fourth floor?"

"I'm psychic," I said.

She believed me, but, in truth, I'd been following her to her classes for several days. I had memorized her schedule, sifted through her mail in the foyer of her dorm, and opened enough of her letters to learn that she was from Vermont. She never knew that I had seen her in the bar many times before, ordering the same drink, using the same line with other young men who were sitting alone.

She moved closer, pushing herself against me. "Why do you want to kiss me?"

"I like to kiss attractive women," I said.

"You're supposed to say, 'Because you're you.' That's the right answer."

"You failed to include me in the riddle."

I did hold her. I did do that. But no act of mine is without meaning. There is always a next event to illuminate the first, and to lend direction to the one that follows.

"Let's walk," she said, and took my hand, tugging me along with her.

We talked about our classes (hers in nursing, mine in premed), about home, about what it was like for us as kids.

"I want to know who you are," she said. "What you care about, what you want out of life."

"Nothing," I said. "It's getting cold. There's some wind."

"Have you ever been in love?" she asked.

"Have you seen the swallows?" I asked, ignoring her.

"Swallows?"

"Up among the buildings along Washington Street. You can still hear them and see them, even at dusk."

"I'd like that," she said.

As we turned the corner, entering a street of shadows, she stopped walking. "Do you hear them? The swallows," she asked.

I listened to the swarm of small birds, their chatter of "Quick, quick, quick," their occasional higher-pitched notes of anxiety.

"There must be thousands of them," she said. "I come down here all the time, but I've never seen anything like this before."

"I thought you were a country girl."

"I am, but this is the city. I've never seen so many birds in the city before."

I started to move away.

"Can't we stay a few minutes? I want to watch them."

Again, I started to move on, but she put her hand on my arm.

"Please wait," she said. "Watch them with me."

I could feel her trembling. I looked up again at the swallows darting in arcs high above our heads.

"It's really cold," I said. "We should be getting back."

Three days later the newspaper reported her death. The medical examiner ruled it a suicide: she had jumped from the roof of her dormitory to the pavement below, he said. She left no note, but the final entry in her diary described her desire to fly among the city's buildings like the swallows. Metaphor is an integral part of the hypnotic, erotic dance just before violent death. That was true for her, and it will be true for Sarah. My nursing student flew from the roof. Sarah will fly from her body.

Sarah reminds me of my nursing student. She looks at me with the same obvious interest. And there are other similarities: Sarah has a Robert (a well-armed ex-husband who, for all I know, still fancies himself in love with her), while my nursing student had a stable of boyfriends, one of whom refused to accept the medical examiner's ruling. He told the police that he had seen me enter his girlfriend's dorm on the day she died. He identified me from photos in the college yearbook.

Men in suits—driving the requisite dark, four-door sedan—paid me a social call. I invited them in, and offered them mugs of coffee (instant, which I kept on hand for unwanted guests).

"Yes," I told them. "I was in the building that day. But I wasn't there to see her. I had stopped by to see a friend, Harold Ford, on the second floor. You'll have to ask him what time. Early afternoon, I think, but I'm not certain. I hadn't seen her in three or four days, nor did I want to see her. She was scary. She talked real crazy."

Harold remembered my stopping by. He wasn't sure what time, but he knew that it was the same day the girl dove off the roof. We talked, joked around, and I left. The cops flatly rejected the idea that I—or anyone else, for that matter—was capable of exhibiting such a relaxed, jovial manner just moments before, or after, hurling a young woman off the roof.

But the boyfriend considered me a malevolent psychopath. He followed me around for days. I tried a gentle, sympathetic confrontation, but he wasn't having any of it. Finally he made his move.

He was carrying a Louisville Slugger when he cornered me in the men's room at the bar.

"You killed her," he said.

"She killed herself."

He took a swing. I stepped back, allowed it to pass, then grabbed the fat barrel of the bat and snapped it out of his hands. His momentum left him teetering in my direction, so I shoved him the rest of the way down. It was a tight fit between the wall and commode, but he made it. I lifted the toilet seat.

"Hands on the porcelain," I said.

He was slow—confused—but complied.

"It's over," I said. "The bowl is there to puke in."

Then I brought down the bat and broke both his hands.

He made good use of the bowl, and never followed me again.

I knew from experience that I would have to be careful about Robert Sinclair. He had a lot more than just baseball bats in his arsenal.

Sarah

My phone rang once tonight, close to eleven o'clock. Hoping it was John, I said "Hello" in the sultry voice I'd been practicing, but it was only Robert.

"Where the hell you been?" he asked, then apologized for swearing.

"Right here."

"Good old Sarah, the homebody."

"Don't start, Robert, okay? I'm not in the mood."

"I seem to remember hearing that before."

"What?"

" 'I'm not in the mood.' That used to be your favorite expression, as I recall."

I sighed. "What do you want, Robert?"

"Why do you always have to talk to me like that? Why can't you be nice?"

"I don't know. Why can't you call me when you're sober?"

Robert laughed. "Before any man takes you on, he needs a twelve-pack and a fifth."

"So what do you want?" Even when he's drunk, Robert never calls without a reason.

"Are you busy?"

"No. But I don't feel like listening to you ramble."

"Aw, Sarah," he said.

I didn't respond.

"Sarah," he said again, his voice soft.

I thought, here we go again. First he gets drunk, then he gets nostalgic and maudlin.

"I'm up to my ass in cases," he said.

I still didn't reply.

"Remember that girl we found dead over at Pine Haven?"

I knew who he meant, but I felt like giving him a hard time. "Pine Haven is a cemetery. *Everyone* there is dead."

"The one who was murdered, then propped up against a tombstone, naked."

"I remember."

"Well, I got that one, plus five missing persons."

"What are you doing working missing persons?"

"They sent the reports over to Homicide when Shorty retired. All the precinct had left was Corbin, and he's on disability for at least six more months," Robert complained, sounding more sober by the minute. But I knew that he had to be soused. Otherwise, he wouldn't be talking to me about his work.

"I was sittin' here tonight, going over those reports, looking for someplace to start," he went on, "when it hit me. Those might not be missings after all. Since when do five stable, employed, respectable women come up missing in less than a year? I think they're dead."

That's how Robert has always been: give him a cold, and he'll call it pneumonia. Now he has some missings, and he's calling them murders.

"Where are you?" I asked.

"The office."

"Do you want me to come and get you?" I didn't want

him driving home drunk. Internal Affairs had already given him three "final" warnings.

"Don't worry. I've switched to coffee. I'm on my second cup."

"Good," I said. "So why did you call?"

"I wanted to ask you about that girl—the one in the cemetery. Didn't you say she was a customer of yours?"

"She came in only once that I remember. What was her name—Harris?"

"Right. Maxine Harris. What kind of books did she buy?"

"Oh God, Robert, how am I supposed to remember that? It was months ago."

"It's been longer than that since we made love, but I remember every detail."

I told him to have another cup of coffee—with Lane—then I hung up on him.

The phone rang again right away. I answered, but only because I was hoping (again) that it would be John. There was no response. Just silence, except for what sounded like someone breathing.

It was late, but I couldn't sleep. I thought reading might help, so I pulled my copy of Rimbaud off the shelf. I noticed that it was pretty beat up; the cover was starting to separate from the spine. I hadn't bought it new. A customer brought it in, wanting to sell it to Harry, but it was too ragged to suit him. When he turned it down, I offered the woman two dollars, and she took it.

I have a special tape that I brought home from the shop. Harry buys it in bulk. It's wide, clear, and strong—perfect for holding a book together. I placed a strip over the spine of my Rimbaud, then I opened the front cover to see how secure the pages were—and that's when I noticed the bookplate glued inside: *From the Library of Maxine Harris.*

John

◆

My next encounter with Sarah was over lunch at a place called Harrington's. It was close enough for her to walk there from the bookstore, but she had to pass from one ethnic pissing ground to another, making it unlikely that she would be seen by anyone she knew.

From the moment she arrived, she was talkative, contributing a wealth of detail to the broad outline I had already sketched of her life. All in all, it was pleasant, although I was annoyed by her attempts to discover more about John Wolf than I wished to manufacture at that moment.

"Where do you live?" she asked.

"Landgrove," I said, naming an upscale suburb in Connecticut.

"That's really out in the country."

"Birds in the morning and all that," I agreed. "Why do you stay in the city? I find it such a dreary place. I'm reluctant even to come in on business when I have to—all the crime, the traffic."

She sipped her iced tea. "I've tried other places, but I always end up back here."

"What other places?"

"Chicago for one. That was a strange time."

"How so?"

"Have you ever been married?"

"Divorced," I lied.

"Then you'll understand."

Sarah told me about her paranoid ex-husband, the keeper of the arsenal, the elusive Robert Sinclair—homicide detective. I marveled at my ability to pick them. She went on about Robert's dalliance with his partner, Lane Frank.

"My doctor's receptionist knew Lane—said she was a nice person, but with a hard edge," Sarah said.

She seemed to drift off into private thoughts, then added, "But she's a cop. I wouldn't have expected her to be running around in ruffles and lace. But even if she had, Robert wouldn't have cared. If she had walked naked into his office, carrying her badge, the badge is the thing that would have turned him on. Cops are like that. They seek each other out, stick together."

"My ex is a psychiatrist," I said. "She'd been involved with a colleague of hers for several months, thinking it was all some kind of intellectual thing between them. She told me about him right from the start—how much they had in common, the long talks they had. By the time she had it all straight in her head, I was seeing a psychiatrist, too, but I was paying mine a hundred bucks an hour."

"Lane's father was some sort of psychiatrist, I think. He's supposed to be famous or something."

"I went to see this guy named Street," I said.

I was watching for a reaction, and she didn't disappoint me. It was momentary—just a change in her eyes—but it was there.

"How did you handle things when you and Robert split up?"

"Not well, I'm afraid," she said. "It's crazy, really. I thought

I wanted to be alone, but once I was, I wasn't so sure anymore."

Alone. What about the kid?

"We didn't have any children either," I said. "It's just as well, I guess."

"Robert and I did have a child," she said, the color in her face draining away. This business of the kid was more of a minefield than Bob the cop.

"Oh," I said.

"We had a daughter," she went on. "But she died."

I think I managed to say most of the right things—sudden infant death, tragedy, loss, and all that. I'm pretty good when it comes to sounding sympathetic. With the mystery of the child solved, another piece of the puzzle had fallen into place. But I still had a lot of unanswered questions, and didn't want to waste a lot of time wailing over a dead kid.

But Sarah had her own agenda. There was a lot of unfinished business surrounding the death of her daughter that she needed to deal with. No doubt she had bent Street's ear about it, and I had accidentally reopened that can of boring worms.

"You'd think in so short a time you couldn't possibly become that involved with someone—an infant who's hardly even a person yet," she said. "But it happens. Her birthday's on the eleventh, so she's really on my mind. I'm thinking about going to visit her. I haven't done that yet. Ever."

"Maybe you should," I said, as if I cared.

"I want to. But I also *don't* want to."

I managed to move the conversation forward by offering to accompany Sarah to the cemetery.

"I don't want to intrude," I said, "but if it would help, I'd be happy to go with you."

"I would like that," she said.

"What about Robert?"

"He usually goes in the morning. If you don't want to run into him, we can wait until afternoon to go. It'll work out."

"I didn't mean that," I told her. "I was wondering how he handles it—the loss of your daughter, I mean."

"He's angry. Sometimes I think that's the only feeling he knows. But I suppose he's just protecting himself."

"You're probably right," I agreed. "I don't know much about police work, but it must be hard on a person—especially if you're investigating murders. I can't imagine having to look at a dead body. You couldn't pay me enough."

"He thinks he's stumbled onto a serial killer," Sarah said. Then she laughed, but stopped, quickly, to apologize.

"I'm sorry," she said. "I know it's not funny—but, to understand why it tickles me, you'd have to know Robert. There's nothing he loves more than a good conspiracy. He's collected all the books about the Kennedy assassination—quotes from them like they're biblical. And now he thinks there's a serial killer slinking in the shadows."

"You mean he's looking for a—I can't think of his name, the guy they executed in Florida—that type of person?"

"Bundy."

"That's it," I said.

"All it is, really, is a lot of unresolved missing person cases and one murder victim. The rest is in Robert's head, except . . ."

Sarah stopped. She was looking at my eyes.

"Except?" I prompted.

"Maxine."

I smiled. "I'm afraid I'm not following."

"Last night I found a book with her name in it. Maxine Harris. She's the one who was murdered. She was a customer of ours."

"I still don't get it."

"I've never known anyone who was murdered. I mean, besides Maxine, and I didn't really know her either. She came into the shop once, and I bought the book from her—Rimbaud, in fact."

Chaos theory—a butterfly flaps its wings in the Amazon, a volcano erupts in the American Northwest—suggests infinite variety, but also an essential pattern, a connectedness, that is found upon microscopic and macroscopic examination. I could say that my selection of victims has been random, and that would be true to an extent. But such a statement ignores what roils beneath the level of the conscious mind.

When I was in Maxine's apartment, I walked around, looked at things, absorbed what the environment had to offer. She subscribed to *Harper's Magazine* and *Utne Reader*. She drank tea—English breakfast—not coffee. A half-written letter to "Ron" told me that marriage was in the cards for next summer in Minneapolis. In the yellow pages of her phone book she had circled "Emily and Others, Used Books Bought and Sold."

A butterfly had flapped its wings.

"She was quiet," Sarah said. "I think she said she'd moved out here from Wisconsin or Minnesota, some place like that. I should say something to Robert about the book, but it probably doesn't mean anything, and I don't think I can talk to him right now anyway."

"I think you should tell him," I said. "It might be a clue."

She laughed. "A clue? What a quaint word. You must read a lot of mysteries."

"I watch the British ones," I said. "On PBS, detectives still find clues."

"It's like a feather blowing in the wind," Sarah said. "They never catch killers anymore."

The next evening was to have been a final, pleasant evening of surveillance. I stood in the shadows of an alley across the street from the bookstore, waiting for Sarah to carry the day's receipts up the outside stairway to Harry in the massage parlor.

The blow came from behind and caught me just above my left kidney. For so large a man, my Mike Tyson lookalike was surprisingly quiet, as stealthy as a jungle cat. The movement of the pipe through the still night air was the only sound I heard. The second blow hit just below my left shoulder, but I never felt that one. I had left my body, escaped, drifted away—knowing that what needed to be done would be done.

I heard Slouch's voice from deeper in the shadows. He sounded almost casual. "Don't let him get to the piece."

When the big man—just shapes, shadows, and motion—stepped closer for the next swing of the pipe, a .38 was in my hand.

My vision blurred, but I could still make out his knees—bent like Barry Bonds's at home plate in Candlestick Park.

I use silver tips plus P—magnum loads that fragment on impact. Typically, the exit wound is the size of a plum. To hit any joint is to render it a hash of muscle, ligament, and fragmented bone. The target always goes down.

The report of my revolver echoed in the alley. My wannabe murderer grunted, wobbled a bit, then fell.

Slouch never should have muttered, "Shit."

I aimed into the darkness six inches below where I knew his mouth was, and fired. I heard him drop.

The big man was sitting, still clutching the pipe, when I pushed myself to my feet. His good leg was folded under him. The other extended out, bent at an awkward angle.

I was close enough to see his face, smell his cologne. He didn't seem to mind, didn't object, when I thumbed the hammer back and aimed at his forehead. He was in shock. When the gun exploded a third time, I watched a slab from the back of his head decorate the wall behind him.

I stumbled past Slouch's body to the back of the alley, where I pulled myself over a wooden fence and headed for my car. I was behind the wheel before I heard the sound of sirens in the distance.

Sarah

I didn't give Dr. Street a chance to say anything before I started in.

"Why did you let me sit here a couple of weeks ago, rambling on and on about John Wolf, without even once mentioning that he was a client of yours?"

He put on his best puzzled expression.

"I don't know what you mean," he said.

"What I mean is that you deceived me. You let me tell you all about someone that you already knew inside out."

"What are you talking about?"

"You. And the games shrinks play. I thought you were different from the others, but you're just as much of a bastard as every other shrink I've ever known. You're all jerks. I think it's a prerequisite for the job."

"Sarah, I don't know any John Wolf."

I felt as if a trapdoor had opened, sending me crashing to the basement. I hadn't yet made up my mind about Dr. Street's competency as a therapist, but I had been certain of one thing: his decency. He had been my ideal, the proof I pointed to whenever telling myself that, yes, there really were kind and honest men in this world. But there he was, lying to me. My god, he even looked as if he believed what he was saying.

"Sarah, it isn't a matter of confidentiality or privilege or anything else. I'm telling you that I don't know anyone by that name."

"I'm talking about the man I met," I said, carefully articulating each word to ensure that there would be no misunderstanding. "The one who came into the bookstore, John Wolf. He told me he turned to you for help when his marriage fell apart."

Dr. Street shook his head. "No, Sarah. I don't know the man."

I stared at him, hating him—and hating myself for ever having trusted him. That first time I went to see Dr. Street, I had settled into his huge leather chair, certain I had no reason to be there, nothing to say. But then I heard myself talking about Dr. Mena—our family doctor when I was a child. Mother had taken me to him that spring when I began napping every day, not wanting to be with my friends, refusing to eat. I was eleven.

He was a large, reddish-skinned man with pure white hair. He laughed a lot, even when nobody had said anything funny. He suggested to Mother that she should let him speak with me in private.

"Children Sarah's age, especially female children, sometimes have secrets they don't wish to share with their parents," he told her.

Then, looking at me, he added, "But Sarah and I are good friends. We can tell each other anything, can't we, Sarah?"

He took me into his examining room and helped me up onto the cold, stainless steel table. He pressed gently on my belly, asking if it hurt. When I told him no, he moved his hand up under my skirt and down inside the elastic band of my panties. As he moved his hand lower, he kept asking, "Does this hurt? This? This?"

Nothing that he did was painful. Some of what he did felt good. Strangely good. So when Mother announced, a week later, that I had another appointment with Dr. Mena, I felt a mix of dread and anticipation. But that time, when he took me off for another private talk, it didn't end up the same way.

I don't know if Dr. Mena put his penis inside me. What I do know is this: he put something inside me. His finger? A tongue depressor? I don't know what it was, but it hurt, and it was large enough or sharp enough to make me bleed. His game wasn't fun anymore. I squirmed away, pressing my legs together. He didn't pursue it; he let the moment pass. But when he walked back out to the waiting room with me, he told my mother there were a few more tests he needed to run. He gave her a slip of paper to take to the lab.

Dr. Mena knew how much I feared needles; how they made me cry. But even so, he ordered the blood tests. I knew that was his way of getting back at me for not letting him do whatever he wanted. I had been bad, and I was getting what I deserved.

One afternoon when I came into the house, my mother was talking to Dr. Mena on the phone. I sneaked upstairs, to listen in on an extension.

"Mono is nothing serious," he was saying. "It just takes time and rest, and then she'll be good as new."

"Thank you for letting me know," my mother said.

"And there's something else."

"Yes?"

"Remember those private chats I had with Sarah?"

"Yes."

"I learned quite a bit about her," he said. "She has a very active imagination."

"I know. We're proud of that."

"I understand. But it is a fine line between fantasy and lies. I think you should be aware, so you can watch for any signs."

"Are you saying that Sarah lies?"

"Oh, no, no, of course not. Only that she is so bright, and given to storytelling."

"She wants to be a writer," Mother said.

"Well, then, I wouldn't worry. I just thought I'd mention it—in case she starts telling tall tales. Be aware that it's just the sign of a good imagination, but one that should be redirected. Into her writing, for example."

The last thing I heard Mother say was, "Thank you, Dr. Mena. I appreciate all the effort you've gone to."

I knew that I must have been a very bad girl. First Dr. Mena had subjected me to needles, then he had told my mother that I lie. I didn't like displeasing him so much. That's why, a year later—when a boy from my class put his hands in those same places that Dr. Mena had touched—I didn't stop him.

There were other boys after that, but none of them mattered. Until I met Robert. He was lifeguarding at the beach that summer between my senior year and my first semester of college. Once I spotted him perched up there on the lookout tower—all tanned and muscular and serious—I started hanging around, asking him questions. Being a pest. Flirting.

"Look," he said, "I'm working."

"I know. Maybe I should go way out where it's over my head. Would you rescue me?"

"This isn't a game."

I reached up and tickled the bottom of his foot.

"Why don't you act your age?" he said, and I could tell that he was truly angry. But when I started to walk away, he jumped down and came after me.

"Hey," he said.

I kept walking.

"I said hey."

I stopped, but didn't turn around.

He came around to the front of me, but I kept my head down. He put one hand under my chin and urged me to look up at him.

"How old are you, anyway?"

"How old do you want me to be?" I asked, smiling.

"At least twenty-one."

"How old are you?"

"Twenty-five."

"I'll be twenty-five in seven years."

"I was afraid of that."

I reached out with one finger and touched his belly, but he didn't seem to notice.

"Do you have a boyfriend?" he asked.

"Yes."

"Oh," he said, looking disappointed.

"You."

He smiled, slow and sweet.

That's how it began. We were engaged by Christmas—and married the following June, about three months after my nineteenth birthday. We didn't have sex until our wedding night. I liked that about Robert—his restraint. It made me feel that he valued me even more than I valued myself.

I thought no one would ever give me that feeling again. Then I met John Wolf, and my stock rose to a record high. That day at Harrington's he brought back memories of how it once had been with Robert. He asked me about my marriage, my work, my daughter. He even volunteered to go with me to the cemetery on Liza's birthday. And he didn't make advances, physically, at all. Not even an accidental brush against my leg. While that was refreshing and flattering, it was also frustrating. I was powerfully attracted to the man. I got wet just looking at him. But I trusted him to know what was best. I willingly let him set the pace.

The day after our lunch date, I was at the bookstore, doing what I always do at closing time. I was carrying the day's receipts up the outside stairway, to Harry. The safe is in the massage parlor, and that's where he keeps the money from both businesses. Just as I reached the top step, I heard a shot.

I went down the instant I heard it, flat on the wooden

landing outside the door. Then I heard two more shots. They sounded like they were coming from the alley across the street.

The massage parlor door inched opened and Harry said, "Gunshots?"

"Over in the alley," I told him.

He opened the door a little wider so I could crawl inside. Right away Sheila started screaming. She thought that I had been hit, and said so into the phone. I found out later that she was talking to the dispatcher at 911. That's why the police headed directly for the massage parlor, not the alley.

When I told them where I thought the shots had originated, one of the officers said, "Nobody else called this in."

"I know a shot when I hear one."

"You got a gun?" the officer wanted to know.

"I was married to a cop."

While Harry argued with the officers about whether I would know the difference between gunfire and firecrackers, Sheila and I led everyone over to the alley—and that's when we found them: two black guys. Dead.

In under five minutes, the scene was crawling with cops. Radios crackling, yellow tape strung everywhere—it was a zoo. I had recognized both dead guys, and knew that John Wolf would want to know their fate. So as soon as everything settled down, as soon as I had answered each investigator's questions twenty times, I returned to the bookstore and dialed directory information.

"What city, please?"

"Landgrove."

"Go ahead."

"I'd like the listing for John Wolf, please."

The operator was silent for a moment, then said, "Still checking."

After another pause, she said, "I'm sorry. We don't show any listing for that name."

"Then it must be unlisted."

"No," she said. "We don't have anyone by that name."

John

◆

When that other Sarah—the one that was my sister—started dating, I used to follow her. She'd get into a Ford or Chevy with a pimply-faced sixteen-year-old who couldn't wait to get both hands in her pants, and they would head for town. I'd get in my pickup and follow.

Sometimes they'd just drive around, stop at the shopping plaza for ice cream, or drive up to the overlook at the power dam and make out. I'd park out of their view, then walk through the darkness—to stand next to the car and watch.

She'd slap his hands away. He'd heat her up with another kiss, then go groping again. She'd say his name in a whiny voice, then slap his hands away again. It was a curious way for all of us to pass the time.

One night, though, she and her bacterial boy of the evening drove up onto the mountain access road. I followed as far as the first parking lot, grabbed a bottle of beer from the case beside me on the seat, and hiked up the switchback trail.

By the time I reached a clearing above them, they had a

blanket spread out on the ground and were taking their clothes off. She wasn't pushing his hands away.

The beer bottle exploded against a rock directly behind them. There was screaming, then he was in his Ford, headed down the mountain—and she was fumbling around in the dark, trying to find her clothes, and muttering, "Please don't hurt me."

"It's me," I said, walking slowly toward her.

"What are you doing up here? Jesus," she said.

In her relief, she had stopped wrestling with her clothes and just stood there, naked. I had never seen her like that before.

"What are you doing here?" she asked again.

She looked like a woman, and she had been doing the things that women do. As I walked closer to her, she became aware, once again, of her nakedness and started getting dressed.

The jagged neck of the broken bottle was on the ground next to her. I picked it up, looking at her face, her neck, her breasts. She pushed her hair away from her face. That gesture, and the way her breasts moved when she did it, caused me to become erect. She didn't notice. She was staring at my hand.

"What's that for?" she asked.

I had never felt that kind of lust before. I wanted to throw my sister down on the blanket and rape her. I wanted to take the ragged edge of broken glass and slash her open.

"I didn't want you to step on it and get cut," I said.

I could feel myself drifting away, slipping off to that place in my mind where I could watch the two of us fuck on the blanket—where I could see myself killing her after I was finished with her body.

"Why are you cutting yourself with it?" she asked. "Stop doing that."

I looked down. I'd been pulling the neck of the bottle across my hand, repeatedly, drawing a new trail of blood with each rip of my skin.

She had pulled on her shirt and was buttoning it. "Please don't tell Dad," she said.

I moved so close to her, I could smell her hair. It was just an instant. I threw the glass into the trees.

She brushed past me on her way to the trail.

"Is the truck down in the parking lot?" she asked.

"Yes," I said, following behind her, watching the rhythmic sway of her ass.

That night on the mountain was the closest I've ever come to reacting. There is no need, ever, to do that. It's better, by far, to simply mold reality into whatever shape I choose.

What I chose for my sister Sarah was entirely visual, not at all tactile. Had I raped her, I would have had to kill her. Otherwise, she would have told her father—our mother's husband. It would have been messy, very messy.

Also, it is contrary to my nature to mix sex with murder, though I do find thoughts of murder titillating—and the act itself an aphrodisiac.

But there was another consideration, one even more compelling than the others. Had I murdered my sister, the earlier incident involving the knife and my family would have been remembered; accusations would have followed, swiftly, and they would have been difficult to deflect. I've always made it a point never to call attention to myself; never to kill too close to home.

But now I have broken my own rule. I've stepped too close to the spotlight. The police will check around the neighborhood. No doubt they will question Sarah—and, no doubt, she will recall our first meeting in the bookstore. While it is unlikely that she knew either of the gentlemen I eliminated, she *had* watched me level a .38 in their direction. That was something she wouldn't forget. She would describe the episode in Emily and Others to any cop who cared to listen. Perhaps she had already phoned Robert—regaled him with every detail. If the police weren't already looking for John Wolf in Landgrove, I knew they would be soon. And they would be thorough.

Any other man might run, but for me the risk is part of the attraction. It is peaking now, and I find it exhilarating. It has never been better than it is now, with Sarah.

Sarah

◆

When I opened my door and found Robert standing there, I didn't say a word, not even "Go away."

"It's business, Sarah. May I come in?"

I sighed. "Sure. Why not?"

He looked wonderful, and I said so—instantly wishing that I hadn't. Now that he didn't have me, Robert behaved just as I used to wish he would: interested, appreciative, flirtatious. I didn't want to give him any encouragement. I had no interest in replaying that old sad song that had been our marriage.

"You don't look so bad yourself," he said.

Searching for a way to change the subject, I asked if he wanted something to drink.

"What I want is some information. You were there at the shooting yesterday," he said.

"Wrong. I was across the street from it, headed up to the massage parlor."

"Tell me what you saw."

"Nothing. I heard three shots. That's it."

Robert flipped open his pocket-sized notebook and wrote a couple of words in it. "The shots," he said. "Were they one right after the other, or was there some time between them?"

"They weren't boom-boom-boom. But there wasn't much time in between. Maybe a little more time between the second and third shots."

"About how long?"

I shrugged. "I don't know. When that kind of thing happens, time is different. It slows down. I thought someone was shooting at *me*. Sorry I'm not much help. But there is something you might find interesting. Those guys came into the shop the other day. I think they were going to rob us, but there was a customer in there, a man. He picked up on the body language right away. He pulled a gun."

"*Who* did—the customer or one of the dead guys?"

"The customer. It was all over in a matter of seconds. The two punks just backed on out of the store. End of problem."

"Who's the customer?"

"I'm wondering the same thing. He said his name is John Wolf and he lives in Landgrove, but there isn't any phone listing in his name."

Robert's eyes narrowed. I knew that look; knew what it meant. "You tried to call him? Is this guy a boyfriend of yours?"

"Jesus, Robert. Do you think I get involved with every guy I meet? I was trying to reach the guy so I could ask him to contact *you*. I thought maybe he'd remember something about those two guys that I don't."

Robert looked truly apologetic. "Sorry . . ."

"Forget it."

"If this Wolf character comes into the shop again, ask him to call me."

"Of course."

• • •

John Wolf called me the next day at work.

"I tried reaching you the other day," I said. "Didn't you say you live in Landgrove?"

He paused before responding. "Yes. But I don't have a phone. I know that's unheard of in this day and age, but I love the peace. That's why I moved to Landgrove—to get away from the world. But I already told you all that, didn't I? How I hate the city, I mean."

So that was it. Directory information had never heard of him because he didn't have a phone. For the hundredth time I thought what an interesting, exceptional man John Wolf was.

"My ex wants to talk to you," I said.

He laughed. "Wants to discuss my intentions regarding you, I suppose."

"No, it's nothing like that."

"Well, I don't mind telling him. I have important plans for you, Sarah Sinclair."

I felt the heat rise in my face.

"So what does he want?" John asked, returning to the topic of Robert.

"There was a shooting in the alley across the street a couple of days ago—two guys shot dead. I think they're the same ones who came into the shop that day you were here."

"I see."

"I told Robert about it—about how you got rid of them by showing them your gun. He wants to see if you remember anything I didn't."

"Okay."

"Would you mind calling him?"

"Certainly I'll call him. What's the number?"

I gave it to him, thinking how odd it felt bringing those two men, my past and my future, together.

"Oh, there's one other thing," I said. "The other day you mentioned a psychiatrist—the one you went to see when you were going through your divorce. Dr. Street?"

"Streeter," he said. "You aren't looking for a shrink, are

you? I wouldn't recommend him. Besides, you can always talk to me."

E and R. What a big difference two little letters can make. It explained everything.

As soon as I awakened on the eleventh (which—since I had taken the day off—wasn't very early), I phoned Robert at his office. My purpose, without being obvious about it, was to confirm what time he would be visiting Liza's grave. I didn't want our paths to cross. I didn't mention that I, too, would be going to the cemetery. For all I knew, I would chicken out, and I didn't want Robert giving me grief about it. Since the day of the burial, he'd been trying to get me to go out there.

"You owe it to her," he had said. Not: "It'll do you good." He made it a responsibility, a requirement—implying that my refusal to go was proof of my failure as a mother; proof that I was the one who killed her. If I didn't go through with the birthday visit, I didn't want him to have that knowledge, that weapon.

"Sinclair," he said when he picked up his phone.

"Ditto," I said.

"Thanks for calling me back so soon."

I glanced down at my answering machine and, for the first time, saw the message light blinking. I'd had the bell turned off, so I didn't know that any calls had come in while I was sleeping. I decided to let Robert go on thinking that I was returning his call.

"What's up?" I asked.

"I wanted to thank you for passing my message along to your friend. I also thought I ought to let you know that he doesn't really live in Landgrove."

"What do you mean?"

"I mean he's playing a game with you, Sarah. The story he gave you and the story I got don't match."

"What are you saying?"

"You figure it out. Maybe he's married. I don't know."

"You always expect the worst from people. He happens to be divorced."

"Look," Robert said, "his lies are between you and him. Let him set the story straight."

"That's what I love about you."

"What?"

"You drop hints. Get me interested. Then tell me to go fuck myself. You never change, do you, Robert?"

"I'm sorry," he said. After a pause, he added, "You know what today is."

"Yes . . ."

"And you know how it gets to me."

"Are you going over to see her?"

"Yeah. In a few minutes."

"Give her my love."

"Right."

After a long silence, I said, "Well, I've gotta run."

"Me, too."

Then I remembered. "Oh, wait. There's something I keep forgetting to tell you. Remember that woman we were talking about—the one in the cemetery, who was murdered?"

"Maxine Harris."

"Yes. She came in the shop once with some used books she wanted to sell. Harry bought a couple, but there was one that was too beat up to put on the shelves. I bought it from her."

"How do you know it was Maxine Harris?"

"I was reading the book just the other night. There's a sticker on the inside front cover with her name written on it."

"You're kidding."

"It's a collection of Rimbaud's work. I don't know how helpful that is, but at least you know she had good taste in poetry."

"Rambo's a poet?"

I remembered all over again how far apart Robert and I are in our tastes. His idea of great literature is *Soldier of Fortune* magazine.

"It looks like she used the book a lot. There's one section that she highlighted in yellow. I'll show it to you the next time you're out at the house."

"Is that an invitation?"

I paused for a moment, considering my options. I knew if I said no, I'd be contradicting my willingness to show him the book. And if I said yes, it might sound like I was offering more than I really was.

"Take it any way you want," I said.

John

◆

I presented my papers to the desk sergeant at the precinct house, a ruddy-faced cop waiting for his heart attack to happen. He glanced at me and made a call.

Sinclair was there in less than two minutes, a reasonable time for a city employee to keep a courier from the British embassy waiting.

"Alan Carver," I announced, extending my hand.

"I was expecting John Wolf," Sinclair said, shaking my hand.

"The undersecretary is in Washington," I told him. "He asked me to deliver this package to you, and to be prepared to answer any questions you might have. I'm sure you can appreciate the delicate nature of the situation."

"Of course," Sinclair said, as he accepted the small parcel bearing the seal of the United Kingdom.

The detective escorted me to a conference room on the same floor. It was a large room, sparsely furnished with a single, chipped Formica table and three vinyl chairs. He sat. I remained standing. He read.

"I think you'll find the information complete. The weapon in question is there—all the necessary papers. The undersecretary does acknowledge his indiscretion, and apologizes. He asked me to assure you that his moving about your city without the proper escort will not happen again."

Sinclair was nodding. He examined the .32 caliber revolver, the license, and the gun's registration certificate. "This all appears to be in order," he said. "Mr. Wolf's letter contains most of the information I need, but—"

"He has briefed me thoroughly, Detective," I said, and waited.

Sinclair scanned the letter again. "His purpose for being in that neighborhood—"

"The undersecretary is an antiquarian book collector. As you can see, the book he purchased that day is included in the package."

Sinclair flipped through the pages of *The Swiss Family Robinson*. He was thinking. In the reality I had shaped for him, he would know that this call was a courtesy, that John Wolf was insulated by diplomatic immunity. He also knew that it was a dead kid's birthday, and he had a grave to visit. He couldn't waste the whole day sparring with an absent undersecretary.

"Were you planning to take this material back with you?" he asked.

"On the contrary," I said. "We wish to be of assistance, just not involved. When you have finished with it, please leave a message at the embassy for me. I'll return and pick it up."

I handed him Alan Carver's card. He stared at it.

"The night of the shooting," he began.

I nodded at the letter.

"He was at a reception with the mayor?" Sinclair asked.

"Easily and, I hope, discreetly verified," I said.

"Sure."

I glanced at my Rolex. "If there's nothing more," I said.

"I'll check all this out," he said, standing. "I'll probably have some questions later."

The man was seething.

I've always been a collector of other people's business cards. With the cards, plus the information I glean from my computer, and an occasional visit to a bank, convention, or embassy, I've been able to assume whatever identities I've needed. I've also educated myself so that I can step into a man's professional life and live it, passably, for as long as I wish.

Later, as I drove toward the cemetery to meet Sarah, I knew that her ex-husband would be tied up for the next several days in bureaucracy, on both the local and the international level. The embassy would accept a message for their courier, Mr. Carver, but they wouldn't tell Sinclair that Alan Carver was on holiday with his wife in the British Virgin Islands.

Nor would they tell him that they had no undersecretary named John Wolf. They would assume, as they had when I called, that he wanted to speak with Jeremy Wolf, and they would provide him with the number at his office in Washington. When I called that number, I was politely given a telephone appointment for the middle of November, nearly a month away—an expedited time frame because I had claimed to be an investigator for the Department of the Treasury with an urgent need for information.

The mayor's office will tell Sinclair that there was no official guest list for the reception. And, if he dealt with the same public information officer I did, she will say, "Your Mr. Wolf probably was there. Both senators were present, and they had twenty or thirty UN types with them. We just don't have a list."

I parked beside Sarah's car at the gate and walked up to meet her at the cemetery office as we had agreed. She stood outside, her light blue dress moving slightly in the breeze. She was holding a small bunch of cut flowers.

"At least the day is beautiful," I said.

She had a map of the place with Liza's grave marked on it. She glanced at it as we walked up to the top of the hill.

The setting was sterile, barren of trees. There were no statues or headstones. Each grave was marked by a flat bronze plate resting in a slab of concrete. We were in the section reserved for children—the Garden of Enchantment.

"I think she's over this way," Sarah said, consulting her map.

When she found the grave, she removed a metal canister from the head of the marker and placed the flowers inside it, then put the canister back in its holder.

I was waiting for her to start in about Liza's short life, Sarah's own role as mother, how Robert did or didn't fit into things. Instead, she knelt and bowed her head. If she prayed, she did it silently. It occurred to me that perhaps the mother should join the daughter. It wasn't just a poetic whim, and it wouldn't have been mere replication. It's just that the opportunity had presented itself. There was a slag pile off to one side of the Garden of Enchantment where a shovel was stuck in a heap of dirt. It would have been so easy to peel back the sod on Liza's grave, dig a shallow hole, make a small contribution to the slag pile, deposit Sarah atop her daughter's casket, and replace the sod. Who would think to look for the missing among the buried dead?

It would have been so easy. I stepped closer to Sarah's back as she continued to kneel. Swallows swooped in low arcs across the hill—splashes of orange and white against the pastel blue of the sky. The day was clear, the top of the hill empty. It would have been a simple matter of reaching out my hands and doing it.

But I had something else in mind for Sarah.

When she stood, she turned and explored my eyes.

"The color changes," she said.

"Others have told me that."

"They're doing it right now. They were gray. Now they're almost blue."

She was finished at the grave. There were no tears.

"I feel as if I could never really know you," she said. "Usually a person's eyes will tell me something, but all yours do is change."

"Doesn't that tell you something?" I asked.

As we began walking down the hill, she said, "You aren't who you said you are."

"Oh?"

"Even the name—John Wolf—you made that up, didn't you? And the way you handled that gun—what are you, CIA or something?"

Not a bad guess. This was the kind of perceptiveness I had expected from Sarah—the side of her that provided the challenge.

"John, or whatever your name is, who are you?"

"John is right," I told her, offering my business card.

"John Wallingford," she read aloud. "Wallingford Antiques, Landgrove. Antiques? Then what is all the mystery about?"

"I hope I don't sound pretentious when I say this, but I am a wealthy man," I explained. "I do most of my business in cash. That's the reason for the gun. I never had to aim it at anyone before that day in your store, but I'm well schooled in its use, thanks to the range I visit twice a week."

"But why the phony name?"

"I wanted you to like me for myself, not my money."

I could see her relax.

"I'm sorry I made you feel so nervous," I told her.

After continuing for a while in that sympathetic vein, answering her questions, I said, "I assume it was fear that made you lie to me about where you live."

"How did you know that? That I lied, I mean."

"It was a point in your favor, actually," I said. "You're a lousy actress."

"Okay," she admitted. "Maybe I *was* a little bit afraid."

"Well, let's have no more of that. I would like to take you out to see Wallingford Manor. We can have dinner, then I'll bring you back to the city to any address you wish."

Sarah laughed. Then she told me her address, and we agreed that I would pick her up at 7:00 on Sunday.

When we reached her car she turned and lingered, as if she expected me to kiss her or hold her. A wave of revulsion surged through me.

"Sunday then," I said.

Sarah

When I arrived home, I noticed Robert's car parked down the street. He must have been waiting for me because he pulled into the drive behind me.

"What's up?" I asked when he followed me up onto the front porch.

"What do you mean?"

"Why were you parked over there?" I asked, pointing down the block.

He looked away. "I don't know. Just a hunch."

"What?"

"Why don't we go inside? I could use some coffee."

I unlocked the front door, then stepped aside to let him enter. He headed straight for the kitchen, trailing fumes of beer. He immediately went about the business of preparing two mugs of instant coffee.

Handing one of the mugs to me, he said, "The mayor's assistant is an old friend of mine. I talked her into faxing me the guest list from a party he had the night of the shootings."

I sat down at the kitchen table.

"I suppose you have a reason for telling me that," I said.

"Something just didn't ring true about your Mr. Wolf. I had a gut feeling that something was wrong."

"You *always* think something's wrong."

"Listen, Sarah, your undersecretary or ambassador or whatever the hell he says he is, is a fake."

"Robert, please start at the beginning."

"John Wolf. The guy who pulled the gun on those goons in the shop that day. He's not who he says he is. And he wasn't where he said he was when they got shot."

I laughed. "I already know that John Wolf isn't John Wolf. He's John Wallingford. Rich. Divorced. An antiques dealer."

"Jesus. What the hell's going on here?"

"He *said* his name was John Wolf, then he said it wasn't. It's Wallingford."

"Shit."

"What's wrong?"

"I didn't even run this guy's gun registration to make sure it was legitimate. I'm losing it."

"What's the big deal? He used a fake name. So what?"

"*So what?*" Robert hadn't raised his voice like that with me for a long time. "A guy tells you one thing one minute, then another the next, and you keep on seeing him? The guy's a psycho. Wake up and smell the Maxwell House."

"I'm sick of your drunken tirades," I said. "I divorced them, remember? Why don't you get the hell out of here?"

He reached out, as if to touch me, but I pulled away.

"I mean it," I said. "I'm tired of going to war with you every time we talk. John Wallingford is the best thing that has happened to me in years, and I don't want you spoiling it."

"I'm warning you, Sarah. There's something really wrong here."

"You're jealous."

Robert hit the table with his fist, causing the coffee mugs to jump. "I'm a cop. He's a liar. There was a double homicide. I think I've got a right to be concerned. This guy is bad news. I don't want him hanging around here."

"He's not exactly hanging around, Robert. I've seen him only a couple of times."

"I need to talk to him."

"You already did that."

"No. He sent some gofer over to the office with a bullshit story about the mayor's party. That, and a copy of *The Swiss Family Robinson*."

The Swiss Family Robinson? I didn't know what Robert was talking about, but his reference to a book made me think of Rimbaud.

"I suppose you want that book I bought from Maxine Harris," I said.

Robert seemed to shift from drunk to sober. "Right," he agreed. "I'd like to take a look at that."

"You can even take it with you—if you promise to return it when the investigation is over."

With Robert following, I went into the living room to get the Rimbaud paperback off the coffee table.

"Gee, that's funny," I said, staring at the empty spot where the book had been just a few hours earlier. "It's not here."

Robert gave me a sideways glance.

"No, really," I said. "It was here when I left this morning."

He didn't say anything.

"This is weird."

"If you want company, Sarah, just come out and say it. You don't have to play games to get me to come over."

He was edging closer to me with a teasing look in his eyes.

I put out my hand, keeping him at arm's length. "Listen, Mr. Ego, I didn't invite you here. You were sitting out front when I drove up, remember?"

He backed off.

"Besides," I said, "I really *do* have a book that belonged to

Maxine Harris. It was here, on this very table, ten hours ago. Now it's gone."

"Maybe Maxine wanted it back."

"You really piss me off."

He left—but not without snickering so loudly, he had to know I'd hear it.

I had some amends to make with Dr. Street. I stopped by his office after work on Friday with a peace offering, hoping to repair some of the damage I had done with that Dr. Street/Dr. Streeter mix up. It was a copy of *Violent Attachments* by J. Reid Meloy. Dr. Street had mentioned it to me once, asking me to watch for a used copy to turn up at the shop. I'd had it for several weeks and was saving it for a special occasion like his birthday or Christmas.

Dr. Street was clearly pleased. "This is an excellent reference," he said. "Thank you very much."

"I read it, though not with the same understanding that you would," I told him.

He looked surprised. "You read it? It's a bit too graphic for most readers."

"But that's what I loved about it."

I took the book back from him and leafed through it until I found what I was looking for.

"Look at this," I said, pointing to a few words on page 108—in the chapter titled "The Psychopath as Love Object." It was a description of a psychopath's romantic partner: "One woman responded to Card I of the Rorschach with the response, 'It's two carnivorous wolves . . . I wish I could see doves mating.'"

After he finished reading, Dr. Street asked me what I had found so appealing about that section.

"It's that woman. I feel like we have a lot in common. I keep wanting to see birds, but instead I see wolves. And even though they frighten me, I'm drawn to them."

Dr. Street looked as if he expected me to say more.

I shrugged. "I don't know how to explain it. It's like there are two forces pulling me in opposite directions at the same time."

"I remember the first day you came to see me. You compared yourself to a bird."

"Yes. The swift. It flaps first one wing, then the other, but never the two at once. It's a being, divided—like the woman in the book," I said, nodding toward the volume I had just given him.

I told him about the birthday visit with Liza, but I had trouble concentrating. I kept thinking about John, about the swallows—how they swooped in low arcs across the hill. And I kept remembering two things about that moment: how I wished that I could fly, and how my feet were sinking more deeply into the grass that covered my daughter's grave.

John

The plan has been in place for years, of course, but tonight I am closer to setting it in motion than I have ever been. It is the method by which I will guarantee my freedom and ensure that I will be able to continue living my life in whatever way I choose. But I'll have to surrender the comfort afforded by these surroundings. I must relocate, and become one of the dozen different identities at my disposal. In some respects the prospect is exciting, but, on the downside, I've grown attached to my space in the country, and am loath to leave it.

It is some comfort to know that I can watch from a distance as the police and the media unearth the story of the psycho medical examiner who kept himself in business. It will be a national story, especially when they discover my land to the north, and begin their excavation—and exhumation. But, alas, I won't be able to join Geraldo on location in Hasty Hills. I will be well on my way to my next challenge, my next adventure.

I telephoned Bernie Lallendorf, the part-time maintenance man at the Hasty Hills municipal building, to ask him to stop by my place on Monday morning. "I have some electrical work for you," I told him. Bernie's always looking to make an extra buck. "When you get here, feel free to walk in. The front door will be unlocked. If I have the stereo on, I won't be able to hear you, no matter how hard you knock."

Bernie thanked me and promised to show up early.

When he arrives, the house will be a bomb, waiting for someone to trigger it. Opening the front door will break an electrical circuit. A switch will close. A priming device will operate. The explosion will leave a crater fifty feet across and ten feet deep.

When the authorities find Bernie's corpse, if there's that much left of him, they'll assume that Doc Chadwick went up in the blast; they'll think they're burying me.

The next day, Saturday, was a workday for me. I drove over to the municipal building, where the county medical center is housed, and took my usual position in the autopsy room, near the array of metal instruments that I keep on a stainless steel table. Looking at the specimen before me, I spoke into a microphone that was suspended from the ceiling by a cord.

"Beginning external examination," I said. "The body is that of a well-developed, well-nourished white female. Her gross appearance is consistent with an approximate age of twenty-five to twenty-seven years. The body measures five feet, nine inches long, and weighs 130 pounds."

For the past five years I've been the chief medical examiner for the county. I've testified in a dozen homicide cases, plus an equal number of civil actions brought as the result of claims of wrongful death.

"The head is covered with shoulder-length brown hair. The eyes are blue. The conjunctival membranes, unremarkable. There is no congestion, nor are there petechial hemorrhages. There are freckles over the face, primarily on the sides of the nose."

Several years ago the county prosecutor called me with questions regarding one of my reports. He wanted to know the possible length and width of the knife that had been used to kill a young woman.

"Can you give me any idea?" he asked.

"I can do better than that," I responded. "The blade is four inches in length, an inch in width at its widest point. It has a short serrated section just below the handle, perhaps a half inch in length, and it has some kind of printing or design on one side of the blade. It's single-edged, by the way. Comparing it with what I have here, I'd suggest that you look for a Buck product, possibly one of those commemorative knives. Any of the hunting and fishing shops around here would carry them."

He was profusely grateful. A similar knife had been found in the home of the man who was about to stand trial for the murder. My testimony would be critical, the prosecutor assured me.

"This creep tried to hide it," he told me. "Stuck it down in the dirt in one of the house plants."

"Not very smart," I said.

Unless the killer wants the cops to find it. Which, of course, I did.

"On the back of the neck in the midline," I said into the microphone, "centered at a point fifteen centimeters from the top of the head, there is an obliquely oriented stab wound which measures two centimeters in length. The right superior end comes to a sharp point. The left inferior end is squared. The wound probes anteriorly for a distance of five centimeters. Subsequent dissection reveals no evidence of injury to the spinal cord."

This one wasn't one of my avocational pursuits. It was a hack job—the result of someone going out of control, flailing away at the young woman's neck, upper back, chest, abdomen. There was one incised wound on her right calf. She was sexually assaulted, then buried in a shallow grave off one of the state roads.

I continued to dictate. "Cause of death: incised and punctate wounds to neck, trunk, and extremities, with insult to jugular vein. Autopsy completed at two thirty-five P.M. Manner of death, homicide."

The state police detective was a flabby guy with a bulbous alcoholic's nose. I knew he wouldn't lose any sleep trying to solve the case at hand. He was just marking time, waiting for his eventual retirement party—complete with gag gifts and free drinks.

"Bad one, Doc," he said.

"I've never seen a good one."

He laughed. "Guess not. What can you tell me?"

"Probably not suicide."

He laughed harder.

"Start pulling the jackets on sex offenders," I told him. "This guy's young, probably less than thirty. The victim put up a struggle. He never had her under control. Not totally. Notice the defensive wounds to the hands and the right forearm. This guy's been violent before, but he's a novice when it comes to murder. Look for priors. Sexual assault, attempted sexual assault. And either he lives or works not far from where he dumped her."

"You're a regular Lucas Frank, Doc," the cop said, referring to the East Coast's most famous profiler.

"I like to think I'm better."

I left the office, feeling lethargic. I was mulling over the pros and cons of using Wallingford Manor for Sarah's swan song. I wasn't yet certain if I would take her there, though I did know that it would be unoccupied on Sunday. I'd done some carving on Mr. Wallingford on Thursday—a favor to the vacationing medical examiner who serves the postmortem needs of Landgrove. I took advantage of that opportunity to explore the gentleman's pockets, searching for items that I might find useful sometime in the future. My fishing expedition netted me several of Wallingford's business cards, including the one I gave to Sarah. It took me less than half an hour to determine the boring cause of Wallingford's death: myocardial infarction. Until his will makes its way through probate, his house will be available to anyone who's able to pick a lock. I had been out there the day he was found slumped over his plate of breakfast eggs, so I knew that Wallingford Manor would provide an ideal setting for what I had planned. But why take an unnecessary risk just for the sake of ambience? Even before I was out of the parking lot, I had decided that Sarah's own home would have to do.

Sarah

◆

Today, Sunday, is one of autumn's masterpieces—a canvas rich in burnt umber, deep gold, and vermilion. Have you ever noticed that it takes dying for flora to reach its peak of beauty?

I awakened early, but remained in bed, thinking about the day before—and my visit to Paradise Mall. I had a precise picture in my mind of the outfit I wanted to wear on my date with John tonight. Something white and virginal, with elegant gold accessories. I found exactly what I wanted at a small shop called Zelda's: a white, ankle-length dress with long sleeves and a high, Victorian-style collar.

When I tried it on, I changed my mind about the gold accessories. I decided they would look too heavy; I wanted more of an ethereal look. I settled on simple pearl earrings.

"You're going to need color somewhere," the sales clerk insisted.

"I don't think so," I said, studying my reflection in the three-way mirror.

"Oh," she said, brightening. "I get it. It's for your wedding."

I didn't argue. The word "forever" had been going through my mind ever since I first met John.

I hadn't been home from the mall for more than an hour when I heard Robert's knock on the front door. I was happy to see him. A mellow, almost dreamlike sense of peace had come over me, and lingered. It was so invasive, so thorough, Robert took one look at me and asked, "What are you on? Xanax?"

"Come in," I said, my voice sounding soft and slow. "I'm about to make some coffee."

At the mall, I had stopped at The Coffee Mill to pick up a Braun coffee grinder and some fresh beans so that I could prepare John's favorite blend—Colombian supreme and French roast. I wanted everything to be perfect if, after dinner, John decided to come back to my place for coffee. Or, better yet, if he decided to stay for breakfast.

"What's all this about?" Robert asked, his glance taking in the array of new purchases sitting on my kitchen counter.

"I've decided to start grinding my own coffee beans," I said.

"My, aren't you the domestic one," he said, his tone making it clear that he meant just the opposite. "So who's the guy?"

I knew what he was thinking. I had put the Mr. Coffee away in the cupboard after Robert had complained one too many times about the quality of my brew. From that day forward, we'd had nothing but instant. And now the Mr. Coffee was back on my kitchen counter. A man like Robert could make a lot out of that—and, for a change, he'd be right.

"Let's try something new," I suggested. "Let's be friends today."

My manner was disarming. Robert was used to our encounters turning into World War III. Although he was suspicious of the change in me, his long-standing desire for a truce between us made him take a chance. He followed my lead.

"I'd like that," he said. "I could use a friend today."

He leaned back against the counter and reached out for me. With his hands on my hips, he urged me toward him. I offered no resistance, moving willingly into a passionless embrace. We could have been brother and sister, father and daughter.

I felt him take a deep breath; his arms tightened around me.

"What is it?" I asked. It was one of those rare moments when I truly cared.

"Maxine Harris."

I leaned away from him, to look at his face, his eyes. "What do you mean?"

"I've spent most of the day getting to know her—going through her diary, some poetry she wrote, love letters from three or four guys. We have cardboard boxes filled with all that's left of her . . . her high school diploma, a college paper she got an A on, photographs. It feels so wrong to be pawing through someone's most personal stuff that way."

He asked if I had found Maxine's book.

I shook my head. I knew that it wasn't just lost; it had been stolen—but I had no way of proving that. There was no sign of breaking and entering, but then why should there be? The locks on my house are the kind you can flip open with a credit card. I had wanted dead bolts, but Robert always said no.

"Let the sons of bitches come on in," he used to say. "Shoot somebody inside your house, and no jury anywhere will convict you. But hit him while he's outside, prying off the door frame, and they'll fry you. The bastard can even sue you. And he'll collect."

"I think the guy who killed her had been stalking her," Robert said.

He was talking about Maxine.

"A couple of days before they found her propped up

against the tombstone, she had written in her diary about a break-in at her apartment," he continued. "I think the burglar and the killer are the same guy."

"You mean he knew her?"

"I don't know. Maybe. But it wasn't a heat of passion type thing. She was all cut up, but it was nice and neat, like a surgeon had done it. Surgery by Buck knife."

The coffee was ready. I filled our mugs and set them on the table.

When Robert sat down in the chair opposite the window, I noticed an unhealthy yellow tint to his skin.

"How have you been sleeping?" I asked.

I know how he is when he's obsessing about a case. He'll go entire nights without a minute's rest.

"How the hell do you *think* I've been sleeping? I just read this guy's love letter to his fiancé—telling her how great their life together was gonna be. The last letter she got from him, he told her how much he hoped they'd have a baby daughter—someone who would grow up to be as much like her as possible. I doubt if I'll get much sleep tonight."

"Tell me about the break-in."

"That was weird shit. I'm not even positive there was a break-in," Robert said. "She wrote about it being mostly just a feeling that someone had been in the apartment, screwing around with her stuff. Panties out of place in the dresser drawer, her jewelry box open when she was sure that she had closed it. That kind of thing. But the lock on her apartment door hadn't been broken, no windows were open."

I felt my stomach tilt.

Robert stopped watching the steam rise from his coffee mug, and looked at me. "Hey," he said, "what's wrong? You look funny."

"Thanks."

"I mean pale," he said, leaning toward me. "What's wrong?"

"I don't know. I feel like I might be coming down with something. It started this morning."

"I'm sorry. I've been running off at the mouth and haven't paid any attention to you. It's one of those headaches, isn't it?" he asked, meaning my migraines.

"I think so."

He stood and came around behind me—to massage the back of my neck. I thought how easily he could have wrapped his fingers around my throat; how effortlessly he could have spared me from whatever it was that awaited me. All the while he was talking, I could feel seeds of anxiety bursting into bloom in my gut. But the sense of dread that I felt—the terrible foreboding—was balanced by an undercurrent of anticipation.

Sarah and John

◆

John had wanted to pick me up at seven o'clock, but when he called to verify our date, I postponed it until eight. I wanted it to be long after sundown, dark, and the house perfect when he stepped inside—the flicker of candlelight dancing on the handblown glass vases, the stemware, the sterling silver tea set.

Bathed, powdered, and perfumed, I would be the focal point in my new white dress; the room would be my frame.

I knew that he would be punctual. At one minute before eight I heard his car in the drive, then the sound of his footfalls on the front steps. I opened the door before he rang the bell.

It plays out like a series of dreams, one after another, projected onto a giant screen in the theater of the mind—with the final scene beginning in silence, in black and white.

He hands me a small, gift-wrapped package.

"A special order," he says. "I was afraid it wouldn't arrive in time, but the fellow at the record store insisted it would. I guess this proves I should have more faith in UPS."

"What is it?" I ask, but already I have the ribbon pulled away and the paper is ripping under my eager fingers.

"It's a single piece of music by a man named Julian Cope," he tells me. "You do have a tape player, don't you?"

Sarah talks. Her mouth moves, but there is no sound.

I drop the cassette into my Magnavox and set the speaker control at the midpoint. The tape has barely begun when John walks over and turns the volume higher.

Recently I returned to Vermont, to the village of Saxtons River. I found what was left of the old house—shutters askew, windows smashed out, sections of metal roof rusting in the waist-deep grass of the front yard. I walked around to the back and up the still familiar incline to my old grove—that trinity of gnarled apple trees. All that remained of my town were a few bits of wood and pieces of metal wire casing.

At the center of the triangle formed by the trees, I brushed away the dirt, lifted a rock from its resting place, and found the knife. It was still wrapped in several layers of plastic, just as I had left it so many years ago. After the "incident," the man my mother told me to call Father had concealed it in his sock drawer. The fool. When they slept, I entered and left that house at will, and I knew where everything was kept. I had reclaimed my knife even before their wounds had healed.

He's telling me about Julian Cope, saying that this is the best work he has ever done. I've never heard of Julian Cope, at least not that I recall. Roger Waters is more to my taste, but I tell John that I love his gift, and "Julian Cope is wonderful."

"Is he new?" I ask, but immediately I see that I have made a mistake. I've seen it before—that look in his eyes, as if I have let him down. It's clear that his opinion of me rises and falls in direct relation to my knowledge, or lack thereof, of the things he cherishes.

Tonight isn't turning out as I had wished. I had wanted candlelight and compliments, perhaps a caress. And I had wanted to hear his voice, to hear him talking about himself and me and us. But the music is too loud, too disturbing. He says this noise, this piece by Julian Cope, is called "Fear Loves This Place."

I wait for it to end, watching him, following his movements around the room as he picks up the artifacts collected at auction sales and put there by my parents. I wonder if he is thinking of them as expressions of my own personality, or if he sees that they are my environment, an explanation for the woman I have become.

The thrumming of an electric bass joins the percussion. The music fills the room—the tape I bought for Sarah, the homemade dub of the one piece by Julian Cope that I wanted her to hear, the one I will leave behind for Robert to find. But the music in my mind is so much sharper, clearer. There's nothing to dilute it, no bouncing around among the knickknacks, the antiques, the debris of a life spent waiting.

He seems distracted—barely looking at me, edging away whenever I come near. What am I doing wrong?

Sarah pours wine into crystal glasses. She's wearing her hair up, enabling me to examine the lines of her neck. Her white dress has a high collar with a narrow band of embroidered birds that encircles her throat. White threads on white fabric.

Her perfume—a foul, cloying scent—seems to shrink the room, making it difficult to breathe.

He's wearing black. A silk shirt, slacks with a crisp crease, wing tips. His hair appears freshly trimmed, his cheek newly shaved. I wonder if he's wearing cologne. I hope I will soon be close enough to know.

I offer my guest a glass of white wine poured from an antique cut-glass decanter. I hope he notices how beautifully the grooves catch the light—multiplying it and reflecting it back, like a prism—turning a dozen candles into hundreds.

Sarah smiles, slices cheese, arranges the pieces on a tray. Her mouth is moving the entire time. In the beginning I had trouble seeing her, holding an image of her. She was elusive. Now I can't hear most of what she is saying, but I know that's a choice, a conscious decision, that I have made.

The music grows louder.

I smile.

I settle down on the brocade love seat near the display case filled with Chinese porcelains. I am hoping that John will come and sit beside me, but he takes the black leather chair instead.

He talks about chaos theory, Albert Camus, Vietnam. And then he tells me about the swallows on Washington Street in Boston, and I tell him about the church I attended as a child. Baptist. I went there because the music was so beautiful, especially "Amazing Grace." I always waited outside the building until services were ready to begin. Someone would pull the rope, and the bell in the tower would ring, calling the parish to worship. I loved watching all the pigeons fly out of the tower. As they scattered across the sky in every direction, it seemed as if the brass of the bell had exploded and splintered. I wondered why the birds never remembered from one Sunday to the next what would happen; why they were always taken unawares. Or maybe they did know. Maybe they accepted their role, and played it.

John moves toward the small table that holds the wine decanter.

"Let me pour it," I say.

But by the time I reach the table, I see that he wants nothing more to drink. He sets down his glass and turns toward me.

I tell Sarah, "It is exactly like a dance."

"Yes," she says, but it is a question.

"This movement of two people toward an event that they both know will happen. Choreography."

The music achieves its crescendo—Cope's pained voice fades, the tape clicks off, the chanting stops—and all is silence again.

A thousand years pass as John reaches into his pocket and withdraws a knife. Look how innocent it is. It could belong to a Boy Scout or a hunter. It's almost a toy. No murderer would own such a weapon. But he does.

Sarah's mouth isn't moving, I slip the knife from my pocket and lock the newly sharpened blade into position.

She looks, first down at the blade, then into my eyes. I know what she sees there.

I imagine my picture in tomorrow's newspaper, a headline about the horror, the grisly mess. I think of the cassette tape—and I wonder if Robert will find it. He will know that it is foreign to my taste, but will he guess that it's a gift from my killer? I wonder, too, about the bowl atop the crystal stem of John's wineglass, and the fingerprints he has left there. Will he wipe them away before he leaves—and, if he does, what will he use? A piece of the white silk slip torn from under my dress? It's a shame about the rug—ancient, handmade in Persia. So many hours of painstaking work marred with blood. If only I could fall to the left, and avoid it. I wonder if I will see Liza. Will she have grown, or will she still be an infant? I will look for her, and for Mother and Father, too. There's so much I want to tell them, and even more I want to ask.

As the hand holding the knife rises toward me, I understand perfectly.

"Maxine," she says.

"How long have you known?"

I think of that first day when he came into the shop—asking for Emily and the others. There is no protection that I could have built around myself, no way I could have avoided this night, this moment.

She doesn't resist. She extends her arm, but it is more like a gesture of invitation than alarm. I take her hand and draw her toward me, allowing her eyes to lock on mine, to study the absence of blue.

The tip of the blade makes contact with my skin, finds its place just above the band of embroidered birds. I feel it puncture my throat, then slide sideways, smooth and swift, following the direction of flight. There is no pain, only a dimming of the light and a sense of wonder.

Both carotid arteries, neatly severed.

She slumps against me, and I hold her—briefly, but tightly—before allowing gravity to claim her.

I am no longer afraid, no longer Sarah.

I feel myself turning into something small and warm and feathered. I am lifting. Rising. Soaring.

I come back to my body, but Sarah's spirit doesn't come back to hers, where it rests in an unsightly heap on the floor. Blood drips from my hands into a small pool on the Persian rug. It has a slight metallic smell with no hint of lanolin.

There is blood on my shirt, my pants, my hands. This world is awash in crimson.

I drop to one knee beside Sarah and brush a fall of hair away from the side of her face. Her profile is almost regal.

If she were alive, if someone hadn't killed her—well, it really doesn't matter. I haven't the time for speculation.

I'll help myself to one of Sarah's towels. I need a shower to wash away the day.

BOOK TWO

Lane

The call came in at 6:30 Monday morning. The victim was twenty-seven-year-old Sarah Sinclair, my partner's ex-wife. Robert Sinclair, who also happens to be my former lover, found her.

Although I'm twenty-five, I'm already assigned to Homicide. That's about five or six years earlier than anyone else in our precinct has ever made it. Robert and I have been partners since I left the academy. That's why, when he put on plain clothes and moved over to Homicide, he began a campaign to get me transferred over, too. It took six months to convince the captain that I wouldn't get in the way and that I'd be good for quotas. Robert knew both points would influence Captain Hanson far more than a recitation of my record (cases cleared, citations for superior service, etc.). Hanson would just chalk those up to the fact that I had a male partner.

In uniform, I'd been a confident cop, comfortable on the street. So far, feelings of confidence had eluded me in the cramped cubicles of Homicide. I was young, a woman, an intruder. The truth was that Homicide wasn't ready for me, and I had my own doubts about whether I could handle the job.

Robert knew that I would be at home. Weekends—from eight o'clock Friday night till seven o'clock Monday morning—we're on call. Also, I had been battling the flu. Barring a call-out for a homicide, my plans were to take aspirin, drink lots of fluids, and sleep. He phoned me direct.

"I'm out at the house," he said, then his voice broke off. I knew that something was wrong; Robert has never been the kind of guy who gets choked up.

"It's Sarah," he said. "Her throat—it's . . ."

I didn't get it at first. I thought he'd called to tell me that his ex-wife had a sore throat. Then I heard a sound, something in his voice and the way he was breathing, and I realized that he was crying, or about to.

"Jesus, Sinclair, what's going on?"

He was silent for a few seconds, then he said, "I walked in and found her. She's dead."

If a case involves family, a cop can't handle the investigation—departmental regulations. But his partner can.

"I'm on my way," I told him.

I arrived at Sarah Sinclair's house just after 7:00 A.M., several minutes ahead of the technicians, police photographer, and medical examiner. The door was open; Robert was sitting in a chair near the body, looking shell-shocked.

As soon as I saw the carnage on the floor, I walked toward him. He stood up and met me halfway. Without a word, we were in each other's arms, and I could feel his tears hot on my neck.

Both carotid arteries sliced open—as if the killer knew exactly where to cut to ensure success. It would have taken her less than two minutes to die, not necessarily from the blood loss, but because the bridge was out. No more oxygen could get to her brain.

Sarah Sinclair was prettier dead than alive. Alive, she wore that uptight, tense expression so many thin, humorless women have.

But dead, she looked serene—at peace. It didn't hurt that she was dressed up for a date. Long white dress. Her gleaming dark hair in an up-do. Wineglasses beside a half-filled decanter on a nearby table. A cassette in the tape player, with the player turned on, and the song—"Fear Loves This Place"—playing over and over. And candles burned down to puddles of wax.

I had wished this woman dead a dozen times, though not lately. It was about three years earlier when things heated up between Robert and me. He was still married, and he'd just buried his infant daughter. He took Liza's death in silence at first, pretending that nothing was different, that nothing of any significance had happened.

He was back beside me in the cruiser the day of the funeral, just a few hours after Liza was put to rest. He showed up for roll call that night just like always, and when we were alone, doing our first tour through the combat zone, he started talking about a missing fourteen-year-old we were looking for. His own daughter was dead, but all he could talk about was someone else's kid—how we had to find her before some pervert or pimp did.

It went like that for weeks, then, gradually, he opened up, telling me about Liza. He talked about going into her room just before dawn, intending to check on her and maybe touch her head or kiss her, but finding her lifeless instead, already gone, without even a tear on her cheek. He said she was just lying there in her crib, looking like maybe she was dreaming. But there was something about the stillness of her eyelids that alerted him and made him check her vitals.

I was surprised when Robert began offering those unsolicited peeks into his personal life, especially since they also involved his inner life. He had an aversion to intimacy, a need to always appear macho. I had never liked him much until he began talking to me, trusting me, telling me about Liza.

Once he got used to saying sweet things about his daughter, he started bad-mouthing his wife. Until then he had hardly ever mentioned Sarah. Most people meeting him for the first time assumed that he was single. It was as if his wife had no role in his life, no connection to anything he considered essential—although, to tell the truth, there wasn't much besides police work that mattered to him.

But when Liza died, Robert became obsessed with finding a place to lay the blame—and it was Sarah's misfortune to be the most convenient shelf.

I didn't discourage him from lashing out at Sarah. I thought sometimes that I should have. But as soon as Robert started opening up, showing me that softer side of him, the side that spoke so tenderly about his daughter, her tiny fingers and intelligent eyes, all my thoughts of him as a boorish, sexist oaf were transformed into desire. A kind of attraction that required me to act, to make some kind of move in his direction, to find out if he was feeling the same thing I was.

"So what are we going to do about this?" I asked him one night as we neared the end of our shift.

"About what?"

"The chemistry. This need to touch."

"It isn't going to happen," he said, and then he was silent.

I felt like a fool, like maybe I had only imagined his interest in me. But even while I was thinking that, I knew it wasn't so. I couldn't be that wrong about a signal as strong as the one he had been sending.

After we clocked out, he tried hurrying to his car, walking fast, several feet ahead of me. But I caught up with him and said, "Look, I'm not stopping off for a beer with you guys tonight. I'm going home."

By then I had gotten ahead of him and managed to block his path, forcing him to look at me. "I'm going to take a shower and go to bed," I told him. "You can join me or you can go home."

He tried to get around me, but I stayed right in his face. "But if you do go home," I told him, "I don't ever want to hear another word about your wife."

He maneuvered around me as if I were an annoying obstacle, and nothing more. I wasn't even certain if he had heard me.

But he followed me home.

A few months later we arrived at that same point most illicit lovers reach. When, after making love, the pain of parting started to outweigh the pleasure of being together, I knew that it was time for an ultimatum. I hated feeling like I needed a commitment. I could almost hear Robert thinking, "Right. Typical female."

But I did it anyway, and was stunned by his response: "Of course I'll tell her," he said.

I had steeled myself for rejection. But there he was, telling me that we were going to be together. Or so I thought. I should have listened more carefully. He had said that he'd *tell* Sarah about us, and that was exactly what he meant.

After his announcement, he made no move to leave her—he might still be there if she hadn't finally thrown him out. She was classy about it; wrote me a polite little note inviting me to come over and help him pack.

Robert didn't wait for my help. A day later he showed up at my apartment with a carload of survivalist magazines, hunting equipment, clothes, and seven or eight guns. It wasn't the joyful moment that I had imagined it would be. Then, about six months after his divorce was final, he returned to Sarah. Although their reunion wasn't permanent, the damage it did to me was. Things were never the same between us again.

For the most part, we ended up like all other cops who are thrown together for eight hours every workday. We got on each other's nerves, ran out of things to say, and served as living proof that familiarity really can breed contempt. The only difference between us and them was that we also slept together from time to time. But it got to where it wasn't happening very often, and when it did, we were barely able to look each other in the eye afterward. So it ended.

What was left was friendship—the indestructible kind that comes from going through a war together. Although the battles we fought were on the streets, not in some slimy jungle, they were just as deadly, and had forged a strong bond between us.

Robert

Sarah is dead.

I can barely think those words, let alone say them. But there are three more words that are even worse: Sarah was murdered.

Hours before it happened, I was sitting in my car a block away from her house, watching the front of the building. No one went in; no one came out.

I was on my own time, and in my own car, so I reached into the Styrofoam cooler on the floor in front and grabbed another beer. Of course, it wouldn't have made any difference if I'd been on duty, in uniform and in a patrol unit. When I want a brew, I have one. They know what to do with their procedure manual.

Sarah always said I had a drinking problem. She was wrong. Only time I ever had problems was when I didn't drink.

For Sarah, life was always a problem, drunk or sober. Who was the guy who said you should never sleep with a woman whose problems are bigger than your own? I should have listened to him. I knew the minute I met her she was crazy in the head. Depressed. It wasn't just a mood. It was her whole way of looking at the world. I put enough of her stories together over the years to figure out that she had been abused, and it had left her feeling worthless. But then the clouds would shift and she'd be all smiles and energy, like she'd grown up with the Brady Bunch. I never knew when I walked in the door who I'd find in the house—the happy Sarah, or the suicidal one. After a while I quit wondering or even caring.

It's a funny thing about marriage. You marry a woman and divorce her, but you never really quit thinking of her as your wife. There's a tie there, something you can't quite cut. At least that's the way it was with Sarah and me. When she told me she was seeing someone, it hit me hard. I didn't even know at first what that feeling was, but then I realized it was jealousy.

When I questioned Sarah about the shootings, I knew as soon as she started talking about this Wolf character that she was involved with him. I could see it in her eyes. The storm clouds lifted. The sun came out. She looked happy, at least as happy as a woman like Sarah can ever be.

The alley incident wasn't the only thing I wanted to talk to Sarah about that day. She knew that I was looking into some murders that I thought might be connected—young women with nothing in common except that they died violently. There weren't many, but more than a precinct our size generally racks up in the space of a year or two. We also had several women listed as missing, most of them not the type to just walk away from their lives. They had good jobs, husbands or lovers, solid reputations. It didn't make sense.

I showed up at Sarah's kitchen door late one night, blubbering about all the dead women littering the city. It was the drunkest I'd been in weeks. She let me in, made me some coffee, and listened to me go over what I knew about each case. She hated that shit. But that night she listened, and when I got to the Maxine Harris case, she recognized the victim's name. She said Harris had been in the store and had even sold some of her used books to Harry, Sarah's sleazebag boss. Just a few days before she died, Sarah had discovered one of them among her own collection—a book of poems that she had brought home from the store. Maxine Harris's name was right there on the bookplate. Sarah said that some of the lines in one of the poems were highlighted in yellow.

I wanted to see that book. On Saturday, the day before she died, I stopped by her place to get it. She wasn't there, so I parked a short distance from the house and watched—for what, I'm not sure. Maybe I thought Wolf would show up. I'd been wanting to get a look at him, to see if my hunch was right. I would have bet a year's wages that he'd be a dead ringer for Alan Carver.

Sarah came home alone. I pulled into the driveway behind her and helped her carry some packages into the house. She acted pleased to see me, but there was something about her manner that bothered me. She seemed agitated or excited, like someone who is expecting something to happen. Someone waiting for something special.

That's how she was toward the end, waiting for Liza to be born. Spacey. Kind of drifting around in her head—loopy, even. When I saw that same look in her eyes again, I knew that it was somehow tied up with Wolf and how she felt about him. It worried me because I knew the guy was a liar. Maybe worse.

When I told her that I had come for the book, she went straight to her coffee table to get it, but it wasn't there. I could see that upset her. She said it had been there just a few hours earlier, and she hadn't moved it. I could tell that she was concerned, that she really believed that someone must have taken it, but I chalked it up to her frame of mind. When we were married I had seen her do a lot of crazy things, like putting the ice cream away in the cupboard or pouring milk on her pancakes. I thought she'd probably find the book about two minutes after I walked out the door.

That's why I went back over to her place last night. I

wanted to see if she had located it yet. When I arrived, Sarah's car was in the driveway, but the house was dark. "Probably out somewhere with her undersecretary," I told myself.

I went back to my apartment, had a few beers, watched the tube, and took a nap. There was no use calling her. She always let that damn answering machine pick up her calls, even when she was at home. So, a little before midnight, I drove back over to her place to see if she was there. The house was still dark. Either she was asleep or she was out somewhere.

I kept checking back throughout the night, but the story was always the same. Then, on my fifth swing past the house, I glanced up at the porch and saw that the front door was standing wide open.

No lights on in the house. Door open. No signs of life. Something was very wrong.

I got out of the car and crossed the street, pulling my 9 millimeter as I crept up the front steps.

I stood close to the doorway with my back against the front of the house and listened. Dead silence.

A quick glance around. The place seemed deserted, so I stepped inside.

I used to call it "Sarah's museum"—a living room filled with antiques, books, and furniture that looked like it would shatter if you brushed against it. Plants to the right of the door, pictures on the wall to the left, and more antiques—small things—on a shelf next to the pictures. A strange, raucous song played softly on the tape machine. The place felt eerie, but that was nothing new.

I never have understood what happened in that house. When I left the last time, I knew I wouldn't be back to stay, but I would be back as often as I could find an excuse. Even though Sarah and I would never be together again, I'd never leave her; not totally. Lane said she understood that. I didn't.

Now there was something wrong in the house—and the cop in me was taking over, absorbing every detail of the place.

There was enough chill in the air that the furnace kicked on down in the cellar. When I heard it, I looked toward the other side of the room where the heating grate was.

Sarah was there—lying on the rug—dressed in white and, I thought, made up like a clown with a great red smile painted across her mouth. For a second I wondered why she'd be doing that, and then I saw that it wasn't a smile, and it wasn't her mouth. It was a gaping wound across her throat.

I moved sideways in the room, thinking that maybe if I looked at the picture from a different angle it would change. It didn't.

It was a joke, but Sarah didn't have that kind of sense of humor. She wouldn't put wineglasses on the table, lay out crackers, dress up, pour blood all over the carpet, and sprawl out on it.

But when I could pull my gaze away from the wound on her neck—when I could see her face, her mouth—it almost looked like she was smiling. No, not smiling, but like she was content, finished.

When the furnace blower started, the smell of death came on strong. My Sarah was beginning to decompose, to dissolve, right in front of my eyes. I backed away.

My cell phone. Who do I call?

I punched buttons until I heard Lane's voice. "Her throat," I said.

Lane was on her way, but I don't know how I knew that. I sat in one of the fragile chairs, the cellular phone in one hand and my gun in the other, staring at what was left of the child I'd met on a beach so many years ago. I was a lifeguard then, protecting swimmers. Sarah was a kid waltzing around in a sexy bathing suit making passes at the lifeguard.

Once when I was drunk I told Sarah how I hated being the guy who finds the bodies. I told her I hoped I'd never have to find hers.

God, how I wanted a drink.

Sarah used to kid me about what I liked to read—gun magazines, *Field & Stream*, *Soldier of Fortune*. I never read novels or poetry. She'd hand me that shit, but I just couldn't do it.

But I do remember something she read to me once. She was trying to teach me to like poetry. All the answers to everything were in poems, she said—all the feelings, all the thoughts, all the attitudes.

What I remember is,

> *It turns, the earth*
> *it turns with its trees, its gardens, its houses*
> *it turns with its great pools of blood*
> *and all living things turn with it and bleed*
> *It doesn't give a damn*
> *the earth*
> *it turns and all living things set up a howl*
> *it doesn't give a damn*
> *it turns*
> *it doesn't stop turning*
> *and the blood doesn't stop running.*

I was going to quote it back to her, to show her I wasn't the dunce she thought me to be. For a while I even remembered who wrote it.

But then I forgot.

And I forgot to quote it back to her.

I heard Lane come in. "Jesus Christ," she said.

"Nobody gives a damn," I told her.

Lane

My first act as officer in charge was to tell Robert to get out of the house. I radioed Fuzzy, one of the few uniforms who seems to genuinely like Robert, to come pick him up. "Take him home and stay with him," I said.

I also knew of Fuzzy's belief that the best medicine for any ailment was 100 proof and bottled by the quart. But there wasn't anything I could do about that.

The house filled up fast. Some of the cops had a reason to be there. Others were just curious. But they were all sympathetic. Even when it's an *ex*-wife, it's like a death in the family. Usually a murder scene sounds like a sick comedy club, with cops wisecracking their way through tasks that would otherwise have them in tears. But not this one. It was as quiet as a church, with all necessary conversations as subdued as prayer.

I told Miller and Towns to dust for every latent in the place, even down in the basement and up in the attic. Anything that wouldn't lift, I told them to package it in paper bags and take it in for fuming.

Hal Levinson, our resident hair and fiber expert, had a go at Sarah's dress even before Dr. Rimlin, the medical examiner, arrived. Working with his magnifying lens and tweezers, Levinson managed to fill up one whole corner of a Baggie with what he called "foreign matter of a consistent nature."

Benny did his thing with the camera, getting plenty of shots before, during, and after Rimlin's cursory examination of the body. I also had him cover the entire living room, coordinating his shots with the crime scene sketches that Sergeant Alsop was making. Then I asked Benny to do a walk-through of the house.

"I want shots of every room," I said. "From every angle."

Benny gave me a look that said I was wasting his time. "What are you looking for?" he asked.

"I don't know yet," I said. "But I don't want to find myself two weeks into this thing, thinking about what I should have done."

Benny shrugged and headed off toward the kitchen.

A little after ten, Captain Hanson showed up. As far as I could remember, that was a first. Hanson's strictly a pencil pusher, an administrator.

"Terrible thing," Hanson said, his voice barely above a whisper. "Just awful."

I nodded, watching Levinson tweeze something from Sarah's ankle.

"How's Robert doing?" Hanson asked.

"Not good. Fuzzy took him home."

"So what have we got here?"

"I wish I knew. Robert says Sarah didn't have friends, but she didn't have enemies either. Says she more or less tiptoed through life, not bothering anyone, never making waves."

"Who found her?"

"Robert. He said she had something he needed for one of his investigations—a book of some sort. He'd been over on Saturday to pick it up, but Sarah couldn't find it. When he came back to see if she had located it yet, he saw her front door standing open."

"Any sign of breaking and entering?"

I shook my head. "No, this guy was invited in. They had a little wine. Listened to some music. Indulged in a bit of romance."

Hanson arched an eyebrow. I pointed to the wineglasses and what had once been candles.

A couple of guys from the morgue were lifting Sarah and placing her on a gurney. It looked so effortless, like she didn't weigh an ounce. She was just a wisp, a feather, barely anything at all. And yet, she was the most formidable opponent I'd ever faced. So many times when Robert pulled me into his arms, I knew that he was wishing I were Sarah. And there wasn't a thing I could do about it, except get out of his way, and watch him go back to her. Trouble is, the only time he seemed to want her was when he wasn't with her.

When Hanson left, I headed for Sarah's bedroom. The bed was a four-poster. The spread was undisturbed, and there were no indentations on the feather mattress. It hadn't been slept in or sat on since the bed was made.

I flipped open Sarah's jewelry box, not certain what I expected to find there. There was an array of antique pins, some miscellaneous rings, and several pairs of earrings. I also took note of a plain gold band. Though it barely fit my pinky finger, it must have been Sarah's wedding ring.

Her dresser—an elegantly carved hunk of walnut—had three large drawers and two small ones, each filled with neatly folded personal items like slips and scarves and sweaters and socks. She kept bars of scented soap in the drawers, a flowery fragrance that I know I will always associate with her.

In her closet she had blouses hanging on the left, skirts on the right, with belts suspended from a hook on the inside of the door, and her shoes lined up on the floor. I went through the pockets of all the skirts, but came up empty—

except for a sugar packet with the name of a restaurant printed on it. Fast Eddie's.

From the top shelf of the closet, I took down several photo albums—but I put them back as soon as I saw that they contained pictures of Sarah and Robert and an infant that I knew had to be Liza.

In the drawer of the bedside table I found a black-and-white notebook, a composition book like the ones students use at school. It wasn't exactly a diary, but Sarah had been writing in it, and making some drawings. I opened it to a page at the center and began to read:

> *America. Antarctica. Europe. Asia. Australia. Africa. It pleases me that the first letter of every continent's name is the same as the last. I find such symmetry satisfying. Comforting. I was born in my parents' house, and that is where I hope to die—my life a circle, with no beginning, no end.*

"Well, Sarah, it looks like you got your way," I said. I put the notebook into my briefcase. I knew I'd want to spend some quiet time with it.

Before I left the crime scene, I told Officer Carey to seal the place and post the usual sign. Then I picked up Sarah's cordless phone and pressed the redial button.

What I heard was a woman's voice saying, "Hasty Hills Municipal Building. May I help you?"

I switched off the phone. "Carey, where's Hasty Hills?"

"Ritzy town up in Connecticut," he said.

When I stepped outside, a light rain was falling. As I walked down Sarah's steps, I noticed a guy leaning against one of the unmarked cars, staring at me. When I moved toward him, his flat gray eyes never wavered, but they seemed to change color—to a deep, cobalt blue. "Do I know you?" I said.

"Robbins," he said, pointing to the ID that was hanging

out of his jacket pocket. "DA's office. I guess I was staring. Sorry. I'm a little spaced out. I've been up for twenty-four hours straight."

"Lane Frank," I said.

"You're the lead, right?"

I nodded. "Why haven't we met before?"

"I'm filling in for one of our guys who's out sick," Robbins said. "Usually I handle white-collar stuff. My degree's in accounting. For fifteen years I've been looking at bank records. But Rafferty got the flu, and I inherited his homicide."

Now *I* was staring. Robbins had the most piercing eyes I'd ever seen. He looked about forty, dark hair flecked with gray, well built.

"Something wrong?" he asked.

"No," I said. "I must've seen you around. You do look a little familiar. Anyone brief you?"

"I'm all set for the time being," he said. "If I have any questions I'll call."

I watched as Robbins pushed himself off the car and walked away down the street.

"It's all sealed up, Detective," Carey said from behind me.

"Oh, thanks, Carey."

"I'll leave one of my boys here, too."

I was nodding, turning back to the street, wondering where to begin.

Robert

Fuzzy Lannehan was directing traffic when I was a kid. He's a sergeant in the uniform division, but he still likes to get out in front of a school in the morning and wave his arms. He's probably the only uniform cop I get along with.

Besides stopping a line of cars and blowing his whistle, the other thing Fuzzy's always been good at is locating and drinking good whiskey. He led me out of Sarah's house and down to his patrol unit.

He hit his lights, but not the siren, as he directed the cruiser into traffic. Then he reached under his seat and produced a bottle.

"Crack that open, Bobby," he said, handing me a sealed fifth of premium Irish whiskey. "It's good for whatever ails you."

I took a long swallow and felt the heat in the back of my throat. My eyes watered and I coughed.

"Take it easy," Fuzzy said. "That ain't like the piss you drink all the time."

I sipped and leaned back in the seat, feeling the heat

spread through my neck and up into my head. "Did you see her, Fuzzy?"

"No, son. I didn't."

When my father died, Fuzzy Lannehan was the only constructive influence left in my life. He kept me out of juvenile hall. He also talked me into going into law enforcement. And Fuzzy had been at our wedding—the only cop there.

"You got any words of wisdom?" I asked him.

"I said 'em all when I handed you that Irish."

"You want a hit off this?"

"You know I don't drink in uniform."

I did know that. Fuzzy could drink most guys under the table, but for all the years I'd known him, I never saw him violate department policy.

I took another swallow and closed my eyes. The picture of Sarah in her sea of blood returned.

"Shit," I said.

"It's just starting, Bobby," Fuzzy said. "Be a while before it goes away—if it ever does."

He parked at the hydrant in front of my apartment building. Once we were upstairs, Fuzzy stripped to his skivvies, and grabbed a pair of my jeans and a baggy flannel shirt off the floor. He was my height, but had about fifty pounds on me—most of it right behind the belt buckle. He zipped the jeans as far as he could, allowed the shirt to billow out over his gut, then found himself a glass and a couple of ice cubes. I handed him the bottle and he poured enough of the Irish to cover the ice.

"You live in filth," he said.

He always said that. It was a ritual every time he came to my place. It was also true.

He handed the bottle back and we both drank.

"When my Monica died, I thought it was the end of everything," he said. "In a way, maybe it was. But I had to go on. I still had one kid at home. I had to work. I had to have a life. But it wasn't easy, Bobby. And it won't be easy for you."

"It isn't like that," I said, thinking at the same time that maybe it was. "Sarah and I already had different lives. Hell, we had different lives when we were still together. It's just that I don't want to think of her the way I found her, but there isn't any way around it. I don't want to think of her dead. I don't want to start to go over there and realize I can't."

Fuzzy nodded, drowning his ice in Irish again.

"We had a crazy life together," I told him, "and we had a crazy life when we weren't together."

There was a knock at the door.

"This'll be Hanson," Fuzzy said as he went to let the captain in.

"Himself," I said. "Think he'll read me my rights?"

Hanson is one of those cops who knows he's going to be captain the day he writes his first parking ticket. He knows it because he's already made a list of all the asses he has to kiss to get there. It has nothing to do with being a good cop—which Hanson isn't and never has been. It's politics.

He also wants five copies of everything. Fuzzy says the captain is the only guy he knows who uses five-ply toilet paper.

Hanson shook my hand, said how sorry he was, and apologized because there were a few questions he had to ask. It was all routine until he asked me why I was at Sarah's house in the first place—what had brought me there so early in the morning.

"I'd been there several times throughout the night, looking for her," I said. "It had to do with a case I'm working."

Hanson looked skeptical, but I didn't give a shit.

"You getting anything from the scene?" Fuzzy asked.

"They were just getting started when I left. Detective Frank's in charge. She'll be in touch."

Hanson started for the door, then stopped. "One last thing," he said. "Before you get too far into that bottle, Lanehan, move the cruiser off the hydrant."

"Right, Captain," Fuzzy said, and followed Hanson out.

When Fuzzy came back upstairs, we had a couple more drinks, then he changed back into his uniform and left.

I was alone. I also *felt* alone, and it bothered me. I didn't finish the bottle, but I'd had enough so that it served as an anesthetic. I was finally numb enough to say it aloud: "Sarah is dead."

I walked around the place practicing saying the words, getting used to them. I stepped over piles of clothes, newspapers, yesterday's boxes from Chinese take-out, chanting, "Sarah is dead." I wanted the words to stop being a feeling; wanted them to become just a sound.

The picture wouldn't fade—Sarah on the floor of her living room, in a blood-red frame.

Then I said the next set of words. "Sarah was murdered."

That brought another picture into focus: the man I knew as Alan Carver standing in the interrogation room, looking down at his expensive watch.

But this time I was emptying a fourteen-shot clip into his face.

I hate funerals. But my being Sarah's ex-husband made me the closest thing to a relative she had, so I made the arrangements. I decided on a memorial service at a small Unitarian church a couple of blocks from Sarah's house, and I wanted to get it over with as soon as possible. I put a notice in the morning paper on Tuesday, in case anyone wanted to attend.

I don't remember much from the service. Sheila from the massage parlor wobbled in on a pair of spike heels, tripping over the carpet. She was wrapped tight in black spandex pants, complete with stirrups, and a flowered orange blouse struggling to cover her chest. She was also carrying a guitar case.

"This is turning into a fucking freak show," I muttered to Fuzzy.

Captain Hanson showed—his malleable, political face baggy and full of sorrow, or the residue of a hangover. I figured he'd be disappointed that he wouldn't get to present a flag to anyone.

When it was my turn to speak, Fuzzy hit me with his elbow. I knew it was coming, but I hadn't thought about it. I had no idea what I was going to say. I went up there and stood and looked down at the floor. "We were divorced," I said. "I think we were closer friends after we split up than during the time we were together."

I looked out at the almost empty room. I could feel the tears forming in my eyes. I never for a minute thought that I'd cry, but the tears did start rolling down both sides of my face.

So many different things went through my mind—stupid little events in our lives. They didn't seem at all important at the time.

My face was wet when I sat back down. Then I heard the guitar, and what sounded to me like the most beautiful voice in the world. Sheila's eyes were closed. Her fingers seemed to find all the right strings by themselves. I recognized the song. I'd never thought much about it—just an old, slow song.

So we
Rise on the wind
Like weakened sparrows
Going home . . .

Sheila just sat there with her guitar and whatever she was thinking. Fuzzy was wiping his eyes with a dirty handkerchief he kept in the inside pocket of the only sport jacket he owned. It was over.

And as I walked out into the sunlight, I knew that it was just beginning.

Lane

I didn't like my last view of Robert, with Fuzzy leading him off to a bottle of booze. I grew seriously concerned when, two days later, he wasn't answering his phone.

I had to talk to him. When Hanson left the crime scene on Monday, he said he was going to catch up with Robert and Fuzzy. He didn't want me questioning my own partner, and elected himself to do it. According to all the textbooks, Robert was the prime suspect. Ex-husband. Discovered the body. Tons of emotional baggage. Quick temper. Heavy drinker. But life isn't a textbook. Anyone who knew Robert knew he didn't do it.

Even so, we had to go through the formalities. Hanson did that. But in his report, which I had just finished reading, he had written one alarming word: suicidal.

I went over to Robert's apartment and was relieved when I heard signs of life on the other side of his door. It sounded like he was dismantling the place.

It didn't take long to establish that Robert had no intention of opening the door for me, so I opened it myself. I've been studying karate since I was four. Except for matches at the gym, I've seldom had to use it. When I do resort to it in hand-to-hand combat, my opponent thinks, for a moment, that I'm asking him to dance. More than one crackhead has done a double take, then stopped to see what my next move will be. And that's when I strike. I've been told that it's a beautiful thing to behold: the graceful lift and dart of my leg, the fall of my victim—it's like a ballet of broken bones. But since I left street patrol, I don't get much chance to show it off. Homicide investigations tend to be passive, with hours spent staring at the same reports, hoping that something new will appear on the page.

Once I got the door out of the way, the first thing I noticed was the mess. Empty cardboard cartons and crushed beer cans all over the floor. Wadded-up bags that looked as if they had once held pretzels or potato chips. Some cheese dip drying in a dish. Cigarette butts everywhere, some in an ashtray, but most just dropped on the floor. The drapes were pulled shut, giving the place a midnight feel even though it was noon. And there were fragments of his tape deck scattered all over the floor.

Robert stood there, looking at me through unfocused eyes, as if daring me to take one step in his direction. He was holding a hammer.

"Look," I told him. "I need you to sober up, and fast. I'm going to clear this case, and you're going to help me do it."

He swayed a bit, like a spring was loose, but I thought I saw him nod.

"Good," I said. "I need to know everything you've got on a guy named Alan Chadwick."

"Never heard of him," Robert said, digging another Old Milwaukee out of the box.

"Come on, Robert. Think. Chadwick. Lives in Hasty Hills."

"I'm telling you I don't know the guy."

"His prints turned up at Sarah's house."

If you ever want Robert's complete—and sober—

attention, just hand him a piece of evidence. It's amazing. He can be falling down drunk one second, and stone-cold sober the next.

"So what does it mean?" he asked.

"You tell me. We ran the latents picked up at the house, but all we got were yours, hers, and his. When we put his prints through the national search, we got the match in Connecticut. There's no criminal record. His prints are on file because he works for the government. The guy's an MD."

"What kind of jobs are there in government for a doctor?"

"He's a medical examiner. I've tried to reach him, but there's something wrong with his phone. A recorded message comes on saying the line's being checked for trouble."

I handed him a Post-it note with Chadwick's address. "I want you to check it out," I said.

He rubbed at the two days' growth on his chin. I knew he was planning out the rest of his day: shower, shave, coffee, Chadwick. Having him follow up a lead was the quickest way I knew to get Robert to rejoin the living.

It was a strange thing about Chadwick's prints. They didn't turn up in just those locations where a burglar or a garden variety murderer would leave them—on her body, in her jewelry box, or on the doorknob. They were on her magazine covers, in her lingerie drawer, on her geranium pot, even on a business card from some antique shop over in Landgrove. You name it—Chadwick had touched it. The way I saw it, our reclusive Sarah had invited someone new into every aspect of her life.

Robert

◆

Lane timed her arrival perfectly.

She got to my front door just as the hammer came down on the metal cabinet of the Sony tape deck. It made a satisfying noise and a dent, but nothing shattered.

I swung again, this time at the front of the machine. Plastic shattered, the sound of the music wobbled, and the deck crashed into the wall behind the shelf.

Lane kept knocking, and I kept ignoring her, wielding my hammer.

The third blow killed it, but I didn't stop there. I don't know how many times I smashed the thing, but I was hammering away long after "Fear Loves This Place" had died.

I remember killing wasps when I was a kid. I'd been stung a few times when I was down at the coal pier diving off the tower. I always swelled up and ached all over, so whenever I had the chance, I killed wasps. And I didn't just swat them, kill them, and leave it at that. I ground them into nothing, repeatedly twisting my shoe on them until there was less than dust. At those times, I could feel my heart going wild in my chest. I wasn't a sadist. I was just terrified, and proving it—with overkill.

I was still beating on the fragments of the cassette when Lane started yelling at me to open the door.

"Nobody's home," I said.

"What are you doing in there? Robert, please open up."

"Go away."

"I can't hear you. Open the door."

"I said, 'Go away.' "

Then the apartment door crashed open and was left hanging by one tentative hinge.

"I'm not impressed," I told her. "You gotta pay for that door."

Bone tired, I rocked on my feet.

"How long are you going to hole up, getting blitzed and feeling sorry for yourself?"

"Wrong," I said.

"Then what the hell *are* you doing?"

She was wearing jeans and a dark blue sweatshirt, standing in front of me with her hands on her hips—all six feet of her. Lane was a woman and a half. A gorgeous one, too—with her auburn hair tied back in a ponytail, and zero makeup on her perfect olive skin.

"I think I'm afraid," I told her.

I glanced quickly at her, then back at the can in my hand. I took another swallow. "Have a beer. Sit down."

"I don't get it," she said.

She grabbed an Old Milwaukee and sat on the overstuffed chair.

The day I found Sarah, my whole body went rubbery. I couldn't even talk. I blamed myself. I blamed her. And I blamed her again for Liza. I hated Sarah—especially that almost serene expression on her face as she lay there in her own blood.

To get through it, I downed just enough alcohol to maintain a permanent buzz, let me sleep a few hours, wake up, and wander around the mall.

I'd been over everything I could remember about the last few conversations we had. Wolf. Carver. Wallingford. Two dead guys in an alley.

My head was a mess. None of this stuff made any sense. Sarah met a guy at work. He pulled a gun on two would-be robbers. A few days later they get blown away by someone with a .38 in an alley across the street from the bookstore. Sarah's Wolf, who isn't Wolf, sends Carver, who isn't Carver, over to the precinct house with a .32 and a line of patter about diplomatic immunity, which, of course, he wouldn't need if he didn't break any laws. But Wolf is Wallingford, Sarah says. Antiques. Landgrove.

Save me a rubber room.

Last night, in my wandering, I drifted into a music store. I wasn't looking for anything. It was well lit in there—lots of people. And there was the tape. "Fear Loves This Place." It was on an album by a guy named Julian Cope.

"I never used to mind being alone," I told Lane.

This shitty apartment was my home. I could fall into the overstuffed chair with a six-pack and watch the Knicks dismantle the Celtics. I could get Rush Limbaugh on the radio and crank it up. Or I could sit in silence, maybe watch the lights come on as the city went dark.

"When I played the tape, that was the first time I thought about him—thought about what he did to Sarah. *Really* thought about it."

I played that one song over and over. I went from buzzed to blitzed. And then my heart started going like it would when I was a kid killing a wasp.

"Fear," I said. "I'm fucking useless. I can't be involved in the case. I know that. And I'm on leave. But I couldn't anyway. Fear."

Lane put her beer can on the table and stood up. "Whenever you sober up, we need to talk. I need information from you, and I've got some things I need you to do in an unofficial capacity."

She started for the door.

"Lane, listen to this."

I pushed the play button on my answering machine.

"Detective Sinclair," the voice said. "Have you finished with my materials? I've finished with yours. It's necessary for me to be out of town for a while, but when I get back, let's do lunch."

There was a long pause, then the voice again. "Please don't doubt me. I always keep my promises."

"Who is that?" Lane asked. "When did it come in?"

"It must have been last night when I was out. I didn't notice it until this morning."

She played the message again.

"English accent?"

"I wanted to question him about the double shooting. When he showed up at the precinct he said his name was Alan Carver, and he was representing the undersecretary, John Wolf, of the British Embassy. But there isn't any John Wolf."

"You've met this guy?"

I finished off my can of beer. "Yeah. I've met him."

She took the tape from the machine. "Did you file a report?"

"It's in my desk. Open cases. Wolf."

"Get yourself together, Robert. I want to see you tomorrow morning. I'll make sure this gets logged into evidence," she said, pocketing the tape.

"I'm on compassionate leave," I reminded her.

"In my office, or I'll come back over here after you," she said.

Lane was gone. I was alone again—just me and the debris I had created. And Lane's debris. I opened another beer.

I remember the night before Sarah and I got married. We sat on the porch at her parent's house and planned the future. We talked until after midnight. Then we went inside to separate rooms. Sarah's mother didn't want us sleeping together until after the ceremony. Or was that Sarah's wish? God, she was so unknowable.

I have to pick up her photograph and stare at it to be able to see her. If I try to picture her in my mind, all I see is a white blur wreathed in blood.

I grabbed my jacket and the box of beers and headed out of the apartment. I pulled the door into a closed position behind me, knowing that any five-year-old could do a B&E on the place if he wanted to.

I was thinking about the medical examiner from Connecticut. What were his prints doing all over Sarah's house? It seemed like a good time to ask Dr. Chadwick that question.

I managed to find my car, which was parked illegally on the street. At least Lane hadn't given me a ticket. As I drove toward the interstate, headed north for Hasty Hills, I scanned the stations for talk radio. I locked into one where a caller was saying, "They're not telling us anything. All these women are murdered or missing, and the police are saying they don't have any reason to think they're connected. I think they are connected, and I think they have a responsibility to tell us what we need to know in order to protect ourselves."

"There isn't any way to protect yourself," I told her.

The host said, "Captain Hanson held a press conference this morning, as most of you listening probably know. Let me just read you something from that. He was asked a question—a direct question—about Maxine Harris and Sarah Sinclair, the woman who worked in the bookstore where a source has revealed Maxine Harris *shopped*—and this is what Captain Hanson had to say. 'At this time we have no reason to consider these cases related, although we are looking at all possibilities. There is no reason to panic. Our investigation is ongoing.' Not much comfort in *that*, is there? We have another caller on the line."

I'm still driving the old beat-to-shit Ford I bought when Sarah and I were together. She laughed at the car. "Eight hundred bucks," I told her. "It's only got sixty-three thousand miles on it. This thing will go forever."

It's over 120,000 now, and still going. Why is it so important that I was right, and that Sarah was wrong? Maybe I needed Sarah to be wrong, to know nothing of the practical things in life, so she'd need me. Maybe that's it.

"I don't know much about serial killers other than what I see on TV," the caller said.

"Welcome to the club," I said.

"They must be sick to do what they do. If they're that crazy, why can't the police spot them?"

"They have to be incredibly sick," the host agreed, "but, from what I've read—and that's not a whole lot—these killers, these *savages* really—believe it or not, they look and act and talk and walk just like the rest of us. They go shopping, pay their bills, join a softball team, get out the votes for the local Democratic party. I had to get that last one in. Couldn't resist it. Theodore Bundy, who killed thirty or forty young women, worked for the re-election of Washington governor Dan Evans."

"Evans is a Republican, shithead," I said.

"That's probably a poor example because Dan Evans is a Republican, but you catch my drift. These guys are hard to spot."

I took the Hasty Hills exit and drove slowly through the quiet little town, down the main street, past the municipal building, and on out into the country. After about three miles I found the place I was looking for—third house on the left after the covered bridge. Except there wasn't any house. Just a crater.

I parked across the street from the yellow crime scene tape and got out of the car. I approached a local constable who had been left to guard the area, and flashed my badge. He looked at the can of Old Milwaukee.

"Off duty," I said. "What happened out here?"

"Doc Chadwick's place," he said. "Was in the Barngreve family for years before Doc bought it. Fire marshal's been all over it. The bomb squad from the city—and some boys from Alcohol, Tobacco and Firearms. Monday morning it just went up. You could hear it clear into town. They found part of a jawbone, but they ain't said it was Doc yet."

The radio in his cruiser squawked and he went to see what was what.

When he walked back toward me, he said, "I've got a ten-fifty with possibly injury out on Fury Road. Stay back from that edge, now. You drink enough of those things, we'll be pulling *your* jawbone out of there."

The constable drove off to tend to his automobile accident.

I slipped under the tape and skirted the edge of the chasm. I don't know what I expected to find. Probably nothing, but I had to look.

I was just starting to move around the lip of the crater toward what remained of the garden when I saw an old man with a cane walking past my Ford. He was headed in my direction.

"Don't get too close to the edge," I called out to him.

"Just taking my walk," he said. "I don't see very well, but I can smell it just fine."

As he drew nearer I could see that he was crippled in some way, and was wearing heavily tinted glasses.

"Arthritis," he said, as if he were reading my mind. "And cataracts. When I get close up like this, I can see pretty good. The doctor says I have to take my walks, but with all the trucks and cars up here the last few days, I went the other way. Too much trouble. Name's Henry. I live down the hill there."

"Robert Sinclair," I said, extending my hand.

"Police?"

"City."

"Why you boys coming all the way out here? Over the state line, and all."

"Curiosity," I said.

"Big bang."

"You heard it?"

"Monday morning," he nodded. "Doc's dead, I guess."

"Constable says they're not sure about that. Did you know Doc Chadwick?"

"Oh, yes. Neighbors for—what?—five, six years? Fine man. Good conversationalist. Intelligent. Of course, I never could understand him doing the work he did."

"Ever meet any of his friends?"

"Doc kept pretty much to himself. I don't remember any friends of his, or any people at all going in and out of his place. Only thing we ever talked about, really, was the old alma mater."

When I didn't say anything, he added, "Harvard. Only thing we had in common. Except he went on to the medical school, of course, and I was in literature."

I nodded, hoping he'd go on, tell me more about Chadwick. But Henry had other plans.

"Well," he said, "I've got to walk on now. Pleasure meeting you, Robert."

"Careful as you go, Henry," I said, watching him start down the hill.

As I was driving back toward the city, I reached for a beer. I hadn't realized how tired I was, or how drunk. I thought I saw Sarah in the road—just standing there, wearing that white dress, looking at me that way she always did. If I'd been in the desert, it would have been a mirage. But out there, on a Connecticut road, it was a ghost. And as long as I was drunk enough to see it, I was drunk enough to swerve to avoid hitting it.

The last thing I remember about my trip to Hasty Hills is the car crashing through a guardrail, headed toward a stand of white birch trees. More ghosts.

Lane

When I left Robert's place, I returned to Sarah's neighborhood, hoping to catch some of the residents who'd been gone when I made my first two visits to the area.

This was tedious work. No one had heard anything. No one had seen anything. Most people just wanted to tell me how horrible it all was, how they'd watched Sarah grow up before their eyes, and now she was gone, and so young, with so much ahead of her, and wasn't it awful about her little daughter, too.

I lost count of how many worried women asked me to recommend a good lock or an affordable gun. One couple said they put their house on the market as soon as they heard.

I parked in Sarah's driveway, and had just gotten out of my car when I noticed a woman—one I hadn't been able to question yet—across the street, waving at me and saying something, which I couldn't hear. I walked over.

"I was trying to tell you that Miss Sinclair isn't home," the woman said.

"I know. I'm Detective Frank," I told her, showing her my shield.

"Terrible thing about Sarah. Have you caught the one who did it?"

"Not yet, but we're working on it. I don't suppose you saw anything out of the ordinary over the weekend—any prowlers or strangers?"

"You mean at Miss Sinclair's house? Oh no. She was the only one who was ever around there. Very solitary. Kept to herself."

I gave one of my cards to the woman. "Well, if you happen to think of anything, would you mind giving me a call?"

She assured me that she would and I was about to walk back down her front steps when she said, "Of course, there was that man the other day."

I stopped.

"What man?"

"The one sitting in his car, watching her house on Saturday. He was parked back a little ways, over there. I remember it was in the afternoon because my sister always calls me between two and five o'clock, to make sure I've taken my heart pills. After we got off the phone, I looked out my window again and saw that he was still there."

"Do you remember what he looked like?"

"I didn't get a good look at him at all. His windshield was filthy. And I don't know one kind of car from another. But I have something that might help."

She disappeared into her house. When she returned several minutes later, she was carrying a piece of scrap paper. "Here," she said, handing it to me. "I wrote down his license plate number. Just in case."

When I got back to my car, I scribbled down the few notes that might require some additional footwork.

"Frustrating case?" a man's voice asked just behind me.

I whipped my head around to see the DA's investigator.

"Oh. You startled me. Robbins, right?"

"Yes. Sorry," he said. "I was in Sinclair's and noticed you were out here."

"Get anything from the scene?" I asked him.

I didn't know what was distracting me more—Robbins's eyes, or his silent approach behind me.

We walked to a diner at the end of the block.

"No, but I've been thinking of the woman in the cemetery. Harris. It seems like these killers follow a pattern. I've read some of the books—the true crime stuff. You're gonna think I'm crazy, but it's almost like you can plot what they do. Where. When. How they kill. There's a logic to it."

"What does the logic tell you?" I asked.

"That there's somebody else on his list. That's easy. But who?"

Robbins reached into his jacket pocket and handed me a book—*Hunting Humans*—by Elliott Leyton. "Read it. Like I said, this isn't my bailiwick. Then again, maybe I've just given you the answer to who's next."

On my way back to the precinct, I called in the plate number that the old lady had given me. By the time I arrived, a printout was sitting on my desk. The plate belonged to Robert Sinclair.

When I got the call from Fuzzy, three hours later, I was still trying to figure out what my partner had been up to, keeping his ex-wife under surveillance only a day before her death.

"Sinclair's been in an accident," he said. "He'll live, but he's got some injuries. You'll find him in St. Paul's ER."

I'd been going all day on nothing but coffee and about ten minutes' sleep. I figured the doctors and nurses could do a lot more for Robert than I could at the moment, and besides, the woman who answered the phone in the ER said that Robert had been transferred to a room on one of the regular med floors. Not intensive care. He was going to be fine.

I thought about going home, grabbing a nap, showering, getting into some fresh clothes, then following up on a couple of loose ends. But I was even too tired to make the drive. I knew that I had something worse than the standard flu. I'd already been through the aches and pains, and the low-grade fever. I decided to stretch out on the couch in the women's rest room, my makeshift bed for the past two nights.

Even though I was exhausted, I didn't fall asleep right away. There was something nudging at the back of my mind, something I couldn't identify—but it made me nervous. And I felt a whirlpool in my stomach, just like I always do when I realize that I'm in over my head.

When I was in college, I watched as most of my classmates prepared for careers in making money. A few of my friends had a different idea. They wanted to teach, or work as community organizers—to contribute something to the quality of other people's lives by improving "the social order." I figured that somebody had to help maintain what order there was if things even had a prayer of getting any better, and I loved the idea of living in a *real* city for a couple of years. The NYPD had a high staff turnover rate, and they were quota conscious, so I called a family friend, Ray Bolton, a detective in Boston.

"You're crazy, and your father will kill me," Ray said.

"Two years and I'll be in grad school," I swore.

So he called a friend in New York, wrote a glowing recommendation for me, and I got the job. Because I'd been on the college track team, I was in better shape than most of the male applicants—also taller—and I'd known how to handle weapons since before I got my first driver's license. It seemed like a natural—something that was right. And, the years I spent in uniform *were* right. I was a good street cop. Quick on my feet, and capable in a confrontation.

But then I followed Robert over to Homicide, and it's

been one frustration after another. I don't think I'm cut out for the mind games that murder demands.

I was in a blurry, floaty fugue—with half my brain cells drifting off to sleep and the other half wide awake, wired, and ready to go. I needed to sleep, to get my head clear—but something still nagged at me, trying to emerge from the fog in my brain. The harder I tried to remember what it was, the more elusive it became. Just as I was giving up the struggle, succumbing to sleep, it hit me. John Wolf. The shootout in the alley. I hadn't checked Robert's file.

I got up and walked down the hallway, back to Homicide. Robert has status: his own phone and his own desk. As it turned out, he also had everything put away, and all his drawers were locked.

I grabbed a paper clip from the communal desk just outside Robert's cubicle and, by unbending it and maneuvering the tip just so, I was able to get two of the drawers open: the wide one in the middle, and the bottom drawer where he kept his file folders.

The middle drawer had nothing in it but two ball point pens, some rubber bands, a telephone message from two Julys ago, and the caps off a dozen beer bottles.

But the bottom drawer held exactly what I was looking for: the dossier on the fictitious Mr. Wolf. I read through all the material—including Robert's report, which was more confusing than helpful. But one note penciled on the file cover did catch my attention: "Check Wallingford."

I went down to the evidence room, retrieved the business card for Wallingford Antiques that I had found at Sarah's—the one with Chadwick's prints on it—and returned to Robert's cubicle so that I could give Mr. Wallingford a call. A woman answered with a simple hello, no company name.

"Is this Wallingford Antiques?" I asked.

There was a pause before the woman said, "Well, yes. But the store is closed."

"What are your hours?"

"No, I mean closed. Out of business."

"Could you please tell me how to reach Mr. Wallingford?"

It sounded like muffled sobs on the other end of the line.

"I guess I've called at a bad time," I said.

"I'm sorry. It's just that my brother John—Mr. Wallingford—has passed away and I . . ." With that, the woman broke down again.

I could hear the phone being passed to someone else, then a male voice said, "May I help you?"

"Apparently not," I said. "I was hoping to speak with Mr. Wallingford."

"I'm his brother-in-law. Are you calling about the ad that was in the newspaper?"

"The ad?"

"The shop we have for sale?"

Sounded good to me. "Yes," I said. "I was wondering if I could stop by and see it."

Wallingford's brother-in-law gave me the address and assured me that it wouldn't matter how late I arrived. They'd be there long after midnight, packing up the items that his wife wanted to keep.

As I hung up the phone, I realized that I was floundering, no closer now to solving Sarah's murder than when I walked into her living room and found Robert looking so sad and so lost. Nothing was adding up. Leads that looked like they might go somewhere ended up right back where they began—like that license plate that had come back to Robert. What did it mean? I was yearning for street duty. That feeling of competence I used to have.

So I did what I always do when I feel most lost. I wrote to a forensic psychiatrist—a man for whom I have the most profound respect. He's prematurely retired, living in a cabin in northern Michigan—where he heats with wood and draws water from a well, yet remains connected to the rest of the world via a Group III fax machine.

He is twice my age, with an IQ that sometimes seems to be triple mine. He insists that he likes people, but I've heard him speak highly of only two or three who are now living.

His heroes tend to be long-departed legends like Milton Erickson, Yeats, Lenny Bruce, and John Lennon. He was in love, once, with a woman named Savannah, but she left him years ago to live on another continent—where she pursues her interest in wildlife. She's a veterinarian, and also his wife, though he hears from her only once each year, on their anniversary.

In the four years since he walked out of his Boston office, never to return, he has refused even to look at case files that are routinely sent to him—the Unabomber, the Tamiami prostitute murders, a series of child killings in California.

Investigators can't believe—or accept—that a profiler of his stature could drop out of the law enforcement loop and mean it. They can understand the need for a temporary rest, a time-out from all the psychos and sickos that kept turning up in his in box uninvited, but no one with such a magical gift could simply close up shop forever. Profiling is in the blood—a skill that takes command of the one who possesses it, giving him no choice but to keep on keeping on. Or so investigators have thought, and hoped, in his case.

But I know better. I know his resolve, and I understand his motivation. It's a matter of survival. He fears that if he opens his mind to one more killer, there'll be no more room for himself. And he's afraid that he'll lose touch with that other side of life—the one he sees in nature, hears in music, and feels whenever the one person he loves most in the world is near.

I know this because I *am* that one person—his daughter, his only child. I also know what his work has done to him, how the lives of the damned have invaded his mind, distorted his reality, turned his dreams into nightmares. That's why I'm always reluctant to ask for his help. I hate the thought of pulling him back into the quicksand that so nearly swallowed him. But this time I had to ask. I had wronged Sarah, and felt that I owed her something. Maybe it was too late for me to apologize for sleeping with her husband, but—with my father's help—I could at least put away her killer.

This is what I faxed to my father:

TO: Pop
FROM: Lanie
Sorry to bring murder to your doorstep again, but, I need help. The victim is a white 27-year-old divorcee, Sarah Sinclair (decree final about two years ago; ex-husband is a 35-year-old homicide investigator; their only child died in infancy).

She was found on the floor of her living room with both carotid arteries cut. I observed, and the medical examiner remarked, that there appeared to be surgical precision—clean, accurate, effective, with the cutting sufficient to do the job, but no overkill.

I noted no obvious after-the-fact display as far as the body was concerned, and all swabs were negative for semen.

Nothing in the house seemed to be disturbed. There were empty wineglasses on a nearby table, beside a partially filled decanter. Candles throughout the room were burned down to nothing.

A tape player was turned on. The music was by a guy named Julian Cope; the piece was "Fear Loves This Place"—which the victim's husband insists would not have been part of her music library. She preferred performers more along the lines of Leonard Cohen, whoever he is.

The only prints in the house belonged to: a) the victim, b) her ex-husband, and c) Dr. Alan Chadwick, an ME from Connecticut, about whom the ex-husband knows nothing. Considering where his prints were found (even in her lingerie drawer), it's my guess that Chadwick was Sarah's secret lover. Maybe he's married, or maybe she was just afraid of what her ex might do if she told him. There is some evidence the ex was watching her house; perhaps stalking her. A neighbor saw him parked nearby on the afternoon preceding the murder.

It may or may not be important to also mention that the ex-husband said the victim was dressed in an uncharacteristic style. While normally she chose conservative, tailored two-piece outfits, such as skirts and blouses, the evening of her death she was wearing an ankle-length white crocheted dress, Victorian in style.

The ex-husband also said that he had seen her hair in an up-do only twice: the day they married, and when he found her body.

The victim worked as a salesclerk in an antiquarian bookstore located in a high crime area. She also had significant income from a trust fund set up by her deceased parents. She had recently been an aural witness to a double murder, a shooting near her place of employment. It's also interesting that she had recently befriended a gentleman who pulled a gun on the victims of that double homicide just a few days before they were killed. Sarah witnessed the incident with the gun, which took place inside the bookstore where she was employed.

In the course of investigating the double homicide, the ex-husband learned that the gentleman with the gun was not who he said he was. Efforts are now under way to pin down a positive ID.

The only other thing I have is an estimated time of death for the woman: sometime between 7:30 P.M. and 9:30 P.M. on the evening before her body was discovered.

As usual, Pop, I am thanking you in advance for any guidance you can provide.

P.S. Had a note from Mom three days ago. She said to tell you that she's well and misses you.

P.P.S. It must be genetic—because I'm also well, and miss you. As always, I love you.

After running that through the department's fax, I folded the originals and tucked them into my briefcase. Then I drove to the hospital to find out if Robert's meeting with Chadwick had produced anything worthwhile.

They had put him on the third floor, right next to the elevators. At least that's where his room was; Robert was nowhere in sight.

A nurse, passing by the open doorway, glanced into the room, saw me staring at Robert's empty bed, and said, "He's down in radiology. Can I get you a cup of coffee?"

I looked at my watch. It was well past suppertime and I hadn't yet had breakfast or lunch. "Yes," I said. "I'd appreciate that."

The nurse returned and said, "There seems to be a problem."

"Robert?" I asked.

"Don't be alarmed. He hasn't taken a turn for the worse, or anything. At least not as far as I know."

"What do you mean?"

The woman was obviously upset. "We seem to have lost Detective Sinclair," she said. "The orderly took him down for a CAT scan, but they weren't ready for him. So Detective Sinclair was left in his wheelchair, in the hallway. But when the technician came out to get him, the chair was there—and, well—"

"Never mind," I said. "I get the picture."

If I knew Robert, he was off chasing a lead. This wasn't exactly the way partners are supposed to work a case—each guessing what the other is up to. But that's what you get when you choose to work with a guy who's been ordered off the case, and is a suspect himself.

"What was he wearing?" I asked, trying to figure what the odds were that he had left the hospital.

"We got him some surgical scrubs. He said he wasn't putting on a dress for anybody, not even the surgeon general."

That was Robert all right.

"Is he going to be in trouble out there?" I asked. "In his condition, is it safe for him to be out there alone?"

"We don't know yet how extensive his injuries are."

"What was the CAT scan supposed to show?"

"Whether or not he has a subdural hematoma."

For the first time, fear set in. "What can that do to a person?" I asked.

"He could lose his memory. Pass out. Even die," she said. "Or he could be fine. He may just have a bump on the head."

I was still trying to decide if I should put out an all-points bulletin on him when the phone rang.

"Robert Sinclair's room," I said.

I heard a familiar voice, "I thought you might be there."

It was Robert.

"Where are you?"

"J. C. Penney's," he said.

"What?"

"The department store. I had to get rid of these green pajamas. They're having a sale."

"Robert—" I started.

"Jeans for twenty bucks. Nine bucks for a flannel shirt. I can fully outfit myself for less than a c-note."

"Your car was totaled. How'd you get out there?"

"Don't ask."

"I wish you'd stop doing that stuff."

"It was just a cruiser, not some civilian's wheels," he said. "Found it parked outside the emergency room door with the engine running, like it was waiting for me."

"I've got a question for you, partner," I said. "How come you were watching Sarah's house?"

"She had a book that once belonged to Maxine Harris. Remember her? I think I told you about this."

"Yeah. Throat slashed. Found propped up against a

tombstone in a cemetery. A guy from the DA's office just mentioned the case. Why would Sarah have a book that belonged to her?"

"It's a long story. The point is, Sarah had the book, and I was waiting for her to come home so I could get it from her."

I heard him pop the top on a beer can.

"Do you know you may be walking around with a subdural hematoma?" I asked.

"Lane, give me a break. I hate hospitals. Besides, there's stuff I've gotta do. You put me on to Chadwick, and I want to follow it up. I feel all right. I really do."

I heard a woman's voice in the background. She was telling Robert that he couldn't drink in there.

"Look, I'm getting hassled. Chadwick's place is a crater. It blew up on Monday. Chadwick may or may not be dead. I ran into this old guy up there, a neighbor. He told me the good doctor went to Harvard. I need to check it out. I've got a gut feeling about this guy and I want to stay on top of it."

"Robert, don't hang up. Don't go anywhere. A nurse told me you could die if you have one of those things in your head."

"I promise you, Lane, I'm not gonna die," he said. "But I've gotta run. I've got just enough time to catch the shuttle to Boston. Maybe if I dig around up there in person, I can turn something up. I don't feel like playing phone tag with a bunch of bureaucrats. If you get anything on Chadwick, leave a message with airport security in Boston. I'll check in when I arrive."

Before he hung up, I heard that same woman in the background, and this time she wasn't complaining about the beer. She was saying, "Hey, mister, are you okay?"

It was 11:00 P.M. when I pulled up in front of Wallingford Antiques. The shop was a small storefront with a blue awning spanning its width. I could see lamps burning inside—their leaded shades giving the showroom a warm yellow glow.

Before I had a chance to ring the bell, an elderly, balding man moved the door curtain aside and peeked out at me. A smile was all it took to get him to open up.

"You're the lady who called about our ad," he said.

Wallingford's sister—a woman with white hair but a young face—was busy wrapping a cut-glass punch bowl in tissue paper. She looked at me with wet eyes, then looked away without speaking. Her husband extended his freckled hand, telling me his name, Brian, and inviting me to explore the shop.

"I'm sorry about your brother-in-law," I told him. "It must have been very sudden."

"His heart had been bad for years," Brian whispered.

So it was a natural death.

Brian wanted to know how long I had been an antiques dealer.

"Actually, I'm not," I said.

His left eyebrow lifted slightly. "Oh?"

I had no idea what I was going to find when I got to Landgrove, but there seemed to be no reason to continue the deceit. "I apologize for misleading you," I said.

I showed them my shield. "I'm a detective, and I'm investigating a homicide. One of Mr. Wallingford's business cards was found in the possession of the victim."

Brian glanced over at his wife. "Oh, dear," she said, putting her hand over her mouth.

"Did your brother keep a record of his customers?"

"My name's Grace," she said. "There's a card file."

"It's pretty straightforward," Brian added, walking behind the counter and pulling open a wooden drawer filled with frayed three-by-five cards.

"Would you check it for a John Wolf?" I asked.

"How was this person killed?" Grace asked.

"Stabbed to death, ma'am."

"How horrible."

"There's no one here with that name," Brian said.

"What about Alan Carver or Alan Chadwick?"

He fingered his way through the cards. "Neither one."

"Sarah Sinclair?"

Brian was at the back of the drawer again, already shaking his head, when his wife said, "Wasn't that the name of the man who was here this morning? Or was that St. Clair?"

"What did he want?"

"He was looking for a feather tree," Grace said. "My brother used to get them in from time to time. They're made of goosefeathers, or maybe chicken feathers. They were very popular in the early nineteen hundreds. The newest ones would date to the nineteen thirties."

"The door wasn't locked," Brian added. "He thought we were open for business. There was one tree here, and this man offered seventy-five dollars for it. So we sold it to him."

I asked him to describe the guy.

It wasn't Robert.

Robert

I caught the last shuttle out of La Guardia. I hate flying almost as much as I hate funerals. But when I have to fly into Boston's Logan Airport, I hate it even *more* than funerals. It's the seawall. The 727 seems like it's just barely skimming over the top, and knowing that some planes have landed short of the runway and disintegrated against the wall makes it all a crap shoot as far as I'm concerned.

I checked in with airport security as soon as I arrived. Lane had faxed what little she had on Alan Chadwick—just his DOB and SS number—but it was enough for what I had in mind.

I picked up a rental car and headed out through the Sumner Tunnel. I found a cheap motel on Massachusetts Avenue, crashed there for the night, then started out fresh in the morning.

People who complain about driving in New York have never driven in Boston. New York is a grid. It's consistent. Stay with the flow of the traffic and you'll get where you're going. Boston is laid out like one of those mazes in a kid's magazine. Everything dead-ends somewhere and you have to start over.

After one street that went nowhere and a couple of one-ways that weren't headed in the same direction I was, I found the Harvard Medical School. The alumni office was just like anything else that wears the Veritas seal—brick, old wood polished to a sheen, leather chairs.

A secretary named Shirley Bright was sympathetic to my problem. I was an out-of-town cop with a dead alumnus of theirs on my hands and no way of contacting any of his family. She wondered why I hadn't just called, why I came in person—and I said the usual: "It's a sensitive matter."

Shirley said she understood. I told her Chadwick's name and gave her his date of birth from the material Lane had sent. Shirley began tapping away at her computer.

"I'm afraid we don't have anything terribly recent," she said. "When he left here he went over to Boston City for a residency in pathology. The last entry says he stayed on as a staff pathologist. That was in nineteen eighty-three. There isn't anything here about family."

Shirley directed me to Boston City Hospital, and said she'd call ahead to let the personnel department know that I was on my way. I thanked her and left.

For starters, Boston City's personnel office was in the catacombs of an ancient building on Columbus Avenue—and it didn't say Personnel on the door; it said Human Resources. Sign of the times. The elevated train rumbled by outside, contributing its share to the constant din.

My secretary this time was named Wanda. That's all her tag said. "This will take time," Wanda told me. "Those old records haven't been put in the computer."

Wanda sighed a lot. I offered to help her search for the information, but she said it wasn't allowed. Authorized personnel only. And she kept having to take phone calls as she plowed through dusty boxes of file folders.

Sometimes when she sighed, Wanda said, "That's such a long time ago."

"What were you doing in nineteen eighty-three?" I asked her, just trying to make conversation.

She thought for a long moment, then said, "I don't want to tell you that. I don't have to, do I?"

I assured her she didn't. Wanda had lost her place, and I had learned not to interrupt.

After I'd spent about an hour and a half skimming through old *Time* magazines, Wanda picked up her phone and punched a few buttons.

"Is he in?" she asked—then, after a pause, said, "No, I don't need to talk to him. I just wondered if he's in."

When she hung up, she turned to me and said, "Dr. Chadwick didn't die."

"What?"

"You said he died."

"That's right. There was an explosion. We need to contact next of kin."

"He's upstairs."

"Who's upstairs?"

She sighed. "Dr. Chadwick. He's in pathology, where he's always been. He didn't even move or anything."

Wanda tolerated my ignorance and directed me to pathology.

Alan Chadwick was a tall, paunchy man with tufts of prematurely white hair that seemed to be glued, at random, to parts of his head. He wore a permanently dour expression, looking out at the world over half glasses. He had large, gnarled hands that appeared to be arthritic.

"As you can see, Detective," he said, "I'm not dead."

I decided to begin at the beginning. "For the past six years or so there's been a man with your name, Dr. Alan Chadwick, with your date of birth and educational credentials—right down to the residency here—employed as a county medical examiner in southwestern Connecticut. Several days ago there was an explosion at his home. We think he may have been killed in that explosion."

"An imposter," the doctor said.

"I see that now," I said. "And there's another part to this. At least two women—probably more—have been murdered in the last few months. One of them was my ex-wife. Just before her death she had begun dating someone new. The night she was killed, she'd been having drinks with somebody—maybe the new boyfriend. His fingerprints were all over her apartment. When we ran them, Dr. Alan Chadwick's name popped up."

"A very clever and homicidal imposter."

"That's what I think. Can you tell me how he could have become you?"

Lane had faxed me a copy of Chadwick's diploma. I pushed it across the desk at him. For this, he looked through his glasses.

"That is my diploma," Chadwick said.

The doctor stood and walked behind his chair where he removed a framed certificate from the wall. He placed it on his desk for me to see. "So is this. Your fax quality is poor, but it does appear to be an exact duplicate of this one. I suppose copies can be obtained through the medical school, but I don't really know how."

I scrawled a few things into my notebook and was preparing to thank the doctor and leave, when he asked, "If you don't mind, how was your ex-wife killed?"

"Her throat was cut."

"I'm sorry," Chadwick said. "When I was in college I dated a girl who was murdered. We weren't engaged or even going steady, or anything like that, but I think I had it in my mind that she was going to be my wife."

"What happened to her?"

Chadwick removed his glasses and rubbed at the bridge of his nose. "It was a fall from a roof. The police said it was suicide. So did the medical examiner. I had seen her a few times with another young man, also a student at the college. I was convinced then, and I remain convinced, that he pushed her from that roof. No one would listen to me."

Alan Chadwick was a few years my senior, yet he looked

decades older. As he talked, even his voice seemed to age. "I took it upon myself to follow this man," he said, "and confront him with what I suspected. Of course he denied it, and he kept denying it. So I decided to beat it out of him. I was never much good at anything physical. I took a baseball bat with me."

Chadwick held up his hands, displaying his oddly shaped fingers. "I started out to be a surgeon, Detective," he said, "but I ended up in pathology and have remained there because of these. You see, he took the bat away from me and used it to crush my career. Now I perform surgery on cadavers, and I teach."

I put my notebook away. "What happened to the guy?"

The doctor shrugged. "He was in and out of college. I don't know if he ever graduated. About a year after he killed my friend, there was another murder—a young woman who lived off campus. She was found in her bed, strangled. I went to the police about him again, but they insisted there was no possible relationship between the two cases. I didn't believe them, and I said so, but nobody wanted to listen."

"I lost track of him when I went on to the medical school," Chadwick added. "I don't know what became of him after that."

Chadwick was an interesting man and his story was intriguing. He obviously had loved the girl—believed she'd been murdered. His belief cost him his hands and his career. His whole life had been redirected because of that incident, and it was clear that he was still haunted by it.

I stood and thanked him for his help. "I'll probably need to talk to you again," I said.

"I'll do whatever I can to help. I don't like having my identity stolen. And I don't like murderers. Perhaps I can redeem myself for what I was never able to do in the Wolf matter."

I was turning toward the door and stopped. "The *what* matter?"

"His name was Wolf. Paul Wolf."

Lane

As I pulled away from the antique shop, I wondered why Robert had wanted to check out Wallingford. Had Sarah mentioned something? Or was Wolf the connection? Did Robert know that Wallingford was dead? I also wondered who might have been out to the Landgrove shop claiming to be Robert. Someone was playing games, but every time I tried to wrap my mind around the questions of who and why, my ability to concentrate went to pieces. Nothing made sense, or if it did, I was too tired to see it.

I drove home. I didn't know what was the matter with me. I just couldn't get myself going—couldn't get any kind of a handle on this case. I understood the importance of time in a murder investigation. The colder the trail, the less likely it is that there'll be an arrest. But I was exhausted. I felt like I did back in college, when I had mono. I knew that I was going to have to make time and get myself to the doctor.

I also realized that I hadn't eaten. I pulled a plastic bag of mixed vegetables out of the freezer and dropped it into some boiling water. I thought maybe an infusion of vitamins might get me back on my feet.

I was wrong. I dozed off for a couple of hours, awakening to the phone ringing. It was Robbins from the DA's office.

"You work late," I said, glancing at the clock. "Or maybe it's early."

"Wondered if you'd had a chance to look at that book yet."

I had to think for a second, then spotted the book on the chair where I'd dropped it. "Haven't had a chance," I said.

"Just wondered."

"Look," I said, "it's not that I don't appreciate your letting me borrow the book. I don't even have time to eat or sleep properly right now."

"No problem," Robbins said. "It's just that—"

"What?"

"Remember what I was saying about his next victim?"

"Vaguely," I said.

I was only half awake, and starting to get annoyed with Robbins's amateurish crime psychology.

"Well, these guys like to take risks, right?" he said.

"I've heard that."

"He obviously had a relationship of some sort with Ms. Sinclair. That's risky. Her ex-husband is a cop, right? He'd know that because he was involved with her. So maybe that adds to his excitement."

"Robbins, I've really got to run," I said. "What are you getting at?"

"The need for more risk," he said. "He could have a cop on that list of his. Think about it, Lane. Good luck."

The phone went dead.

Robbins was just too strange. He might be a wizard at accounting procedures, but I didn't need him dragging me awake to share his theories of criminal behavior.

But, by the time I was sipping my coffee, I realized that Robbins had gotten under my skin. During the days that Wolf spent with Sarah, Robert might have dropped in at any time. That was risky. Then, after killing Sarah, he called and left a message on Robert's machine. Now someone was drifting around the edges of this case. He'd been out to Landgrove, posing as Robert Sinclair and shopping for a tree made of feathers.

Robert could be a target. But this guy preferred women. Shooting the two men in the alley seemed incidental—like they were in his way. So, I could be the target. That's what Robbins had been getting at.

As fast as that thought went through my mind, it was followed by another—a memory. I was sitting with my father at the breakfast table. I'd had a nightmare, and Mom had come into the room and sat on my bed until I'd gone back to sleep. She must have briefed him, because, without my saying anything, Pop looked up from his newspaper and his plate of herring and eggs and said, "Fear is useful, Lanie. It teaches you something about itself. And it teaches you something about *you*."

Reports had piled up on my desk in my absence. The fibers that Levinson found on Sarah's dress matched a carpet produced only by Bigelow, a new line that had been on the market less than two months. There had been only one installation in our area; it went down a week earlier at a clothing store. I could easily picture what had happened: Sarah had tried on the dress in the fitting room. When taking it off, she let it fall to the floor and stepped out of it. That's how it picked up all those particles that Levinson had identified.

I waited until 9:00 A.M., then called the shop. I got a clerk on the line (the same one who had waited on Sarah), and learned that, yes, Ms. Sinclair had purchased a dress there recently. "She was a regular," the clerk told me, "but this time, she was shopping for her wedding gown."

Wedding gown? I made a mental note to tell Dr. Rimlin to hurry up the pregnancy report, and to thank him for the toxicology results that he had placed on my desk. The only thing significant were traces of the antidepressant Tofranil PM. Rimlin's opinion was that Sarah probably had been on a therapeutic dose, then had taken herself off the medication several days before her death.

Benny had come through with a stack of photos five inches thick. I went through them quickly, but since I didn't yet know what I was looking for, I decided to move on to the memo from the scientific evidence unit. I recognized Miller's signature at the bottom, so I knew it had something to do with the fingerprints. But all he wrote was, "Call me. We've got something odd here."

I picked up the phone again, this time pushing the buttons for Miller's extension. His voice mail came on. I hung up without leaving a message.

While I was still sitting there, wondering if I should try to reach Miller at home, I heard the fax machine switch on.

It was Pop's response:

TO: Lanie
FROM: Pop

I spent the morning on the lake, locked in a mind game with that wily largemouth bass I've been after since last year. For weeks he had me convinced that he was gone—departed to another hole across the lake, or dead. Yesterday he hammered my favorite yellow spinner on the first cast and snapped the line. I just wasn't expecting him to hit. Today I could see him making passes behind the red and white spoon I was using. The water roiled in great swirls, but that was all.

Tomorrow is another day. He doesn't know that I have the advantage: more line, more lures, and all the time in the world.

I never have understood why you won't go to medical school. You could have a great career (even go into psychiatry if you want), meet eligible young doctors, raise a brood of interns, and be miles away from those street-sweepings you surround yourself with.

Think about it. You get yourself in at Johns Hopkins and I'll write the check. That's the commercial message for this episode of *Father Wants to Know Best, But Daughter Won't Let Him.*

Your fax tells me volumes (as you will see, I still have my sources here and there). Robert Sinclair. Good potential as a detective, but he hasn't made much use of it. A bit paranoid for my taste. Heavy drinker. And a bigot.

How did you get by that one? I know you like to "pass" from time to time, but when he moved in with you (sources again) he must have noticed the photos of your marvelously mocha mama.

Lt. Swartz from your department also faxed a summary of the case(s). I did some work for him a few years ago, and now he's trying to seduce me into this case. Only reason I looked at what he sent was because he said right at the start that you were in charge. I faxed him a note this morning requesting copies of the usual. It should arrive by helicopter tomorrow afternoon, and the bastards better not scare my fish.

I want it understood that I have no intention of getting involved in this case beyond what I can contribute from the comfort of my armchair. I'll skim the case files when they arrive, give you my impressions, then get back to more pressing business. Fishing.

I already have a few observations to pass on, for what they're worth:

You don't need me to tell you that Sarah Sinclair wasn't this killer's first victim. Start with a 50 mile radius and collect all unsolved homicides, missing persons, untimely deaths, etc., regardless of MO. Skip VICAP. That whole program was put together by a bunch of anal retentive clerks. Send a fax (I love this thing) to the relevant departments. Victims will be female, 18–40 years old. You will have at least a dozen, probably 20+. Not only was your victim not his first, he's been at it for a while.

My initial take on your Sarah is that she had drinks and pleasant conversation with the man who killed her. Her new gentleman friend—the one who pulled the gun in the bookstore (he *did* do the shooting, by the way; I've never been a fan of coincidence) is the man you're after. He fancies himself an artist, a stage director. He selected Ms. Sinclair well ahead of time, engaged her in a parody of courtship, and, when he had amused himself to the max with the details of her life with the risk he was taking, he cut her throat.

Remember, even Ted Bundy made an exception—the young woman in Utah he followed for several days and tried to date; he even told her that he was a student at the law school. The sheriff's department in that jurisdiction refused to share their case materials (eventually lost them, I believe). Then Colorado and Florida happened. Antone Costa on the Cape was another one. Two of his suspected victims were young women that he'd had relationships with. There were others, but they do appear to be exceptions—the kind that Quantico always seems to fall on their faces over.

This "gentleman" is very bright, clever, devious, etc.—all the qualities we've been groomed to expect in our serial killers. But he's got more of everything, and he's been at it longer (he's in his early 40s). You probably won't pin down a positive ID. Or, if you do, it won't give you much. He has more people he can be than Laurence Olivier.

Let me have a look at what they drop in the lake tomorrow and I'll see if I can be of any further help.

P.S. Leonard Cohen is (gulp) my age. Maybe a little older. A poet. A songwriter. A brilliant performer. I'll fax you a twenty; go buy a CD.

P.P.S. Julian Cope is a different kind of genius. I guess all artists at one time or another get around to wrestling with their concept of God. Cope's tune is from an entire work *(Jehovakill)* devoted to that theme. The killer's preference for this piece should not be interpreted as evidence of his grandiosity (although there's plenty of that). He doesn't want to *be* God. He wants to destroy Him.

P.P.P.S. If you write to your mother, tell her to send you the twenty for the CD. Then she'll owe me only $86.50 from our last poker game. Besides, it's easier for her to get to a post office in Zaire than it is for me here. She knows I love her; you don't have to tell her that. I don't want her to think I'm easy.

P.P.P.P.S. I love you, too. Which is why I now fall back into paternalistic mode. When we track down this one, let the SWAT team take him out, and you watch from a great distance. I sense no hesitation in this man. Given the chance, he would kill us all.

Well, that was that. If Pop said it was the gentleman who pulled the gun on the guys in the bookstore, then it was. He's never wrong about this stuff, though I can't even begin to figure out how he does what he does. If he had been a lousy profiler, he'd still have his practice in Boston. He wouldn't have had to run all the way to the Michigan woods to escape the killers who keep breaking into the sanctity of his mind. But at least Michigan is a better out than the one that I had feared he might take. There was a time when I would visit his apartment every three or four days, just to do a sweep of his medicine cabinet. I even got rid of his ant traps.

I did what he said. I papered the entire state of New York with faxes, asking about murdered or missing women in the target age range. Then I sent inquiries into the New England states, and Pennsylvania. If I hadn't been so tired, I would have checked our local records, too.

I got worn out just thinking about my schedule for the following day. I might get some feedback from Pop. Robert might let me know what he found out at Harvard. And I had a long list of people that I wanted to talk to: Sarah's boss at the bookstore, the girl upstairs at the massage parlor, everyone at Fast Eddie's, Miller from the scientific evidence unit, and Hanson.

Actually, I didn't want to talk to Hanson. He wanted to talk to me. At least that's what the note on my desk said.

So, the next day was going to be a big one. But there was no way I could head home without sending Pop a quick reply.

TO: Sherlock
FROM: Found Out
How long have you known about Sinclair and me? Parents are supposed to teach their children that adultery is wrong.

It really was wrong, you know. Why do I always have to learn my lessons the hard way?

As for "passing," I didn't—not on purpose. But Robert is one of those bigots who's also misinformed. He thinks if you're not white, you gotta look black.

He didn't find out about Mom from a picture. It was when I mentioned her sickle-cell anemia. He laughed and said, "Only niggers get that." I looked him in the eye and said, "Yeah. So what's your point?" And that's the first he knew.

Thanks once again for setting me on the right path. I'll focus on the gentleman with the gun. You're right: he does seem to have multiple identities. Who knows how many?

Let me know the minute you've read the stuff Lt. Swartz sent over.

Lanie

P.S. An interesting tidbit fell into my lap tonight. Sarah had been planning to get married. The dress she died in is the one she bought for the ceremony. But here's the oddest part: nobody knew that she had a serious relationship going. I've never met a woman yet who can keep something like that a secret.

P.P.S. What do you make of all those fingerprints that ME from Connecticut left all over Sarah's house? Any way he could be tied up in this?

I was ready to leave for the day, when I had one of those hunches that I just can't leave alone. I called the Landgrove PD.

"You had an untimely up there," I told the dispatcher, after explaining who I was. "Antiques dealer named Wallingford. Was an autopsy performed?"

After telling me that Mr. Wallingford was one of Landgrove's most respected benefactors, she said that she didn't know whether an autopsy had been performed. But she did know the name of the ME who, in the absence of their own medical referee, had been called to Wallingford's estate.

Dr. Alan Chadwick.

Robert

◆

Thursday night I got back from Boston with less than two bucks in my pocket, and not much more in my checking account. Friday was payday. I stopped by the precinct first thing in the morning to pick up my check.

When I walked in, I saw that the suits were there—FBI special agents from Quantico, the Bureau's Behavioral Sciences Unit. The chief suit was an agent named Dexter Willoughby, a three-piece bureaucrat cut from a mold they keep in a vault at the Smithsonian. If I hadn't already had a headache, he was exactly the kind of guy who could have given me one.

Willoughby and Hanson were standing in the hall deep in conversation. "There's a meeting of the minds," I told Fuzzy.

"Hey, Bobby. How's the head?"

"Solid as a rock."

"I figured," he said. "What's up in Beantown?"

"Red Sox ain't in the world series. Where's Lane?"

"Conference room. You guys have a briefing with the feebles at eight-thirty," he said.

"Doesn't anybody remember that I'm on leave?"

Everybody was wearing plastic security tags. I hadn't seen that happen since Clinton threatened to visit.

"Is Dexter Willoughby really that guy's name?" I asked.

"They don't tell me shit," Fuzzy said, then grabbed his allotment of parking tickets for the day and headed out.

This trip one of the feds was a pantsuit—nicely wrapped. But I couldn't help thinking that a night in the sack with her would be like fucking my accountant. And I'd have to pay taxes on it.

Lane and Ms. Agent were side by side, with Lane towering about six inches above her federal friend. What the little woman didn't know was that all the power dressing and power lunches in the world wouldn't do her any good when dealing with my favorite Amazon. I waved to Lane.

"Hang on," she said to the agent, and came over by the door where I was standing. "You're alive."

"I'm doing," I said. "Look, I've got a lot to run by you."

"We have a briefing with the feds in about ten minutes. The woman is Special Agent Walker. There are a couple more of her colleagues around. I don't know how long it's going to take. Maybe after that."

"Who brought them in? Hanson?"

"They brought themselves in. They've been working three unsolved cases up in the Albany area. Same MO as our two."

"Weren't you running some checks, too?"

"There were nineteen sheets on my desk when I got in this morning. I haven't had a chance to look at them yet. That's not counting our two and the Bureau's three. We're looking at five states."

Five states—maybe two dozen victims. I wondered what the hell we were dealing with.

"You and I aren't going to have any time to talk," I complained.

"Maybe after the briefing—"

"I'm not going to any briefing, and I won't be around later."

"Hanson says—"

"Fuck Hanson. I met Alan Chadwick."

Lane's eyes opened wide. I knew I had her attention.

"He's a pathologist at Boston City Hospital. Early forties, but he looks sixty. Pathetic kind of guy, but I liked him. Our Chadwick was an imposter—managed to get his hands on this guy's credentials. The diploma, the transcript, the residency, everything."

The room was starting to fill with detectives. Hanson and Willoughby moved toward the portable podium at the front.

"Our Chadwick didn't die in the explosion," Lane said.

"I didn't think so."

"ATF pulled a fairly intact finger from the debris, but it didn't match up with the Chadwick prints on file with the state. We're still checking out who the dead guy might be. I had a fax from the Hasty Hills PD saying they have two possible missing persons—their medical examiner, who's the guy they know as Chadwick, and a handyman at the Municipal Building who hasn't shown up at work all week."

"What do you have on the guy who calls himself Chadwick?"

"He owned a piece of land north of Hasty Hills. State cops found some mounds out there, also some sinkholes in the soil. Could be a burial site. They're up there doing methane probes right now. He also signed a death certificate on your guy over in Landgrove."

"My guy?"

Hanson was clearing his throat, rapping his knuckles on the table, while Willoughby looked with barely concealed disgust at the coffee urn and two trays of dunkers Hanson's secretary had set out for our guests.

"I have to get out of here," I said. "I've got some calls to make."

Landgrove rang a bell, but I had to leave before Lane

could try to talk me into staying. Hanson loves to throw parties about as much as he likes to see himself on the six o'clock news. He'd be pissed that I didn't attend his affair, but I figured Lane would cover for me. Technically, I wasn't on duty anyway.

The Paul Wolf angle couldn't be more than a bizarre coincidence. It sounded as if everybody but the doc agreed that Chadwick's girlfriend had jumped to her death. Besides, our Wolf's first name was John. But I couldn't leave it alone. It's the kind of thing that would nag at me if I didn't check it out.

I went back to my cubicle and got on the phone. Directory assistance had a number at Harvard for an office dealing with student affairs. I tried that one first. Judy Newton at that office gave me Helen Trammell's number at alumni. Paul Wolf hadn't graduated. Helen directed me back to Judy. Judy connected me to a dean named Harvey Hesselman. Harvey educated me about confidentiality, court orders, and lack of jurisdictional standing. I placed another call to my friend Judy.

"Harvey doesn't understand me," I told her.

She laughed. "I don't want to get in any trouble. I could lose my job."

"I don't want that to happen," I said, "but I think you can help me without putting yourself in a bad position. If you can get a look at this guy's file, just memorize what you can out of it. Don't try to write anything down. If all you can get is his date of birth, that would help. And call me."

I gave her the number at my desk, and my home phone.

"I can't promise anything," she said.

"I wouldn't ask you to. I appreciate anything you can do, Judy."

I had a feeling that Judy wouldn't let me down. Regardless, the legal affairs people would have to start the wheels turning to obtain a court order. Even Harvard isn't immune.

I wandered over to the desk that Lane shares with two other investigators when they're not off sick or on disability.

Her nineteen victims had become twenty-one. I read the top one. Rebecca Holbrook, twenty-eight, separated, mother of two, climbed into her Volkswagen one morning three and a half years ago. She dropped the kids at day care, then went off to her job at a bottling plant. Rebecca never got there. She vanished—disappeared from the face of the earth. Her car was found on a bus route almost midway between the day care center and the plant. There were no suspects.

I wondered if Rebecca Holbrook was residing just north of Hasty Hills.

The second sheet was more recent. Ten months ago, Susan Cullen, twenty, was a cashier at a convenience store in a town of 15,000 in Connecticut. She was supposed to work until 11:00, then close the store. Shortly after 9:00 a regular customer came in for his newspaper and six-pack. The place was empty. Susan's body was found floating in a river a week later. The cause of death was ligature strangulation—a leather thong was still in place, knotted so tightly around her throat that it had disappeared into her skin.

The number of cases involving strangers killing strangers is skyrocketing. Almost a quarter of all homicides in this country are of that variety, and most of them are committed by serial killers. But the numbers don't impress me. The names and the details do.

Silvia Chambers, thirty-six, strangled. Lydia Hall, thirty-one, bludgeoned. Ann Waters, twenty-one, strangled. Miriam Spender, twenty-five, stabbed. Connie Snow, twenty-nine, missing, foul play suspected. Some of the cases went back to the 1970s. Most were of more recent vintage.

Not all these cases were related. They couldn't be. But I was starting to think that a sizable number were—and, once we sorted it all out, we'd discover that this case spanned a lot of years and a lot of communities, bringing horror to a lot of families.

How could Sarah have been so comfortable, so relaxed with this guy? She could be a little spacey. There were times when she was an absolute flake. But at the end, she was like a young girl falling in love for the first time. It wasn't that Sarah was *that* bad a judge of people. It was that this guy was so good—sexy, suave, a smooth talker. My name's this. No, my name's that. And she bought it.

Wallingford. Sarah said that he was from Landgrove. What the hell did that mean? Lane said Chadwick had signed a death certificate in Landgrove. "My guy," she said. If Wolf said he was Wallingford, and Wolf turned out to be Chadwick, maybe he'd signed his own fucking death certificate. Jesus. I needed a drink.

The fax machine started cranking. I reached for the sheet. Make it number twenty-two. Catherine MacKenzie, thirty-eight, found with her neck broken in a stall in a men's room at the airport. Possible suspect: white male, graying brown hair, blue eyes, six foot, educated, tried to pass himself off as a bank official. Said he had a delivery for Ms. MacKenzie, and managed to get into her apartment building. But she had called the bank, knew he was a fraud, so the place was crawling with cops. He smelled them and ran—all the way to the airport, where MacKenzie had a flight booked to Heathrow the following morning. Sounded like the brass balls of an Alan Carver to me.

I added the sheet to the pile and went back to my cubicle. After sending off a formal request for information on the suicide and the homicide *my* Chadwick had told me about, I gave him a call. He was between patients, he said—one on the table to his right, and one on the left. I was starting to like this guy.

"What else can you tell me about Paul Wolf?" I asked him.

"It's been so long," he said. "And no one was ever interested. I remember I wrote down things about him. I kept a notebook, but I haven't seen that in years. I don't even know if I still have it. I know he enjoyed inflicting pain. Oh, I provoked him. I stalked him—I guess that's the word they use now. I asked for what he did to me. But I know he enjoyed doing it. I felt like he wanted me to keep coming after him, so he'd have an excuse to do something else to me."

"Do you remember where he was from?"

"I want to say up north somewhere, but I'm not sure. My girlfriend was from Vermont. That may be why I want to say that."

"What about other people who knew him?"

"He was a loner. If he had friends, I never knew it. He was premed but, like I said, he wasn't much of a student. I don't remember who told me that. He played games of chess in his head. No board. No pieces. Complete games. He'd tell people he could do this and get them to bet that he couldn't. Sixty or seventy moves sometimes."

"Did he have a job?"

"Not that I know of. He had a scholarship to begin with, but lost it."

Again I thanked Chadwick and told him to call if he thought of anything else. He said he would.

Lane showed up just as I got off the phone. "Feel briefed?" I asked her.

"They're going to do some of their magic down in Virginia and report back later. There's a chance of this and a chance of that, but we can't be sure of anything."

"Well, they're real busy making movies," I said. "Got to sell the product."

"We're supposed to maintain an upbeat posture with the press. Put pressure on the killer. Make him think we're getting close to him."

"Lane, he knows we haven't got shit. This guy is surreal. How many fucking identities does he have?"

"Willoughby wants us to start rating our leads," she said, "using some kind of numerical system that'll go into the computer easy."

"Well, this guy does gobble 'em up like Pac-Man. Besides, we need a good computer game around here to break the monotony."

"What about the Harvard Chadwick? You said you had more."

"Lane, I'm gonna tell you something. But I don't want to hear one word about my paranoia."

Before I had a chance to tell her about Paul Wolf, Hanson and Dexter Willoughby walked up.

Right away, Hanson began giving Lane the bad news. "Detective Frank," he said, "since the Bureau will be working these cases, we won't be using any outside consultation. I told the lieutenant to send a fax up to your father to let him know we appreciate his assistance and to explain the situation. The Bureau has a suspect in the Albany cases. We'll be working that angle, too."

While Hanson was running his mouth to Lane, I had a chance to size up Dexter W. The dude was wearing hotshot shoes—real leather, with all those little curlicues punched in it. And they were small because his feet were small. Actually, *everything* about him was—well, not small, really, but dainty. He was neat in an undersized sort of way, like a miniature. And he was perfect. There wasn't a single wrinkle in his suit or on his little pink face.

But on closer examination, I saw that Dexter Willoughby did have a flaw after all. His briefcase was too big. It looked like what I'd use for a weekend trip to the NCAA basketball championship. I figured he lugged his procedure manuals around in it.

"You have a suspect in the Albany cases?" Lane asked, but the two men ignored her.

Hanson finished saying his piece, then Dexter spoke up. Even his voice was dainty. "This is a complicated matter," he said, in what seemed to be a signal for Willoughby and the captain to walk away.

Once they were out of earshot, I said, "Fucking profound. Somebody write that down."

"*What* suspect?" Lane said, though not necessarily to me. "If we're supposed to work this case, it'd be nice to know who he is."

"It's a complicated matter," I reminded her.

"I have to fax Dad."

I turned back to my desk and stared at it. A single sheet of yellow, lined paper contained all the sense I was able to make out of the case so far. The rest of it was a question mark, and I had just started to ponder that when my intercom buzzed.

"Sinclair."

"The methane probes were positive," Lane said. "Looks like he had his own graveyard."

"But he didn't bury them all there," I said. "Why?"

"Sounds like a question for Special Agent Dexter Willoughby."

"He's got his own suspect," I told her, and clicked off.

And that's why cases don't get made. Nobody tells anybody shit, especially not when the feds are flocking around like vultures at a leper colony. Investigations have lives of their own. They're reactive. You do all the shit the manual says—check this, cross-check that. Then some dude calls in and says he saw the boyfriend carrying a gun, leaving the crime scene two minutes after the shooting. So you react. You put all your resources into that lead. Turns out it wasn't the boyfriend; it was a plumber. He wasn't carrying a gun; it was his pipe wrench. It wasn't two minutes after the shooting; it was two weeks before. And you've pissed away all that time and effort, but you do it again, with the next call.

Kojak solved them all. Even though Joe Friday talked like a computerized voice mail, he cleared 'em in half an hour. Always by the fucking book. It was a joke. TV was killing us. At least on *Homicide* some of them get left hanging, and the assholes who don't like the show complain because it's too realistic.

I felt bad for Lane. It was her first case as lead and here I was doing as little communicating as anyone else around the shop. She'd set all the right stuff in motion—analysis of physical evidence, neighborhood door-to-door, background information, a list of the latest wackos released from mental hospitals and the prisons upstate—but none of it would mean shit until something flew in from left field.

The feds just made matters worse. Their presence pisses off the drones, puffs up the brass with self-importance, and shuts mouths. Willoughby had his own suspect. I doubted if he or Hanson would ever get around to briefing any of us who were doing the legwork. But hey, who gives a shit? They've probably got the wrong sucker anyway.

Lane

As soon as I arrived at the precinct on Friday, Hanson motioned for me to come into his office, reminding me that he wanted us to have a talk.

"Let me grab a cup of coffee first," I said—but he told me no, there wasn't time. The feds were due any minute for a briefing on the Sinclair/Harris cases, et al., and I was to be the lead presenter.

"Have a seat," Hanson said, closing the door behind me.

I settled onto the wooden chair farthest from his desk.

"There's a delicate matter we need to clear up, Lane," he began. "In a situation like this it's standard practice. You know that. I have to ask you where you were from three o'clock Sunday afternoon until you reported to the murder scene Monday morning."

"This is about Robert and me, isn't it?"

"You and the deceased weren't exactly friends."

"You think I killed her. Is that it?"

"I just want to get your story on the record."

"My *story*? Captain, you know where I was. I was on call from Friday night till Monday morning."

"Dispatch doesn't show you out on any calls all weekend, until the one Monday."

I wanted to walk out, but I knew that Hanson would call it a female thing if I did. "There weren't any calls," I said.

"The problem is, Lane, the log doesn't even show you dispatched to the Sinclair scene."

"I called in when I got there."

"But how did you get there? Who notified you?"

"You know who notified me. Robert did—when he found her."

"We need to clear that up for the record. The polygraph will take care of it, and then we can put all this behind us."

Hanson stood up, smiling—as if he thought we were the best of friends—and gestured toward the door. It was time for the meeting with the feds.

I walked out into the hall. I was a suspect. Someone was playing with my head. Robert was doing his own thing. And this case was going nowhere.

There was one bright spot in my morning. A fax from Pop was waiting in my in box. Once again he mentioned Robert. All I could do was hope that nobody else in the department had read it.

> TO: Found Out
> FROM: Pop
> Ever since you were a child I've told you that I know more than everything. You've never believed me. I've known about your dalliance with Robert Sinclair since before it happened. Parents are like that.
>
> I hope that one of the lessons you've learned is that you can't take care of Robert. He has to wrestle with his own demons—the ghosts of his ex-wife, his child, and the ones that rise up with the fumes from his various

bottles. You can lead a horse to water, but you can't make it say no to a fifth of Wild Turkey.

Your man with the gun and all the identities (possibly/probably including that of county ME; Lt. Swartz did mention Chadwick, the explosion, etc.): You will find more identities. He wasn't concerned about leaving his prints around because he knows they won't ever lead anyone to him. He destroyed the house because it would reveal too much about him. He has studied those of us who study people like him. I'm sure he's read all the books, and probably attended a few seminars. Some of us may have even met him (those of us who bother to attend those god-awful things).

I went over the material the good lieutenant dropped on me. Your wolfman is charming, suave, attractive, deliberate, very cool. He develops his dramatic scenes for murder in fantasy ahead of time (sometimes it's days in advance—as it was in this case; other times it's only hours). Also, well ahead of time, he could have drawn for you the tableau depicted in the crime scene. All of which, of course, reveals his first weakness: rigidity. He might say that he can't be stopped. But I would say that, once in motion, he can't stop himself—other than to make a few minor adjustments. He must carry out his fantasy/plan.

This "rigidity" translates into a number of things. He gives obsessive attention to detail, can't tolerate imperfection. He has to be in absolute control. He's an organizer and a collector, like Christopher Wilder, that fellow who terrorized the country several years back. After Wilder was killed in a shoot-out in northern New Hampshire, Florida police found a copy of the Fowles book *(The Collector)* on his shelf. No, I don't know what he collects, but if he is your ME, his collection wasn't in that house. He has another, more permanent residence (and identity), one that he has never compromised.

He requires not only respect, but adulation. Like any narcissistic psychopath, however, as soon as he receives his praise, he dismisses it, and dismisses anyone stupid enough to be suckered by him. But even so, when he isn't worshiped, he's enraged.

Although it galls him to create his works of homicidal art, display them, and not be able to take the credit, he is sufficiently in control to recognize his own need for anonymity. His rather smooth exterior masks a turbulence inside. He has to go away for a while and hide, but that bothers him, too. No doubt he can busy himself with his collection—but not for very long. He has a thirst for risk and excitement.

I suspect that he had (has?) a sister—probably younger (these are crimes of control, power, manipulation; an older sister would have thumped him one). His mother was inadequate, but indulged him. This would be the most common family arrangement, with father, if present in the home, aloof and removed, except in matters of discipline, which would have been quite physical. Mom failed to protect him from Dad—she was caught in her own bind (Defy her husband? Unthinkable!). And I suspect there was a blowup (at least one) when the wolfman was a mere cub. Think about it. Read Laing's *Sanity, Madness, and the Family*. There has to be tension in the familial relationships. Study physics, dear daughter, and chaos theory: turbulence eventually explodes. We're talking about an adult who believes that he has a license to Cuisinart the world. Primal learning supersedes all other education.

So what did he learn? His preferred status in the family disappeared when little sister squirmed her way out of the womb. The sex/aggression fusion evident in the crimes requires that he was old enough to jerk off when she was born (self-reinforcement). Mom might ignore the stains on the sheets, but Dad would beat the piss out of him, further reinforcing the equation of sexual exploitation and violence. We're so civilized I could puke.

I don't think that Sarah Sinclair was planning to marry. While there was something ceremonial about her dress, the setting, etc., the ceremony was more likely his. She does sound like something of a romantic—one who was swept off her feet by this fellow—but marriage? I doubt it. I can understand the confusion. Sarah would have used extravagant words when speaking about what, to any other woman, would have been simply a special date or a significant moment. Sarah seems to have done nothing in moderation. When she withheld herself from relationships, she did it with a fierce determination. And when she opened herself to her killer, she did it with abandon. But her marriage had failed. Why fly into another?

Something about this man summoned forth a side of Sarah that had lain dormant for too long. Maybe there was no stopping him. But there was no stopping her, either.

Sorry to be so clinically distanced about all of this. If you come up with any more information that you want to run by me, feel free, but keep in mind that I cannot and will not become physically involved in your manhunt. I'm counting on the vast resources available to you law enforcement wizards to bring him to ground. I have no desire to pierce my soul with another fishhook in order to lure out the land sharks this culture creates with such abandon.

Pop

P.S. Please advise about other unsolved cases. You must have collected a few by now.

P.P.S. Examine the photo marked #011. Sarah's house is neat. No doubt she vacuumed in anticipation of the evening. You'll need a magnifying glass in order to see what I believe to be a blue jay feather just beyond her fingers, next to the table.

P.P.P.S. Please send me a copy of Sarah's journal. She has much to tell me.

Before tucking a copy of Sarah's journal into the manila envelope I had already addressed to Pop, I stuck a Post-it note on a page that I knew would interest him:

John is unlike any other man I have ever known. He says things that seem, on one level, to make sense. But when I think about his words, I realize they lead nowhere, say nothing.

Today he went with me to visit Liza's grave. I told him how much I wished that I could go back and undo the mistakes I have made. "I would be a better mother," I told him. "I would hold her more, kiss her, and tell her I love her."

He nodded and said, "The hummingbird is the only bird that is able to fly backward."

I wonder where his mind goes to retrieve such thoughts. I want to visit that place. I want to understand it.

Sinclair came in just before showtime with the feds, but refused to attend. I didn't push it because he looked worse than I did. I was hoping that he also smelled worse. He reeked of Old Milwaukee, and something else that I couldn't identify.

Maybe it was getting a whiff of him that made me feel so queasy. Whatever it was, I was rocky on my feet and I felt terrible. So when Special Agent Walker cornered me after the briefing to tell me that "we girls" should work together, share whatever we dig up, show "the boys" who the real sleuths are, I didn't even try to be tactful. I gave her a flat no. She wanted me to turn over all my files, but she had no intention of giving me anything. That's the way the feds operate. They're real good at taking, but just try to pry anything out of one of them.

I hadn't told Robert the one piece of essential news that had come across my desk that morning. It had arrived by fax during the briefing: a jawbone found in the debris of the Hasty Hills explosion, with three teeth still intact, had been matched up, via dental X rays, with a fellow named Bernard Lallendorf. He was the missing handyman I told Sinclair about earlier. According to the report, he was employed at the Hasty Hills Municipal Building, the same building that I had reached when I pressed the redial button on Sarah's phone. It was also the building where our pseudo Chadwick's office was located. Someone up there had noticed that Lallendorf went missing the same day the crater turned up where Chadwick's house used to be.

God, how I hated this case. All it did was make me dizzy. I had to quit letting fatigue, my bad mood, and my upset stomach get in the way of the investigation. I swallowed my frustration as best I could, and went searching for Robert to update him on the jawbone. But he was nowhere to be found. I had no idea how long it would be before he'd check in again, so I copied the report and left it on his desk. I left the same information on his answering machine, and told him that Hanson had asked me to take a polygraph.

Robert wasn't even supposed to work the case. Because of his rank, Swartz never acted as lead anymore. I had walked into it. God, how I wanted to walk out of it. I was in over my head—wishing I could be back in uniform, but no longer sure I could handle even traffic, B&Es, or domestics. That's what this case had done to whatever confidence I once had.

For the first time in two months, I also wanted the comfort of Robert. I remembered the last time we were together. Robert and I got dressed and ate breakfast in silence that morning, not even looking at each other. It was a relief when we finally climbed into our separate cars for the drive to the precinct—and, once there, immediately fell back into our "cop mode," bantering and biting just like always. Anyone watching us would figure that we hated each other—or were in love.

I knew that Robert and I couldn't be. But it didn't make me want it any less.

A ringing telephone pulled me back to the present. It was the one on Robert's desk.

"Detective Sinclair's office," I said.

"Is Detective Sinclair in?"

"He's on temporary leave. Perhaps I can help you. This is Detective Frank."

"My name is Henry Street. I was Sarah Sinclair's psychiatrist."

"I'm heading up that investigation, sir."

Street cleared his throat. "I'm afraid I'm more than a little uncomfortable," he said. "I keep remembering how Susan Forward went public after Nicole Simpson was murdered, and all the criticism she encountered."

I didn't say anything. If the man knew something that could help us, I certainly wasn't going to bring up professional ethics.

"I'm wondering how I might assist you," Street continued. "I know that you can gain access to Sarah's records through the appropriate filings with the court, but there's someone else you might want to take a look at—and I'm trying to figure out just how I can guide you toward him. It's someone I learned about several years ago. A case in Vermont."

I waited.

"Are you still there, Detective Frank?" he asked.

"Yes."

"And are you interested?"

"Intensely."

"Then let me grapple with this. I'll have to get back to

you. Meanwhile, you may want to get the proper wheels turning regarding the records I have here at my office."

This was going to be touchy. I wasn't too sure I wanted to see the outpourings of Sarah Sinclair's heart, especially if I was mentioned in those records. And I didn't think Robert ought to get his hands on that stuff, either. But it was my job, just as her journal was required reading. So, as soon as Street and I had said our good-byes, I got in touch with the DA's office. I told an assistant DA what we needed and where to find it, then, on impulse, asked if I could speak with Robbins.

"I haven't got time to switch you around," she said. "Why don't you call back and ask for his extension."

Just as I was hanging up the phone, Miller was at my desk.

"Did you get my note about the fingerprints?" he asked.

"I tried to call you last night. What's up?"

"We got another match on those Chadwick prints. They come back to an Eric Randolph, a guy who spent eighteen months as a cop in Contra Costa county, California, in the early seventies."

"You're kidding."

"A*nd* to Lester Walden, who drove an armored car for a few months in Denver, Colorado, during the mid-seventies. Lieutenant Swartz gave the company a call. According to their records, Walden just dropped out of sight. Didn't report to work one day and that was it. Denver has two unsolved cases from that time period similar to ours."

"Jesus."

"And there's one more. This one's a criminal match. A case that dates back to the mid-sixties, in Vermont."

"Vermont?"

"Right. But it was heard in juvenile court. I doubt if we can get the name. The file is sealed."

"I think I love you, Miller," I said. "We just had our first piece of good luck."

Miller dropped the reports on my desk and left, not even

asking what I meant. I looked up Street's office number and gave him a call. He answered his own phone.

"This is Detective Frank," I said. "Was that Vermont situation you mentioned a juvenile case, by any chance?"

"You do work fast, don't you?"

"And would it have anything to do with a fellow named Chadwick?"

No response.

"How about Wolf?"

I thought I heard a slight intake of breath on the other end of the line.

"John Wolf?" I asked.

"The weather isn't perfect, but it's certainly getting warmer."

"John . . ."

"Cold."

"Wolf."

"Hot."

"Does the first name begin with an A?"

"Brrr."

"B?"

"Brrr again."

"Listen, could we get together and go through the alphabet? I could be there in a half hour."

He agreed, but not with much enthusiasm.

On my way to Street's office, I stopped at Radio Shack, where I bought a fax machine to install in my apartment, along with a switcher box so I wouldn't have to put in a separate phone line. Maybe Hanson didn't want Pop on the case, but I did. I also didn't mind the idea of communicating with him in a more private way. There was no telling how many pairs of eyes were reading his faxes before I did.

Street was seated in his office, with the door open. As soon as he saw me in the reception area, he stood up and came toward me, a smile on his face and his hand extended in a warm welcome.

"Detective Frank," he said. "This is a genuine pleasure. I've heard a great deal about you."

I must have blushed because right away he fell all over himself apologizing.

"I meant from your father, not Sarah," he said. "He and I trained together with Dr. Herman up in Boston, then kept in touch over the years. I understand he's retired now."

"Somewhat."

"And how is your mother—Savannah, isn't it?"

"Still curing animals in Africa."

"Well, come in, sit down," Dr. Street said, ushering me into his office. "May I get you a Pepsi?"

"No thanks," I said.

"Pineapple juice?"

"Nothing for me, thanks."

"Punch?" he asked, almost spitting the "p" at me.

"We aren't by any chance looking for a Peter Wolf, are we?"

Street laughed. "Cold," he said.

"The only other male name I can think of that begins with a P is Paul."

"Really?"

"Is that it?"

"If you're too warm, I can turn up the air-conditioning."

"Are we talking about the mid-sixties here?"

"I think sixty-four is a comfortable temperature, don't you?"

"Vermont?"

"Wonderful climate."

"Please," I said. "No more games. I really need to know about this guy."

Street rose from his chair and walked to the window, where he stood with his back turned toward me. He stayed there for what seemed like several minutes, though I suppose it was less than that. Then, still not looking at me, he said,

"Sarah Sinclair met someone shortly before her death—someone who claimed to have had some sessions with me. She said his name was John Wolf."

"Then it's John, not Paul?"

"Hold on a minute," Street said, turning to face me. "She *said* John, but the name meant nothing to me. And then this thing happened, and I couldn't get that conversation out of my mind. The last name—Wolf—kept rolling around in my head. And then I remembered. Paul Wolf. Saxtons River, Vermont. A troubling case, a terrible case, really—and I couldn't help wondering if that was the fellow she met. He'd be about the right age."

"He was a patient of yours?"

"No. His case was part of my training, something one of my mentors used when illustrating the rights of minors, the limits of confidentiality—that sort of thing. I talked with the presenter afterward. We became friends and that case came up in conversation several times later. It stuck with me, at least in part because it was so brutal. I don't know how Sarah's fellow happened to know my name. I don't even know if the Wolf that she met is the same one I knew about. But I did feel that it was worth mentioning to you."

Street explained that the case had fascinated him because it focused on the requirement to report an explicit threat. The question was, "Can a threat be reported if it's made by a juvenile?"

"This was before Tarasoff in California, when there were no real guidelines," he said. "This young man had specific plans to kill a dozen different people. The therapist and social services people screamed confidentiality, so the youth's rights were protected. Then one of those people he named was killed in precisely the way he said he would do it. He was in a private school at the time, technically in state custody, but he had a history of leaving the place whenever he felt like it."

"Was he ever tied to the murder?"

Street shook his head. "The investigation produced

nothing. I also remember that when they removed him from his home, they searched his bedroom. There were small bones, feathers, crudely cut pieces of animal pelts—shoe boxes filled with the stuff. Curiously, there was no odor. Everything had been cured in some way. He was an extremely primitive but exceptionally intelligent young man. That can be a deadly combination, especially in someone with no regard at all for other people."

"Since we're exchanging confidential information," I said, "fingerprints found in Sarah Sinclair's house matched up with someone in a sealed file in Vermont. A case from the mid-sixties. A juvenile."

"Perhaps I can find the notes I took when the Wolf case was presented to us. I know I wouldn't have hung on to them, but my mother was a pack rat, saved everything, absolutely everything. My first tooth, my first bib. Thank God she had the sense to throw away my first diaper. I'll see what we've got in the attic. I was so outraged by the case, I may well have written home about it."

As I was leaving, Dr. Street took my hand and held it in both of his, staring into my eyes the entire time.

"Please remember me to your father," he said. "And forgive me for the silly game I put you through. It's just that these ethical quandaries always confuse me."

"As far as I'm concerned, we never spoke."

"Thank you," he said, his hands still holding mine.

Until we were standing toe to toe, I hadn't realized just how much taller than I he was. At least six inches. It felt wonderful being able to look up to a man for a change. We made plans to talk again as soon as he'd had time to sort through all those boxes his mother stuck in the attic thirty years ago.

I felt drained. After leaving Street's office, I intended to go back to the precinct to see what had come in during my absence, but I was exhausted. Far too tired to think about interviewing the folks at the massage parlor and Fast Eddie's.

I used my cellular phone to call Carol, my doctor's assistant. She gave me an appointment, and I said I'd be there. We'd had problems with that in the past—missed appointments—but I knew that I'd keep this one. Whatever was wrong was slowing me down. I was losing time I didn't have.

Robert

After cashing my paycheck, I picked up a case of Old Milwaukee and took it back to my place. I opened one of the cans as I listened to my phone messages. The first one was from Lane, telling me to put my beer down and take notes. There was a handyman's jawbone in the wreckage at Chadwick's place, Hanson wanted her to take a polygraph, and Special Agent Walker was pumping her for information. No surprise about Chadwick. And I guess it was no surprise about Hanson. He'd be wanting me on the box, too, I was sure.

I finished my beer and fell asleep in the chair. I seldom dream. If I do, I usually don't remember the plot. But this one I remember.

For some reason I want to say it took place in Maine. I've never been there—I've seen pictures, received postcards—but I've never been there.

There were stunted, scrub pines that seemed to grow up out of a broad expanse of flat rock. There were bushes low to the ground—bayberry, my dream said—and lichens all over the rock. And there was a man—the man I had known as Alan Carver—sitting on a small boulder, smoking a cigarette.

He was fifty yards away when I first saw him, his hand moving down from his face, a puff of smoke billowing up and away from his head.

He was older than I remembered. His long hair had gone totally gray and he was bearded. I approached him in a friendly, sociable way, thinking it unusual to find anyone out in the middle of nowhere. I waved to him as I walked up, watching the wind blow back through his hair. His hand came down from his mouth, but no smoke emerged. Instead of a cigarette, he had a .38 in his hand.

Everything about him was different, but I knew who he was because of the eyes. They were the eyes of Alan Carver, the eyes of John Wolf. They turned yellow—glowing—as he raised the weapon and aimed at my chest.

I awakened in a sweat, with a throbbing headache. I riffled through my junk drawer in the kitchen, looking for codeine, Darvocet, even an aspirin if that was the best I could do—but then I remembered. All that stuff was over at Sarah's.

It was early evening. I figured the Old Milwaukee had knocked me out around four. I'd spent the afternoon waiting for the phone to ring.

Somebody tentatively knocked on the door frame. My semi-shattered door is a bit intimidating. I moved it aside on its single hinge.

"If this is any indication of what the rest of the place is like, please don't invite me in," she said.

It was Special Agent Walker, wearing a forest green pantsuit, sharply creased.

"I have a friend with big feet," I said.

She stepped inside and I slid the door back into position.

"He wanted in pretty bad," she said.

"She."

"Then it's not just me. You really are irresistible."

I'd never had a special agent of the nation's premier law enforcement agency come on to me before. Since most of them are guys, I'm particularly proud of that. But this was different. She also had rings on a significant finger.

"How do you feel about adultery?" I asked her.

"I think only adults should do it," she said, catching my glance at her hand. "The gold band was my grandmother's. It keeps some of the wolves away."

"I think I'm going to feel used," I said.

"Consider it a role reversal."

She slipped out of her jacket and tossed it on the chair. Her blouse was a lighter green, silkier, clinging in the places where it should.

"Is there a rule that says a woman can't size up a man the way men do with women all the time?" she asked.

"I can't say I'm totally comfortable with the idea of being treated like an object, Special Agent Walker."

"Susan. I've never liked it either."

"Beer?"

She took the can, didn't want a glass. She was folding herself neatly into a corner of the couch when the phone rang.

"I waited until I got home," Judy Newton said.

I grabbed a pen. "Good idea," I said, watching Susan Walker recross her legs.

"Paul Wolf's date of birth is December twenty-third, nineteen fifty-two. He's a Capricorn, by the way, if you're into that. They tend to be very dependable, organized, somebody you can rely on to get things done. He wasn't like that when he was a student here. He came from a private school in Vermont—was on scholarship there. He had a scholarship here, too, but he kept losing it. He was premed. Finally he dropped out. His home address was a rural route in a place called Saxtons River, Vermont. I ski at Killington, so I remember seeing that place on the map, but I couldn't tell you exactly where it is."

I thanked Judy, assured her that no one would ever know where I got my information, and promised her dinner at Jacob Wirth's the next time I was in Boston.

"I'm almost married," she said.

"Then I'd better hurry."

We both laughed and hung up.

Susan Walker sipped her beer and watched me.

I was thinking about Alan Chadwick—the real one. His girlfriend had been from Vermont. I wondered if there was any connection.

Here I was with a randy FBI agent in my pit of an apartment, my ex-wife barely gone to ashes, and the remnants of a very bad dream. I knew I should probably bring Lane up to date on Paul Wolf, and what I was doing, but something—or somebody—kept getting in the way.

As soon as the question formulated itself in my mind, I asked Susan Walker, "Who's your suspect?"

"Was the call about the case?"

"An angle I've been following, yeah."

"I know I'm not that unappealing. You just can't stop being a cop."

Maybe I was wrong. Maybe she didn't remind me of my accountant.

"Can we peel each other and talk at the same time?" I asked, loosening the buttons on my shirt.

She got up from the couch, walked over, stood up as tall as she could, and kissed me. She also slipped a condom into my right hand. I don't know where the hell she'd been keeping it.

"I suspect Robert Sinclair in the bedroom with a club," she said.

We were shedding clothing and stumbling into the bedroom. We fell into the bed. While I was trying to remember the last time I had changed the sheets, her tongue tied mine in knots and the hand wearing Grandma's ring wrapped itself around my club. So much for trying to pump a cop.

I watched Susan walk back into the bedroom wearing my bathrobe and carrying two cans of beer. "Well, you lived up to your billing, Sinclair," she said. "No fuss, good fuck."

"Really, Special Agent Walker, I think you're setting a bad example for the young women of America."

"What? They're getting it whenever they can."

She handed me a beer.

"So who's your suspect?" I asked.

"You mean I didn't even manage to distract you?"

"I'll show you mine if you show me yours."

"We already did that."

The phone rang.

"Well, at least they waited until we were done," she said.

It was Alan Chadwick. "I hope I'm not disturbing you."

"Not at all," I said, slipping my hand inside the robe that Susan had let fall open.

"I found that notebook," he said.

I was drawing a blank.

"I kept those notes about Paul Wolf. I still have the notebook. It was strange. When I got home I just went right to where it was. I didn't really want to read all that again. I kind of skimmed it. But I did follow him around for a long time. Everything I found out about him I wrote down, because I was sure the police were going to want to know about him. They never did."

"I'd like to see it," I told him.

"I thought you would. I have it packaged. Just need your address."

I gave it to him.

"He was from Vermont," Chadwick said. "Saxtons River. She was from Springfield, just north of there. He could have known her before, although she insisted she didn't know him. Said she met him at a bar near the college. Later, of course, I wished that I had asked her more about that meeting. The other young woman who was killed—the one who was strangled a year later? She used to hang out at the same bar. I know that's a tenuous connection, but—"

"Do you know where she was from?"

"No. I don't remember. Why don't you read through this. My handwriting isn't too bad." He laughed. "Then if you have other questions, I'll try to answer them for you."

"More work?" Susan asked when I hung up the phone.

"Look, you've been through all those classes on the minds of killers—all that profiling shit, right?"

"I prefer not to think of it as shit."

"Simple question, Susan. Are the victims ever connected? When one of these guys gets going—Bundy or Gacy or Ramirez—whoever they are—"

"Sometimes the victims share characteristics. Hair parted in a certain way, gay lifestyle—"

"I don't mean that. I mean *connected*. A leads to B leads to C leads to D. That kind of thing."

"I don't know of any cases like that," she said. "Sounds pretty unlikely. Sure, these guys plan everything out, but they're still pretty impulsive. They troll for whatever happens to be out there. If that's your angle—that they're connected somehow—I think you're wasting your time."

"Probably," I agreed.

But I couldn't get it out of my head. The dream.

"How about a group shower and some dinner?" Susan asked.

"Sounds good. Why don't you start and I'll join you. I have to make a call."

"A quick call," she said, as she headed for the bathroom.

I tried Lane's number and got her machine. "Yeah, I got your message. We have to talk. I'm gonna be tied up tonight. Maybe we can connect in the morning."

Connect.

Lane

I stopped at the office late Friday night. I was hoping that a solid lead might have dropped out of the sky and landed in my in box. While I was there, I reread Pop's most recent communiqué. That's when I noticed his reference to the feather near Sarah's hand in photo #011. I had let that slip right by me the first time I read it.

That juvenile case from the sixties involved feathers—they were found among the animal parts stored in the shoe boxes in that crazy kid's bedroom. And now a feather shows up in a crime scene photo. What the hell was going on? Was I seeing connections that weren't really there?

I called Hal Levinson, our hair and fiber man, knowing he'd be in. There's a rumor that he doesn't even have a home. He takes sponge baths in the men's room in the basement, and keeps clothes in the trunk of his car. I think it has something to do with a divorce or gambling debts. Maybe both. He picked up on the first ring.

"Levinson, this is Lane. I have a question about the Sinclair murder scene."

"Shoot."

"Did you find any feathers over there?"

"One. *Cyanocitta cristata.*"

"English, please."

"The plume of a blue jay."

"What'd you do with it?"

"What I do with all the feathers. I collected it, identified it, and filed it."

"*All* the feathers? How many do you have down there?"

"We're in a strange business, Lane. I've picked up everything from raw chicken livers to uncut diamonds and hula hoops at murder scenes. Feathers are among our more ordinary finds," Levinson said, sounding bored. My guess was that he was holding the phone with one hand and writing a report with the other.

"How long have you been with the department?" I asked.

"Eighteen years, in February."

"And how many feathers have you bumped into at murder scenes?"

"I don't know. Maybe eight, ten. Maybe more."

"*Indoor* murder scenes?"

"Right. Dozens more if you count the outdoor scenes, of course."

"You've never considered that odd?"

"What?"

"Finding feathers indoors."

Levinson took in a deep breath, probably steeling himself for the lecture he was about to deliver.

"Listen, Lane, they could be from anything."

"Like?"

"A feather bed."

"Yeah," I said. "Sears is running a big sale on mattresses stuffed with blue jay feathers."

"They aren't always from blue jays," Levinson said. There was an unpleasant edge to his voice that made me wonder if maybe I *was* making a big deal out of nothing.

"Believe me, Lane," he added, his voice softening, "the feather's a red herring."

"Prove it."

"Prove it isn't. I'm telling you, this is routine stuff. I talk to people at conventions all the time. We swap war stories, and I think everyone on the Eastern seaboard has at least one unexplained feather story to tell."

I hung up feeling like Levinson's argument about the significance of the feathers could just as easily be seen as support for my point of view. Maybe feathers kept turning up because there was a crazy out there using them as his calling card. His signature. And maybe Pop was the first one to notice.

I wanted to catch up with Robert. We had a lot of ground to cover. He had left a message on my machine saying that he was going to be tied up for the evening, so I thought that I'd call and talk to his tape for a while. When I dialed his number, I got a busy signal. I kept trying at fifteen-minute intervals for nearly two hours. By then I was worried. I called the operator and asked her to check the line; she said there was trouble and she'd report it.

I didn't like the sound of that. Besides worrying that Wolf-Chadwick-Carver might have paid Robert a visit, I hadn't forgotten the nurse's warning that a subdural hematoma could kill a person. I decided to check on him.

It seemed pointless to knock. All I had to do was set the door aside and walk in. Sinclair's living room was empty and I didn't hear the TV in the bedroom. The phone was off the hook. I put the receiver back where it belonged and turned to leave.

Just then, my partner, completely naked, stepped out of the kitchen carrying some slices of pizza on a large white plate. He was headed for the bedroom.

"I have an idea," Robert said. "Why don't you drop by

unannounced, walk right in, and make yourself at home? It's really a bad time, Lane."

Sometimes I have to be hit with a two-by-four. "I need to talk to you," I said.

"Let me call you later."

Just as I was beginning to wonder why he kept glancing toward the bedroom, I found out. A woman, wrapped in Robert's robe, appeared in the doorway.

"Oops," she said, but she didn't look embarrassed.

"I think you two have met," Robert said.

"Yes, of course," I said.

Susan Walker backed into the bedroom and closed the door. Earlier that morning, at the precinct, Walker and I had been standing together, talking, when Robert rolled in. She noticed him right away—and, thinking back, I realized that she did sort of perk up at the sight of him. "What's his story?" she had asked me. I explained that he was my partner. "What kind of guy is he?" she wanted to know.

"I'll be running along now," I said.

Sinclair followed me out into the hallway of his apartment building, with nothing more than a slice of pizza shielding him from an indecent exposure arrest.

"Hey, Lane," he said, trotting after me.

I had come to his apartment to discuss the case. At least, that's what I had told myself. Maybe I'd been looking for something else, too, but I'd lost on both counts.

Robert

I walked back into the apartment, grabbed a beer, and sat down on the carpet in the living room. Susan walked out and wrapped a blanket around me.

"I didn't know you and your partner were involved," she said.

"Neither did I. It's been a long time."

Susan was pulling on her clothes. "I should get going."

"Yeah. It's late, I guess."

"After midnight. I've got a briefing at eight. Can I call tomorrow night?"

I stood up and pulled the blanket tighter. I felt a chill and my head was pounding. "Yeah, let's do something."

We kissed and she was gone.

I sat on the sofa and called Fuzzy. His voice was sleep sodden.

"It's me," I said.

"It's late."

"I think I've got one of those hangovers that start to come

on when I stop drinking too early. I'm going out, hit a few bars. Want to join me?"

"I was dreaming," Fuzzy said. "It was a nice dream. I don't want any nightmares. Besides, I'm on duty at four. See you tomorrow."

"Good night, Fuzzy."

The line went dead.

I dressed, grabbed my keys and wallet, and took the three cans of beer remaining from a six-pack. I slid the door into place as best I could, which was becoming a bad joke.

My car was beside its hydrant. I got in and headed for the waterfront, wondering what Lane was so amped about. It had been over between us for months.

I found a place called the Sea Breeze. It was right across the street from the river, which smelled like a men's room in a bus station. The Sea Breeze itself smelled even worse, but it was just what I wanted. I sat at the bar and ordered a Wild Turkey boilermaker.

The bartender—short, fat, and smothered in tattoos—said all he had was Old Crow.

"Good enough," I said.

There were maybe five guys still drinking. One guy had passed out at his table, and a few hookers were grabbing a drink before heading out for one more trick. There wasn't much talk, just chain-smoking and serious drinking. I tossed mine back and ordered another.

I knew what I was doing. Running from Sarah. Running from Liza. Playing at being a cop. Anything to duck reality.

I knew it, but I couldn't stop it. You live a whole life that way, what are you supposed to do? You can't flip a switch and suddenly become sober and responsible. It's bad enough dealing with shit on the run. Who wants to stand still and do it?

The headache was receding. Nothing like finding the right medicine.

A hooker walked over and stood at my elbow. "Twenty in the car. Forty at my place," she said.

I looked at her. Nineteen? Twenty? Somebody's daughter. "Honey, I just want to drink."

"I know you," she said. "You're a cop. Bert, this dude's a cop. What are you letting fucking cops in here for?"

Bert was the bartender. "You a cop?"

"I just want to sit here and drink," I said.

"Finish your drink and get the fuck out," Bert said.

"He busted me," the whore told him. "Couple years ago. Him and a big dyke cop."

"Look, I don't want any trouble."

By this time, two more Sea Breeze patrons had moved toward me.

"I'm gonna finish my drink, then I'll walk out of here," I said, slipping my 9 millimeter onto the bar.

They stopped.

"Give me an excuse," I said. "Please give me an excuse."

I looked at the clock behind the bar. I couldn't read the time, but it had lights that kept twinkling—like they were drops of water going over Niagara Falls. Over and over again.

"I don't need an excuse," I said, and fired four shots into the waterfall.

There was a geyser of sparks and shattered plastic, the smell of cordite. All the assholes were under tables or running for the bathrooms.

The place got real quiet. I didn't bother with the drink, just sat for a few minutes, then walked out. I made it through the door and into the parking lot before I went down to my knees. I thought I'd been slugged from behind, but I was alone in the lot, on all fours on the damp asphalt.

I crawled to the old Ford and pulled myself up by the door handle. I felt like I had to get somewhere, but I couldn't remember where.

I got behind the wheel and started the car. Then I fished a pint of Wild Turkey out of the glove compartment and removed the cap with my teeth. The old amber liquid did the trick—or at least part of it. I don't know how long I drove, or what route I took, but it was after three in the morning when I pulled up at the precinct house.

I managed to find my cubicle and slip in without anyone noticing. At that hour there weren't many people around anyway.

I took a sip from my pint and called information for Saxtons River, Vermont. "The police department," I said.

"They have no listing," the operator said. "I can give you Bellows Falls or the state police."

I took both numbers and started with the small-town department.

"No one in the department goes back that far," the dispatcher said when I told her I was interested in a case from the 1960s. "Charlie Murdock was chief for years, but he's dead. You might be better off trying the state police. They're just up the road from here."

I tried one more approach. "What about the name Paul Wolf? That mean anything to you?"

"Paul Wolf? Why didn't you say so. I was a substitute teacher at the school when all that happened. It was the only thing people talked about around here for months."

She sounded happy to talk. There wasn't much going on in Bellows Falls at 3:30 in the morning.

"What exactly happened?" I asked.

"Paul and his mother, Alice Wolf, lived alone in an apartment in Bellows Falls. She was a waitress at a diner there. Nobody was real sure who Paul's father was. Eventually, Alice met a man named Edward Corrigan and moved in with him in Saxtons River. Corrigan had an old house there that he was always working on, but never really made livable. Paul was a loner. Corrigan had no use for him. People were pretty sure the stepfather batted Paul around, but Alice never complained. She went to church and prayed a lot, but never tried to get help for Paul or any of the family. Then Alice got pregnant. The baby—Sarah—was the apple of Corrigan's eye. She was his baby. And Sarah was a real cutie, don't misunderstand me. But things just got worse for Paul. It seemed like Corrigan hated him even more after the little girl was born."

The sister's name was Sarah. Was I finally starting to make some connection?

"I'm not real clear about why it all happened that night, but Paul went after Corrigan with a knife. Alice grabbed him from behind. Paul cut them both pretty bad, but they managed to get the knife away from him. Mental health was involved after that, and Paul was sent away to some private school. He was home for a while the summer before he left for college. He was so bright. It was such a waste. He left here that summer and hardly ever came back. I heard he didn't do so well in college down in the city. Then, of course, there was the army. He was killed in Vietnam. His ashes are buried right up the hill here. But somewhere in there—I'm not sure exactly when—he started going by another last name. He was convinced he knew who his real father was. I don't know where he got the idea. He thought it was Gary Pease, a local guy who died in a logging accident the year Paul was born. That's why he took to calling himself Paul Pease."

"What about Sarah?" I asked.

"She married and moved away. I don't know who she married or what her name is. I think she cut off all contact with her parents about the same time Paul was shipped off to Saigon."

I sat at the computer terminal and put in a request for information. The army did have a record for Paul Pease. He was killed at Pleiku in 1972, three years before the last American soldiers came home.

I did the paperwork necessary to get his complete file and his fingerprints.

"I don't care what his fucking name is, he ain't dead," I muttered to myself. "There's an explanation for all this shit."

"You're not going to find it," Hanson said.

The captain had walked in behind me, right after addressing the 4 A.M. roll call.

"You don't work this case," he said. "That's department

policy. You don't work *any* case when you're on leave. You *are* on leave, Detective, and you don't come off leave until you've been through alcohol rehab. Twenty-eight days and a clean bill of health, or you start looking for something in warehouse security. Leave the nine on your desk."

After Hanson said his piece, he walked out.

I placed my weapon and badge on my desk, then wandered down the hall. Lieutenant Swartz was standing outside an interrogation room in front of the one-way glass.

"What's up?"

"Willoughby's been working the guy most of the night," he said, gesturing at a slightly built, fiftyish guy wearing Coke bottle glasses. "You smell like the inside of a cheap bottle."

"Who is he?"

"Name's Wayne Purrington. He's already confessed to doing the three prostitutes up in Albany. There's two more in Troy the Bureau hadn't even connected to him. He's been down our way since just before Harris was done. Won't talk about Sarah, but says he *might* have done Harris. Says he doesn't remember."

I studied Purrington's sallow complexion, sunken cheeks, missing teeth, balding head, long, bony fingers—he was dressed in jeans and a flannel shirt, looking like he belonged in a dump like the Sea Breeze.

"He didn't kill Sarah," I said. "He didn't kill Maxine Harris either."

Swartz agreed. "But Willoughby's gonna get a confession out of him anyway."

"And when Purrington gets a lawyer, he'll recant. This is all bullshit."

Again, Swartz agreed. "I'm keeping the investigation going, Sinclair. Lane's going to handle it. You get your ass into rehab and take care of business. You not only smell bad, you look bad."

I nodded at him, might have said, "Thanks," then continued wandering down the hall—with my head banging like a pile driver and the whole world going blurry on me. Swartz was right. I did need a little R&R somewhere. But first I wanted to find Fuzzy.

Somehow I managed to get to the coffee machine, and there he was.

"Fuzzy, you went through rehab, didn't you?"

"Twice," Fuzzy said. "I guess it didn't take. I'm so close to retirement now, they don't bother with me anymore."

"What's it like?"

"Food's good. Too much talking, though—all this shit about a higher power. See, I've had this understanding with God ever since I was a kid. When He's ready to take me, I go. No argument. No pleading for more time. I just go."

Fuzzy was getting revved up—maybe from the coffee, I don't know. He was also going in and out of focus. Too much to drink and not enough sleep. Or maybe I needed a drink.

"This body ain't no temple," Fuzzy said, "as you can plainly see. When it needs Irish whiskey, it gets Irish whiskey. And I've put enough stout through my kidneys to rain out a Yankees game. Now, I had these rehab dudes—most of 'em found Jesus curbside—telling me to give myself up to a higher power. I already had that worked out. And I kept getting the steps mixed up. There must be a dozen of them fucking things."

Fuzzy's voice faded, my eyes wouldn't focus, and my head was pounding like a son of a bitch. I saw Fuzzy put his coffee down and start to reach for me. Then the lights went out.

The room was white.

And God—all seven feet of him—was very clearly black.

"This ain't heaven," I said.

"No, mon," the grinning giant said. "Don' be heaven, but be nice gig."

"Hospital?"

He nodded.

"Are you really that big, or are you standing on something?"

"I eat only the right foods, mon. Grains. Fruit. Built me a very healthy body."

"Why aren't you playing for the Giants?"

"I play no silly game with puny guys. I'm in an elevator one time standing eye to eye with Shaquille O'Neal. He's not used to that, now. No football. No basketball. I *bowl*."

"Reach out and knock the pins down, huh?"

"*Break* the pins, mon. Another hospital pay me five hundred dollars to play for them this year. Next year I renegotiate. Maybe this place gets wise."

I was enjoying the big guy, but I had other things on my mind—namely, finding a way out. "What is this place?"

"Same one you break out of before. But not this time. You and me, we have a good time. I tell you the story of my hero's life—Bob Marley—you fall asleep. Then I listen to my music."

He held up a Walkman and a set of ratty-looking earphones.

"You sleep some more," he said. "That way you stay out of four points."

"Four points?"

Still grinning, he held up a leather strap. "Four-point restraint. They keep you in bed so you shit in a pan. You want to shit in a pan?"

"I want to go to sleep."

"Good. Then I tell you about my hero, Mr. Bob Marley. Humble beginnings, that mon."

"What's your name? And what are you doing here?"

The grin disappeared. "I'm Lymann Murr. I'm hired as a special to make sure you don't wander off. We understand each other?"

Just then Hanson appeared at the door and started in. For a big man, Murr was quick. Hanson's face was about level with the guy's breastbone.

"Who are you?" Murr asked.

Hanson was nonplussed. "Hanson. I'm the captain."

"Show some ID," Murr said.

Hanson did.

Murr wasn't impressed. "You're not on the list," he said.

"I'm the captain—his boss," Hanson said.

"Go away," Murr said. "I don't like violence."

Lane came in then, and walked around Murr and Hanson.

"Lymann," she said, nodding a hello.

"Hey, Lane. You want this guy in?"

Lane looked at Hanson. "Probably not a good idea right now, Captain," she said. "The doctor's on his way over, too. We'll all have to leave."

Hanson retreated.

"I stopped and picked up your mail," she said, tossing it on the bed. "I also fixed your door."

"Look, about last night."

"Lymann, tell the little white man to shut up."

"Lady said shut up, mon."

"And it wasn't last night anyway," Lane said. "You lost a day."

I've been drunk enough to miss out a few hours before, but never anything like this. I knew I'd been down at the waterfront. There was a hooker. I remembered bits and pieces, but couldn't put the whole picture together.

"He keeps threatening me with a bedpan," I said. "That your idea, too?"

"That's for shooting Bert's favorite clock. He says it was an heirloom."

I looked at her. "I did that?"

She nodded. "You walk away from treatment, you face charges. That's the deal."

I fumbled through the mail that I hadn't bothered to pick up for days. Bills. Ads. And a small package with no return address, just a postal cancellation from White River Junction. I couldn't read the state abbreviation.

"I picked up all your notes," Lane said. "Also got that notebook Chadwick sent you."

"Good. Where's White River Junction?" I asked.

"Vermont," Lymann said. "Other side of the river from Hanover, New Hampshire, where I went to school."

"You went to Dartmouth?" Lane asked.

"Studied music. I play synclavier. Bedpans aren't my only gig," he told her. "I thought you knew everything about me, cuz."

"Cuz?" I said.

"I'm Lane's mama's sister's boy," he explained, grinning. "That makes us cousins."

"Nice to know we're keeping my confinement all in the family," I said, as a book slipped out of the wrapping and onto the bed.

Rimbaud.

I opened the cover and stared at the bookplate: *From the Library of Maxine Harris*.

"This is the book that Sarah told me about," I said. "The one I had gone to her house to get."

My head was finally starting to clear. "Wolf's name is Pease," I said. "He has a sister named Sarah."

I told Lane what I remembered from my conversation with the dispatcher in Vermont—that Wolf had grown up in Saxtons River, tried to kill his parents, and was believed to have died in Vietnam.

"Somebody has to get to the sister," I said, pushing the blanket off and starting to get up.

"He's had enough," Lymann said, putting me right back where I was.

"There were notes and some stuff from the army on your desk," Lane said.

"That's what you need," I told her.

"I'll take care of it. You're here for the duration."

I leaned back, looking again at the volume of poetry, thumbing through the pages until I saw the highlighted lines. I read them aloud to Lane:

The wolf howled under the leaves
And spit out the prettiest feathers
Of his meal of fowl,
Like him I consume myself.

"Christ, what are we dealing with?" she said.

Lane

I flunked my polygraph.

One question did me in: "Do you know who killed Sarah Sinclair?"

My voice was saying, "No," but my head was saying "Yes." I knew that Wolf/Carver/Chadwick/Pease was our killer. I couldn't even tell anybody what he looked like, but I knew that he did it. So when I said no, the needle jumped.

Fibs (that's what we call the guy who runs our polygraph; his name is Gibbs) asked me the same question during three different trials, and each time it activated an emotional response. After the third try, he said, "Sorry, Lane. This isn't working out."

I didn't even wait for Hanson to call me in. Monday morning, while he was out at a city council meeting, I walked into his office and put my badge and gun on his desk—along with a note reminding him that department policy required that I be placed on *paid* suspension.

Before I left, I gathered up everything that I thought I might possibly need: Xeroxes of all the scientific evidence reports, the packet of faxes I had received from surrounding police departments, the stack of crime scene photos Benny took. To avoid being brought up on charges, I stuck a handwritten note in the case file, signing them out to an unreadable name.

I also picked the lock on Robert's file drawer again. He had told me about the book and the gun that "Alan Carver" dropped off. I wanted the gun. Now that Hanson had my 9 millimeter, I wanted something with more firepower than the .22 I kept at my apartment.

Robert had known that the whole embassy story was a fraud, so the paperwork on the gun *had* to be fake. He'd even yelled at Sarah, telling her what a fool she was to fall for all the lies this Wolf character was telling her. But then it was days before he ran the serial number on the gun.

I found the report in Robert's in basket, so I knew that he hadn't seen it. The .32 had come back registered to Dr. Alan Chadwick of Hasty Hills, Connecticut. There was also a second gun in Chadwick's name—this one a .38 (probably the gun he used on the two guys in the alley across from the bookstore).

I tucked the .32 into my cosmetics bag and headed home, where a fax from Pop was waiting. I sat down to read it while I waited for some coffee to perk.

TO: Lanie
FROM: Pop
Getting fired from a job that I've never accepted is a significant insult. But I see that despite my dismissal from the case, Lt. Swartz continues to view me as part of the team. And apparently he sees you the same way, despite your suspension (bad news travels fast). No wonder I like Swartz. The only authority he seems to respect is his own.

If I were to join this renegade investigative unit that you and Swartz have going, I suppose that you would be my boss. But then it's always been that way, hasn't it? We need to talk about your managerial skills. I've already done a few hours' work for you, but you haven't even mentioned a benefits package. I'll want 100% insurance, of course (including Rx and dental), and automatic vacation whenever the fishing looks promising. Any problems with that?

Although Lt. Swartz is continuing to fax information, he has warned me not to communicate with him at the office. He says I'm to run everything through your fax machine at home. He apologized for the inconvenience, but says it's a necessity—"because Hanson suffers from rectocranial inversion." I'm going to push for that to be included in the new *Diagnostic and Statistical Manual.*

To business. Another photo for you to consider: #119 from the Harris case. It's not a crime scene shot (she was found in a cemetery); it's from the search of her apartment. Again, use a glass. Look at the saucer under the jade plant. If I'm not mistaken, that's an epaulet feather from a red-winged blackbird. Your wolf has many signatures.

A friend at Cambridge PD checked for me on that strangulation homicide that the real Dr. Chadwick mentioned to your partner. No photos, but they still had the inventory taken at her apartment. There was a feather. It meant nothing, however, because she worked part-time at the Peabody Museum there. Also, re Chadwick's young friend who fell (or was pushed) to her death: the final entries in her diary do refer to flying like a bird, but they are not the words of someone suicidal or psychotic. Quite simply, she was enchanted by the swallows that fly up among the buildings in Boston's business district. A "strange new friend" had taken her there. She wrote that she wanted to learn more about him, and she pondered what it would be like to fly like the swallows. It was rather charming, really—not the end of the world, more like the beginning of something.

Wolf's signatures change. They don't represent the kind of linkage cops like to see. Because he knows about investigations, *he* changes.

Some victims are displayed; some are left where they fall. Some (apparently) are buried north of Hasty Hills. He enjoys manipulating the crime scene (before, during, or after the fact?). He puts things in, takes things out, or just moves things around. It's not always the same.

I fear that all of your various pieces of evidence will lead nowhere. You'll have names, places to check—and you have to do this, of course—but you won't find him, and he knows that. Your federal friends will be content to focus on their suspect, waiting to see if there are any more killings with a similar MO, but I can't accept that. They consider all the Wolf/Chadwick material to be a low priority right now because the information they feed into their databases doesn't include the subtleties—this killer's hallmark—that can be seen only in a close reading of the individual crime scene reports.

There *is* linkage. It may not be a conscious thing with Wolf (although I fear that it is), but it's there. Rebecca Holbrook was the young woman who disappeared on her way to work at the bottling plant. A year before her disappearance, a man was killed in an industrial accident at the plant. Alan Chadwick, MD, was a member of the inspection team that spent three days evaluating the plant's safety and medical response procedures. Coincidence?

A few months before her disappearance, Ms. Holbrook attended her tenth high school reunion in Pawtucket, RI. A secretary at that school, Paulette Carson (who had no connection to the reunion or Ms. Holbrook), was found strangled in her apartment.

Unsolved. No feather. But there was an audiotape in her cassette player that close friends insisted she would never have bought: *The Teardrop Explodes*—another Julian Cope incarnation. Coincidence?

Ms. Carson was originally from Ansonia, CT—the same town where Susan Cullen disappeared from a convenience store ten months ago. She's the one who was found floating in the river. No music. No feather. But someone had broken into her apartment, fingered his way through a few drawers, helped himself to a bowl of soup, and walked away with a book—a collection of poetry. Coincidence?

I'm beginning to get a feel for this gentleman. I don't like it. Never do. Something nags in one of the far corners of my mind. When it decides to make itself known, I'll advise.

With the help of a friend at Social Security, I was able to locate Paul Wolf's half-sister: Sarah Humphrey, 492 Devil's Kitchen Road, Casselberry, Florida. Phone: (407) 555-6073. Go see her.

Pop

P.S. I would have expected Wolf to blow out the candles at Sarah's house. Why didn't he?

The coffee was ready, but I sent off an answer to Pop before pouring it.

Pop,
If you know about the suspension, you know about the polygraph. I walked out before Hanson had a chance to track me down. I don't have time to deal with him. I've got a killer to catch. Rather, *we* do. So I'll be camping out at Robert's for a while. Right now, he's getting checked out physically, then he'll be transferred to Tranquil Acres for 28 days of withdrawal and soul-searching.

You're supposed to tell *me* why our boy didn't blow out the candles. My guess is that he hung around, enjoyed the house for a while. We know that he took a shower. Luminal lit up the bathroom, especially the tub. Remember, by the time he was ready to leave, the candles had burned themselves down to nothing. More evidence that he was comfortable there?

Yes, I'll go to Florida. The timing of your request (read "demand") that I pay Sarah Humphrey a visit is perfect. The less I show my face around this town right now, the better.

Also, I'll call Lt. Swartz and let him know that I'll find a way to get your faxes to him. I know he'll continue to work with us.

Keep on loving me. Think you can do that?

Lanie

I wanted to tell Pop about Robert, about my need to be close to him—and about Susan Walker. But I've never been too sure how much Pop knows about matters of the heart. I don't think Mom ran off to Africa simply because she was crazy about chimps. I think she got tired of the way Pop kept retreating from her, going somewhere deep inside his head. Sometimes she had a look on her face, like she felt abandoned—even when Pop was right there, in the same room. That's why, after Mom took off, I didn't blame her. I blamed him.

But then, maybe I didn't know my father as well as I liked to think I did. Maybe he had a romantic side that he kept hidden around others. I have suspected that he has a woman with him in Michigan. One time when he made it out to a post office, he mailed me a picture of him sitting in a boat, fishing. It took two days for it to occur to me that someone else snapped that picture. But who? He has never mentioned anyone else being there, not a single soul, in any of his faxes.

After sending off my missive to Pop, I downed a glass of orange juice and an oatmeal cookie, then headed for Sarah's house. My car (a big Buick named Karen Ann) is a relic from my college days—a gift from Pop. Since I've always had use of one of the department's cars for any serious driving I've needed to do, I haven't bothered keeping Karen Ann tuned up. She doesn't even ask to have her oil changed. But I thought she could use some exercise, so I drove her over to Sarah's place.

I hadn't turned in my key to the lockbox on Sarah's front door. I wanted to pull a photo of Sarah out of one of those albums on the shelf in her closet. I didn't intend to linger—just grab a recent photo for ID purposes—but once I started turning pages, I couldn't stop. I looked at picture after picture of wedded bliss. For a marriage that was, in Robert's words, pure hell, it certainly looked a lot different on paper. His arm around her in one picture, hers around him in another. Both of them grinning at their infant child in still another.

I needed to see Robert. There was so much about this case that I wanted to run by him. I also just wanted to sit there with him, to be in the same space that he occupied. I knew that I was feeling vulnerable, and being around that guy had always been an antidote for that feeling.

As soon as I arrived at Robert's room, I sent Lymann on an errand. Then I closed the door and sat down on the edge of the bed.

"I've got news," I told him.

"I heard about your suspension."

"I'm lying low. If you want to reach me, I'll be at your apartment."

"Tonight?"

"For as long as I need to be there."

Robert was looking at me in a new way—like he was appraising me.

"What?" I asked.

"Tell me about the polygraph. Where'd you screw up?"

"When Fibs asked if I knew who killed Sarah. I know, and you know. It was Wolf."

He seemed to relax.

"Yeah. I'll probably fail mine, too," he said.

There was a tap at the door, then Special Agent Walker stuck her head inside and said, "Hope I'm not interrupting anything."

"Hi, Susan."

That's all Robert said, but the words were beside the point. I was staring at his face. I saw his eyes, how his whole expression changed when he looked at her. I'd never seen that look in his eyes before—except maybe in the pictures of him and Sarah and Liza.

I got up off the bed and mumbled something about having to run.

"Not on my account, I hope," Susan said.

"No. I have to get some sleep. I have a doctor's appointment in the morning."

"You okay?" Robert asked.

"Yeah."

"You sure?"

"It's nothing. The flu, maybe mono. I'm just run down."

As I was leaving, I could hear Lymann telling Susan that she wasn't on the list of approved visitors. She followed me all the way to the parking garage, but she was in stilettos; I was in sneakers. She didn't catch up with me until I was unlocking my car door.

"We've gotten off to a rotten start," she said, "but I want you to know that I'm still hoping we can work together on this."

She offered me her card, but I didn't take it. The look on her face might have been genuine hurt.

"I'm sorry," I said. "I really am. I know I'm being a bitch. I don't have any claims on Sinclair. It's been over for months."

"That's what he told me," Walker said.

"Yeah," I said, feeling even more alone than I had earlier.

"I'm going to tell you something that I haven't admitted to anybody else. Maybe not even to myself," Walker said. "Becoming a federal agent is an experience in brainwashing. Everything we do, we do for the company. Right or wrong has nothing to do with it. We're told that our job is to gather information, period. But I don't buy that. I should have been a cop, like you. I need to make arrests, see results. So if there's ever anything I can do for you that's, well, off the record, let me know. It'll be just between us."

"I'm on suspension," I said.

"I know."

"I failed my polygraph."

"I know that, too. And I know that isn't going to keep you out of this case."

"Okay," I told her. "I'll keep your offer in mind."

But when I drove away, I didn't head straight for Robert's apartment. I knew she might be tailing me. I drove to Fuzzy's place instead. When he opened the door, I walked right into his arms. That hug was the best thing I had felt all day.

I ended up spending the night on Fuzzy's couch, remaining in the house even after he took off for work at 3:45. About 8:30, I got up, took a shower, put my dirty clothes back on, booked a flight to Florida, then drove over to the Women's Center.

Carol's diagnosis was a post-flu, secondary infection—"walking pneumonia." She gave me a prescription for an antibiotic, and I had it filled as soon as I left the clinic. She also ordered bed rest, but that I couldn't do. I just had to hope that the medication did its job fast.

Robert

The docs had me pumped full of something that felt worse than booze. I couldn't think—couldn't get a handle on anything.

"I didn't think Lane would care about me and Susan," I told Fuzzy. "I figured that she and I were all over. She was looking for commitment—all that shit. I couldn't handle it, and that was that."

"She might not have known how she was feeling," Fuzzy said.

"We could've talked about it at least."

"And what would you have said? That you're ready to rush off to the altar?"

I rolled over on my side. "Not that," I mumbled.

"Bobby, some day you're gonna get by you and Sarah and Liza. Then maybe you'll look at what it means to be in a relationship. Monica and I had twenty-eight years of it—some good, some bad. It was work, Bobby. To make it go that long, you have to work at it. And I miss her, too. We were gonna move to Phoenix when I retired."

"Sometimes I think that Lane and I could have worked things out," I said.

"Why not now?" Fuzzy asked. "Why are ya talkin' like there's no chance now? Get by it. Think about *her*. Think about the two of you, if you want to."

"You got anything to drink, Fuzzy?" I asked.

"I'm off the stuff," he said, and got up and walked across the room. "Hey, Lymann, wanna play some cards?"

Lane was jealous. But she was the one that broke things off. I hadn't known that she still wanted there to be something going on between us.

"What time they putting me in storage?" I asked.

"Soon as the doctor checks you out, we go," Lymann said.

"Tranquil Acres?"

Fuzzy laughed. "You know where it is? Up above Hasty Hills."

"I can't stand it," I said.

"You see the morning paper?"

"It's around here somewhere. I can't read. It blurs."

"Purrington confessed," Fuzzy said. "Says he did Harris. He's probably getting arraigned right now—one count here. They'll have a separate arraignment on the five up north."

So I end up in a rubber room, and Lane holes up at my place. She can't bring Wolf down alone, and Hanson will isolate her. He's got Purrington. No one can fault him.

"Hanson's picture in the paper?"

"Him and Willoughby," Fuzzy said.

"Case closed," I said.

After the doc cleared me for takeoff, Lymann strapped me into a wheelchair and rolled me down to meet Fuzzy with the car. My favorite sergeant wasn't kidding: he headed north on the interstate, toward Hasty Hills.

"You really quit drinking?" I asked Fuzzy.

"Yeah."

"Just like that."

"When you went out on me, Bobby, we were talking about God calling *me* home. You shoot the shit out of the

Sea Breeze, I figure you're getting a person-to-person, collect. I didn't want to see you go, and I'm not in much of a hurry either. Sobered me right up."

I watched the mile markers go by. The road was familiar. I wondered how many times Wolf had driven up and down here.

The night Lane kicked in my door, I told her the truth. I was scared. And I was scared going to the drunk farm, too, but in a lot of ways it was a relief. I wanted Wolf dead, but the shape I was in, I wasn't the man to do it. Lane would do whatever she could. Swartz would help her. And maybe in a month we'd at least know where the bastard is.

Fuzzy left the interstate, but continued north on a two-lane road through woods and rolling hills. He had to slow down when we passed a state police operation—the dig on Wolf's, aka Doc Chadwick's, property.

"You hear anything about that?"

"Staties ain't saying much," Fuzzy said. "Last I knew they were up to eleven."

Eleven more dead.

"Willoughby and Hanson gonna tie that to Purrington, too? He just happened to choose this land for his mass grave?"

"You want my opinion," Fuzzy said, "I think they're afraid to open this up—afraid of what they'll find. Another Zodiac or Green River killer. Maybe another Ted Bundy. Thirty victims? Forty? Fifty? And they can't catch him. Hanson would be back on a beat, and Willoughby would be running for the senate in Virginia. Lucky thing Purrington was in town when the manure hit the fan."

"Somebody's got to stop this guy," I said.

The car picked up speed again. I leaned back in the seat and figured it was time to let go. There wasn't anything I could do.

Lane had done everything in the world for me—kept me alive. I was so hung up on Sarah, I just never saw it. For me to be with Lane meant I wasn't with Sarah, and that meant I was at least a little crazy, a little brittle, a lot blind.

I remember that first night when Lane blocked my way in the parking lot. She was telling me then that she loved me. I figured she just wanted to get laid. So I followed her home.

Somewhere in all those months of drunken calisthenics there was a lot more than good sex. And I missed it.

When Fuzzy shook me awake at the entrance to Tranquil Acres, I felt as if I'd had my first real rest in years. I'd fallen asleep somewhere along the way. I was weak, tired, and maybe getting my first hint of what would be, to me, an altered state of consciousness—sobriety.

"All out for the Ho-Ho Hotel," Fuzzy said.

Lymann opened the car door for me.

"Fuzzy, tell Lane I said I'm sorry. For everything. Tell her that."

He nodded. "Good luck, Bobby."

We shook hands.

Lymann helped me out of the car and to a standing position.

"Walk or ride?" he asked.

"You keep an arm on me and I think I can walk," I said. "You going through the program, too?"

"Ninth time for me, and I don't even drink."

"I won't give you a hard time, Lymann. I promise."

"I know that. No way you outrun the mon."

"Ain't that the truth," I said. "Ain't that just the truth."

Lane

◆

I'd started taking the antibiotics. Carol knew I couldn't climb into bed and stay there, so she told me to at least take it easy for a couple of days. But I had work to do. Even though I still felt tired and weak, I decided to trudge on. I had to.

I had been the lead investigator, and I still considered it my case, my responsibility. As much as I had disliked and even feared Sarah Sinclair because of her power over Robert, I owed her. And Robert couldn't do anything. I knew he wanted to be right in the middle of it, but he was out of circulation and going to stay that way for a while. Hanson was wearing blinders—so certain that everything was going to wrap up neatly with Purrington. I had no choice. I had to keep working it.

Number one on my list was a visit to the massage parlor above the bookstore where Sarah worked. Harry wasn't there, but Sheila was on duty.

"Harry won't know nothin' anyway," Sheila assured me. "Sarah didn't like him—never talked to him, except to tell him how much he shorted her check each week."

"How did you and Sarah get along?" I asked her.

"So-so. She was always floating around in that dream world of hers. Only time she really talked to me was when she wanted something. Like that day she borrowed my blazer."

"When was that?"

"Not long before she was killed. Her blouse got dirty when she was cleaning the shelves in the bookstore, and she had a date right after work—no time to go home and change. You know, now that I think about it, I never got my blazer back. I suppose it's evidence or something, huh?"

"I'll look into it, Sheila," I said. "Sarah had a date?"

"Yeah. With some new guy, a customer."

"A customer of yours?"

"Nah. The bookstore. I saw him go in there one time, but he wasn't the type to frequent a place like this. Too clean. Seemed to have a high opinion of himself."

"You got all of that out of just one glance?"

She smiled, missing the skepticism. "In this business, you learn to size up a guy pretty fast," she said.

"What about Sarah? What'd she say about him?"

Sheila lowered her voice, as if confiding a secret. "I could see it in her face, in her eyes," she said. "They were all lit up, kind of manic, when she told me about her date."

"Did she tell you the man's name?"

"John," she said, shrugging. "John Fox, I think. Or Lamb. Some kind of animal, anyway."

"Wolf?"

"Yeah. That's it. But he didn't kill her."

I looked up, my pencil poised above my notebook.

"I'm pretty good when it comes to reading a guy. This one wouldn't have dirtied his hands. I'll bet he gets manicures twice a week. Besides, if he had killed her, he wouldn't be hanging around in this neighborhood, would he?"

"You've seen him?"

"He had on sunglasses, so it was hard to tell—but the hair was right, and the shape of the head. He drove by this morning. I'd forgotten to lock my car door, so I went back downstairs to do it. That's when I saw him."

"Did he say anything? Do anything?"

"He slowed down, glanced at the store, kept on going. I really didn't pay that much attention to him. He's not my type."

"What kind of car was he driving?"

She shrugged. "I don't know. They all look alike to me. It was a dark color is all I remember."

I thanked Sheila for her help, then drove over to Fast Eddie's, the restaurant whose logo was on the sugar packet I found in Sarah's skirt pocket. I asked a waitress if the owner was in. Without a word, she went to get him. A fat guy emerged from the kitchen, wiping his hands on a Holiday Inn towel.

"Hi," he said, "I'm Fast Eddie."

"Have you ever seen this woman?" I asked, showing him the picture I had removed from Sarah's album.

He stared at it for several seconds, then looked at me and said, "Who are you?"

"Detective Frank, Homicide. I'd appreciate it if you'd take another look at her."

"Don't need to. That's the girl who come in here with Doc."

"Doc?"

"I don't know his real name. Doc's what everybody calls him."

"Who's everybody?"

"The women he brings in."

"He's a regular?"

"Regular enough. Orders a combination—French roast and Colombian supreme. I'm always glad to see him because I have to make it special. He pays a buck fifty a cup. I'll pour it all day for that kind of money."

"How long has it been since you've seen him?"

"When he was here with her," Eddie said, indicating the photo of Sarah.

"How did Doc treat her?"

"It's funny you should ask that," Eddie said. "With this woman there was something different."

"What do you mean?"

"With the others, he always kept his distance, leaning back in his chair like he was pulling away from them. But with her, he reached out and touched her hand."

"That was unusual enough for you to notice it?"

"I always pay attention to stuff like that—you know, the way people interact. I like to study them. Maybe I shoulda been a shrink, huh?"

"What about her? How did she react to him?"

"I think she dug the guy. She talked a lot, smiled even more. Made a big deal out of the coffee, too—probably because it was his thing. And she gushed over the cheesecake, but everybody does that."

The whole time I was talking to Fast Eddie, I kept thinking there was something I was missing, or something I should be remembering. It didn't hit me until much later—after I was settled in at Robert's apartment, going through the stack of crime scene photos. When I reached the one showing Sarah's kitchen counter, I took a closer look. There were two packages sitting there.

I picked up the phone and punched in the numbers for the photo lab.

Benny was annoyed. "What happened to the Sinclair crime scene photos?"

"Someone signed them out, I think."

"Yeah, and I think I'm talkin' to her," he said. "Hanson went ape-shit."

"Sometimes Hanson forgets that we're all on the same side."

"What about the polygraph?"

"Benny, I don't have time to fight with Hanson right now. Besides, all his money's riding on Purrington. Meanwhile, the real killer is still out there, and I'm the only one looking for him. If I don't find him, he kills again. It's that simple. Benny, I think I'm finally making some headway. I need your help."

"Don't put me in this position, Lane," he said. "I'm not supposed to talk to you. None of us are."

"So don't talk to me. Call Fuzzy and tell him what I need to know."

Silence.

"Listen," I said, "this is all you have to do. Print photo number one twenty-six again, but this time enlarge it so we can see what it says on the labels of those two packages."

More silence.

"*Please,*" I said.

He hung up on me.

Twenty minutes later Robert's phone rang. I let the answering machine pick up the call, but I monitored it. When I heard Fuzzy's voice, I reached for the receiver.

"Hi, lover," I said.

"How ya doin'?"

"I've had better days. Did Benny call you?"

"Yeah," Fuzzy said, "but I don't think this is gonna help you much. All he said was two things."

"What?"

"French roast and Colombian supreme. Said he couldn't read the brand. What is that shit? Dope?"

"Coffee."

"Women," he mumbled, then hung up.

If I'd had any doubt that Chadwick—or Wolf, or whatever he called himself—was a welcome guest in Sarah's house, it was gone now. She'd laid in a stock of his favorite coffee beans, as if she had expected to be serving him his morning brew. I was more certain than ever before that the good doctor had been her Sunday night date. Just like Pop had said.

By sunset I was starting to feel hungry. I opened Robert's refrigerator, hoping to find something edible, but the smell was so sickening, I slammed it shut. I didn't find much in the freezer, either. Just three ice cube trays, two of them empty.

And a small tree.

I backed away, staring at the tiny, imitation pine. It was about five inches tall, with small red berries stuck to the tips of the branches. It rested on a wooden, cross-shaped base that enabled it to stand upright.

"A feather tree," I said.

Someone claiming to be my partner had been at Wallingford Antiques and purchased an antique feather tree. Was this for Robert? Wolf had called Robert. Or did someone know that I would be staying here? As I grabbed the .32 out of my cosmetics bag, I realized that my whole body was trembling. Robert's apartment wasn't safe anymore. Everything that had been so familiar about the place now threatened me.

I was shaking like I did when I was a kid and had a bad dream—when Savvy would hold me tight at night, and Pop always had something to say in the morning. "Whether the source of your fear is real or imagined," he said one time, "the only power fear has over you is what you allow it to have."

I walked to the door, slipped the chain in place, then checked out the bedroom. I made sure the locks were secure on all the windows, pulled every shade and drape in the place, then returned to the kitchen.

I was still standing in front of the open freezer when the phone rang. I let the answering machine take the call. When I heard Fuzzy's voice, I picked up.

"I ordered you a pizza," he said, "but don't let the delivery guy charge you for it. I put it on my credit card. The tip and everything. He's bringing you some Pepsi, too. They don't deliver beer."

I could hear somebody knocking on the door. "I think he's here now, but I'm not wild about letting him in. Something strange is going on, Fuzzy. Stay on the line."

I put down the phone, closed the freezer, and pulled back the hammer on the .32. Then I opened the door with the chain still in place. It was Special Agent Susan Walker.

"I thought you might want some company," she said.

Under any other circumstances, my answer would probably have been no. But I didn't want to be alone, and at least Walker was a cop. I told her to hang on a second, told Fuzzy that everything was okay, then let her in. The pizza guy arrived two minutes later.

"Your current address is just between us," Walker told me. "I know Hanson's looking for you, but that's not my problem. You know that I think it's bogus anyway."

I must have believed her. Either that, or I was desperate to trust someone. "Listen. I want you to hear this."

"What is it?"

"The innermost thoughts of Sarah Sinclair."

Walker sat cross-legged on the floor while I stretched out on the couch and began reading aloud from a handwritten poem that I had found tucked inside Sarah's notebook:

Autopsy

A polished bone, stronger than I thought.
Hair, prettier than I remembered.
I expected the brain to be worn smooth,

but it is wrinkled, with folds
that catch the dust.
I pick up a handful of teeth,

searching for the traces of the words
known to have traveled past them.
Nothing.
I drop them into the kitchen sink

to hear the sound they make.
A Morse code?
No. Nothing.
Perhaps the hands will tell me

what I need to know.
Narrow.

Nails neglected; cuticle untrimmed.
No. There is nothing to be learned here.
The lips: just a fever blister

of psychosomatic origin.
No sign that kisses
were ever placed there.
This, then, must be it:

the packing paper that keeps
each part from rubbing
and irritating the others.
Dozens of papers wadded into balls:

letters, poems, grocery lists.

I spread them flat—

and read the cause of death.

"You know, right after Sarah was murdered, Robert told me he was scared," I said. "Maybe that's why he started drinking more. Now I'm the one who's getting scared."

I told her how it looked to me—that Willoughby and Hanson weren't investigating anything until they finished with Purrington. "There's somebody else out there," I said. "And there's going to be another victim. We all know that Sarah was seeing this guy Wolf. But we can't find any Wolf. Whoever killed her was there that night for a date—candles, a little wine. Can you see her spending the evening with Purrington? His victims up north were sexually assaulted and practically hacked to death. Neither Maxine Harris nor Sarah was raped, and both were killed with a surgical precision. The postmortem cutting on Harris was a clinical job. Sound like Purrington?"

"All I can do is talk to Willoughby," Walker said. "I can't promise anything."

"That would be a start," I said.

I wanted to tell Walker more. I wanted to take her into

the kitchen and show her Robert's freezer—to educate her about the many identities of the elusive Wolf, to shower her with feathers. But I didn't know how much influence Susan Walker had, or how far I could trust her.

Walker had been gone for five minutes. I lifted the miniature tree out of the freezer and placed it on the table. It looked like it was made out of plastic, but one touch of the small, delicate branches confirmed what it was. When had our phantom gotten in? Before I fixed the door? No. It was after. Locks didn't deter him, either. "What are you telling me that I'm not hearing?" I said.

I was getting ready for the shower—had my sweater peeled off and was starting on my jeans—when the phone rang. I thought it was probably Fuzzy calling to say goodnight, so I didn't wait for the machine to kick in. I picked up the receiver and said, "Hi, sweetie."

There was a single intake of breath on the other end of the line, then a long sigh.

"You should have followed my advice," a man's voice said.

The voice was familiar, but there was a different quality to it. "Robbins?"

"It's too late now," he said.

"How did you know where to find me?" I asked him.

There was a click, then a dial tone.

I started checking the phone book, then realized that I had no idea what Robbins's first name was—if that was even who had called. So I dialed the twenty-four-hour line at the DA's office. I explained who I was, that Robbins was filling in on the Sinclair homicide, and that I had to talk to him.

"Sinclair is Mandell's case," the clerk said. "We don't even have a Robbins."

I hung up. There had to be a mistake. Maybe she didn't know Robbins because he was in white-collar crime. That's a separate unit. But why wasn't he at least in her directory?

I fell back on the sofa, staring at the feather tree. I closed my eyes, but then I saw feathers floating through the air like huge, wayward snowflakes. It was one of those illusions that are fueled by exhaustion—when you're in that half-conscious state, neither asleep, nor fully awake. Then, in a more dreamlike state, I was at a reception in the country outside London. A man with eyes as blue as the sky and a sharp English accent asked, "Would you care for a cup of tea?"

I sprang upright. "Jesus. The only thing missing is the English accent."

I'd listened to the voice on Robert's answering machine—the tape I should have logged into the evidence room. I had left it on the bookshelf in my living room.

I didn't want to risk going back to my apartment—for all I knew, Hanson had someone watching the place—but nothing could keep me away, either.

I wanted to hear that voice again; I had to know whether Robert's English diplomat was the same guy who had been drifting around the edges of my investigation. I needed something that would start to clear away the confusion.

I was looking for reassurance that I knew I wouldn't find. Robbins was right; he should know. I *was* next.

I reached my neighborhood a few minutes later. The street looked quiet. Nobody on foot. No unfamiliar cars parked nearby. But I drove on past anyway. When I was certain that no one was following me, I left my car two streets over and walked back. I cut through a parking lot, then turned into the alley on the north side of my building.

The darkness was almost impenetrable—relieved only by the ambient lighting from the street a hundred yards ahead of me. The stench of decay wafted out of the blackness as if rising up from something rotting under the cinders and asphalt.

I pulled the .32 and moved down the center of the alley. Pop once told me, "Fear is the best amplifier of sounds." He was right—a rat scavenging a midnight snack from the trash, a homeless drunk shifting his weight beneath his cardboard quilt, the city's debris moving through the streets and alleys at the whim of the wind.

I jumped up and grabbed the fire escape ladder, certain the clattering could be heard all over the city. I climbed up to my living room window, then used my Swiss Army pocketknife to peel away the glazing. I lifted out the pane and leaned it against the railing behind me. Sliding through the opening and onto my couch took only seconds.

I knew better than to turn on any lights. If anybody was watching the place, I didn't want to advertise my presence. I felt along the shelves of the bookcase until I located the cassette. Then I took it to my recorder, dropped it in place, and fumbled around until I found the play button.

Soon my caller was saying, "Detective Sinclair, have you finished with my materials? I've finished with yours." It had to be the same guy. *Had* to be.

But was Robbins Wolf?

I popped the tape out and slipped it into the hip pocket of my jeans. I wasn't going to have time to consider Robbins as Wolf. Something about the apartment wasn't right. Perfume—a heavy scent that I'd never use. Someone had been there. Fear was even tighter on me now than it had been in the alley. I just wanted to grab some clothes and get out of there.

Still leading with the .32, I made my way into the bedroom, groping along the wall until I found the closet door. When I opened it and reached inside, I managed to grab some pants on my first try.

There was just one problem. Somebody was wearing them.

Robert

At first I couldn't sleep. Then I couldn't sleep without dreaming. Then I couldn't dream without drinking. Fifths of Wild Turkey, quarts of Jack Daniels, cases of Old Milwaukee floated like angels with brand names through the clouds of my head.

I figured Fuzzy was a veteran at this sort of thing, so when he came in to visit, I told him about it.

"Me, I had some winners," he said. "In one of 'em I was riding a horse. Can you see me on a horse? I've never been near a fucking horse. It was Trigger, Roy Rogers's horse. You know they got that sucker stuffed and standing around somewhere? I don't mean like a museum or anything. It's in their fucking living room. Maybe it's Dale Evans. She always wore weird chaps. She'd do something like that. Anyway, it *was* a palomino I was riding. I'm sure of that. And I rode pretty good for the full-figured dude I am. Had a good fucking time, Bobby."

"Fuzzy, mine ain't like that," I told him.

"Don't mean nothing," he said. "It's just the weird shit

your head does. One of the times I went through rehab, the shrink said you dream more when you get sober. The other time, the same shrink said research showed that alcoholics dream more when they're soused. I think he had his head in the bottle, too."

Fuzzy was no help.

The doc said it was normal.

Lymann was even less help. "I never dream," he said. "Once I have reality under control, maybe I'll try it."

I was tired from lack of sleep. Then I was exhausted from sleeping. I had no idea what was going in through the hose they had stuck in my arm, but it had me fogged out. I always liked Jimi Hendrix's "Purple Haze." Now I knew what it was.

They gave me a little blue pill on top of that "to help you relax and get some sleep."

I'd been a kid again, met the folks, revisited Christmases and Thanksgivings, B&Es I did when I was eight, somebody's funeral when I was nine. I held Liza again. And I held Sarah again. I dodged bullets, ducked knives, greeted ghosts, ran from priests demanding my confession.

But the one that shot me upright in the dark room, snapping out the IV line, bringing Lymann rocketing out of his sleep with leather straps in hand, started out like the drunk dream I'd had about Maine. It might have been the same scrub pine growth, the same clearing with a few scattered chunks of granite, and the man who called himself Carver—black suit and British accent—smoking the same cigarette.

There were other people around this time. Some I recognized. Most I didn't. And there was a group behind me applauding.

Then it changed. All of us were indoors—my high school auditorium, then a TV studio. The applause was coming from the audience. They still clapped their hands, but now they also screamed out numbers—three, one, two, two, three. I was a contestant on that old quiz show, *Let's Make A Deal*, only Fuzzy was the host.

"Bobby, you gotta pick a door," he said.

I looked at the doors. The set was like a grammar school play I'd been in, except that back then the doors were the covers of giant, plywood books. I was Tom Sawyer, complete with a straw hat, ragged jeans, bare feet, and a shank of oat grass stuck in my teeth.

"You gave away what you had for a chance to look behind the doors," Fuzzy said.

TWO. ONE. THREE. ONE. THREE. TWO. TWO.

"Got any of that Irish?" I asked him.

"Might be behind one of them doors, Bobby."

Then one of the doors popped open—number three—but there was nothing behind it.

I was telling myself that I wanted to wake up. I couldn't. But I could see through the doors. Sarah was back there, and Lane, and Carver-Wolf. They were moving around, shifting from place to place. Who would be behind which door?

TWO. TWO. TWO. TWO.

"One," I told Fuzzy.

The audience sighed in unison. The door opened. There was Wolf with his nickel-plated .32. This time he didn't raise it toward my chest like he did with the .38 in my Maine dream. He turned toward door two.

Fuzzy was gone. The audience was silent. Wolf smiled, and door two slipped open. Lane.

Wolf's arm moved upward. He pointed the gun toward her, then pulled back the hammer.

That's when I came up, the IV went flying, and Lymann landed on me with his straps of Spanish leather.

"I'll stay still. I'll stay still," I told him. "Just let me call Lane. I have to call her. I have to warn her. Lymann, don't fucking do this. Wolf is going to kill her."

Lymann Murr did his job. He never spoke a word, didn't even need the lights. After I was restrained, he called the nurse. She reinserted the IV, shot my ass full of something, then left.

"I have to call Lane," I told him. "Wolf is going to kill her."

He put the phone on my chest. "Touch-Tone," he said. "You get one hand free. Play with anything else, I break the hand. Okay?"

"Deal," I said.

I tried her number. I tried my number. No answer. I punched both numbers again, then her extension at the precinct. No Lane.

"Lymann, you gotta get to her."

He removed the phone, rewrapped me with leather, then pulled up a chair beside the bed. "You will be sleeping soon," he said. "I will continue to call my cousin. I take your fear seriously. But no wolves will bite Lane. She wouldn't like that. Now I tell you more about Bob Marley, his hard life in Jamaica, the words he sings to my people."

Lymann might have said more. He probably did. But I was out.

Lane

As soon as I touched her, I knew that my visitor had been dead for a while—long enough for rigor mortis to set in. I used the penlight on my key chain to get a look at her face. It was Sheila, still wearing the same red spandex pants and metallic gold sweater she had on when I interviewed her earlier at the massage parlor.

I no longer cared whether Hanson had anyone watching the place. I switched on the light.

Sheila's arms had been pulled behind her back and were bound at the wrists with gray duct tape. Another piece of tape covered her mouth. One of her red spike heels still clung to her foot; the other had fallen on top of one of my slippers on the closet floor.

Sheila's killer had screwed a quarter-inch steel eye hook into one of the joists in the closet's ceiling. Then he ran a length of half-inch, yellow nylon rope through the eye to form a hangman's noose, taking the time to make it perfect. Thirteen wraps.

The inverted V-shaped bruise on her neck and the

petechial hemorrhages in her eyelids told me that she was still alive when she was put away so neatly in my closet.

I don't know how many dead bodies I've seen during my career—enough that it no longer fazed me. But my reaction to finding Sheila went off the scale. My legs didn't want to work, but I managed to move from room to room, checking every area where someone could conceal himself. I had the hammer back on the .32, ready to fire at anything that moved. I switched on all the lights as I went, satisfying myself that I was alone. Except for Sheila.

Then I called Swartz at home.

"I've got a problem," I said.

"I know. Hanson was in a huddle with someone from Internal Affairs all afternoon. They're talking about going to the DA for a warrant on you if you don't come in."

"I've got bigger troubles than that," I said.

"You went into Sarah's house, Lane. You're suspended. That makes it trespassing and tampering with a crime scene."

"Listen to me. I have a corpse in my closet. A woman named Sheila. I was talking to her just this morning."

"Jesus," Swartz said. "Lane, stay there. Don't move. I'll call this in, then I'll be right there."

"That won't work. Hanson already wants to haul me in. Now I have a body in my closet. Look, I've got to get out of here."

Swartz was silent for a moment, then asked, "What are you going to do?"

"Find the guy who did this. Before he does it to me."

I tucked the .32 into my waistband, grabbed the clothes I needed, and snatched up Robbins's copy of *Hunting Humans*. Then I hurried back to Robert's place, arriving just as a transmission from Pop was coming in. It wasn't like him to be up so late.

TO: Detective Frank, Semiretired
FROM: Pop, Retired

My question about the candles in Sarah's house was rhetorical. There could be many other explanations, of course, but yours and mine are pretty much the same. It wasn't just that he felt safe lingering there. It provided him with a sense of absolute control. Preliminarily, you concluded that there was no staging, no arranging of the body, etc. I concur, but there was something he did after he killed the young woman. It may not even be detectable, but he touched her somehow, maybe lifted her dress and replaced it—I don't know. But I do know that he did something.

Not only did he linger in Sarah's house after killing her (some killers bathe their victims, by the way; do their nails), he had been there before, alone. That's when he left his prints in every cranny. Maxine Harris suspected a B&E. Sexual curiosity? Power at its most perverse? Some aspect of his ritual? Maybe all of the above. Check Sarah's phone records; I suspect that he conducted business at her expense. Perhaps he made toll calls to Hasty Hills to see if there were any fresh corpses awaiting his expertise. He believes he's invulnerable. No one can stop him. My guess is that you should be looking for calls to the courthouse, the PD, the municipal building—wherever Connecticut houses its medical examiners' offices.

Why did Wolf take such a risk, entering a neighborhood where he would soon commit a murder? Because Sarah's nest would have been irresistible to him. He wanted to *feel* the place, to be in secret violation of her personal life, to finger her most intimate possessions, to examine her books, the food in her refrigerator. He wanted the smell of her, without the bother of her presence. He wanted to inhale her, hold her in his lungs.

I've come across another Connecticut case: Annie

Maxwell—strangled, then discarded in a horse stall. In his statement to the police, her husband said that Annie had been bothered for years by dreams about a man coming to kill her. He was someone real, someone she knew from college. They met at a warehouse fire, of all places. She saw how fascinated he was by the flames, the destruction, and asked why he wasn't afraid. "I was born this way," he told her. They talked, went back to her place, drank, listened to music—the usual college thing.

Annie said he was a very cynical fellow, angry, always mumbling about the emptiness of people. He intrigued her. She pursued him. He cautioned her that she had no idea what risks she was taking. She never mentioned his name to her husband, but said that during a game of some sort he had confessed to the murder of a coed. Annie kept up her part of the game, but she was convinced that he had told her the truth—that he really was a killer (there had been a coed killed a few months earlier). She was equally certain that he knew she knew.

Annie Maxwell was at Radcliffe when Wolf was still loitering around Cambridge.

There is no coincidence. Events conspire to make fools of us only when we allow them to. The people from Quantico observed a pattern in Albany. They failed to see it a few miles away in Troy. If their approach is that impaired, how can they see the design in two decades of events? In the face of chaos, all science must redefine itself. Anyone so presumptuous as to claim knowledge of a unified science of human behavior is destined to become the snake that eats its own tail. That is thinking at its reductionist worst.

Linear thinking, clinical distance, logic—flush 'em all. When a plane crashes and we're told that the cause of the crash is wind shear, we're being told that there was an undetected movement of air so rapid and so powerful that it threw tons of metal and humanity to one side. With all our instruments, our gauges, our computers, how could something so powerful be missed? We put men on the moon. Did we bring them back? I'm not so sure now.

Wolf appreciates our limitations. He uses them to his advantage. Think of this man—conducting autopsies, serving as a medical consultant, attending conferences—and no one ever suspecting that he'd never even attended medical school. From his lair in Hasty Hills, he ventured into the world, then retreated, hidden in his cloak of respectability. For years the arrangement was perfect for him.

He had to kill Sarah Sinclair, no matter what the cost. Of all the deaths over all the years, hers was special. It was different. We need to know why. Sarah will also be the link to his next victim. Based on what we know, that person may be dead already.

Lt. Swartz has determined that Wolf/Chadwick spent a great deal of time away from Hasty Hills, time that cannot be accounted for. I believe that he has another life, another world, another identity—one he visits just often enough to maintain it (in the event he needs to slip back into it permanently someday). Or maybe he has always intended to end up there. That's where we will find him. This man is methodical when it matters (his other identity, his "collection"), and sloppy when it doesn't matter (fingerprints).

When you talk to his sister Sarah, ask her about the sexual episode(s) between them when they were growing up. Don't ask *if* it happened—it happened. Probably it was something voyeuristic. Later, he acquired his social skills in a similar fashion—watching others, and mimicking them.

And ask her where he is. She may not know—she may not even know what name he uses—but her guess would be a good one. I have my own. The fabrication of what would become his personality was based on fear. That's where he came from. That's also where the rigidity and the need for control come from. He fancies himself invulnerable and all-powerful, and he certainly has operated that way. But he came from fear. Why else create a personal world that can exist only when all that is called order or structure is what you impose on it? And, to borrow from Julian Cope, what place would fear know best? I believe that we'll find Wolf at home. In a very real sense, he never left.

Detective Sinclair was kind enough to have Lymann FedEx the real Dr. Chadwick's notes on the young man he knew as Paul Wolf. Chadwick had labs in the buildings near the Peabody Museum; he saw Wolf entering or leaving there a half dozen times. Once Chadwick followed him inside and watched as Wolf stood in a room of mounted birds, staring first at one, then another. He touched the glass enclosures, as if transfixed. Chadwick wrote: "He had the strangest expression. Looked like he was somewhere else entirely. I could have said his name and it would have echoed in those vast hallways without his noticing. I think now that he should have seen my reflection in the glass. Perhaps he did. Nothing matters to him except that which is in his own mind at the moment. Why is it that no one else senses the violence that's pulsating inside this man?"

Interesting stuff.

Pop

I grabbed a sheet of blank paper and began writing as fast as I could.

Pop,

I'm in trouble. Just stopped by my apartment and found a corpse hanging in the closet. Sheila, from the massage parlor above the bookstore where Sarah worked. There's the connection.

Also, Hanson's trying to arrest me.

And I'm scared to death. This guy who said he was from the DA's office has been on the edges of the investigation since day one. I don't have time to write out an explanation, but I think he's Wolf. Connections. Am I next?

You said in your fax that you think Wolf has gone home. But he *has* to be here. Sheila couldn't have been dead long when I found her—I interviewed her just a few hours earlier. Please find a phone and call.

L.

While I waited for Pop's response, I thumbed through Robbins's book. He hadn't highlighted or underlined anything, but I found a slip of folded paper tucked inside. It was a receipt for dry cleaning a blazer. Sheila's receipt—the blazer Sarah Sinclair had borrowed for her date with John Wolf.

Robbins was Wolf.

That first day, right at the crime scene—where only hours earlier he had ended Sarah Sinclair's life—he stood on the sidewalk in the rain and waited for me to walk out. There were cops all over the place, but that didn't bother him. He was back in a couple of days. Coffee, he said. Read this book, he said. He had given me the answer, and I had missed it. Now Sheila was dead, and I was next.

The fax clicked on.

Lane:

Get out of that apartment now. Go to a hotel. I've been going over every shred of information I've accumulated on Wolf. I'm getting a grasp on him, developing a sense of the essence of this man. If anything, I have underestimated him. His leaving a corpse in your closet dictates what I must do now. Forget everything I ever said about doing this from my armchair. After each kill, he cools off for a short time. I don't know how long. He would go home where he feels safe, and where he maintains his permanent shrine to himself. I'm going to Vermont. You're going to Florida—and, after you call and brief Swartz on your meeting with sister Sarah, you're going to check into a motel on the beach.

And stay out of New York.

Pop

I weighed the risks of going back out onto the street, and figured I'd be better off staying put. Holding the .32 in my hand, I curled up on Robert's couch.

I dozed on and off, but after only a few hours I was fully awake—tired, but feeling somewhat better, and more in control in the daylight. The medication seemed to be doing its thing. Now I had to do mine.

My plane wasn't leaving until a little after ten. I decided to call ahead, just to make sure that Sarah Humphrey would give me the time of day.

"I'm going to be in Florida a little later today," I told her when I had her on the line, "and I'd like to stop by and have a talk with you."

"You're a cop?" she asked.

"Right," I said.

"What's this about?" she wanted to know.

"Your brother."

There was silence on the other end of the line. I decided to wait it out.

After several seconds, Sarah Humphrey asked, "What's he done now?"

"Possibly nothing. I'm still trying to determine that. I'd like to stop by and ask you a few questions. Routine background stuff, that's all."

"Do I have to do this?"

"No."

She sighed, then said, "Yes, I do. I've been expecting this call for a long time. I'll be home all day."

Before leaving for the airport, I left a message on Swartz's voice mail outlining the Robbins angle. Then I dialed my home number and entered the remote access code for my answering machine. There were five messages: three from Hanson telling me to get down to his office, and one from Robert, saying that when they got through wringing the alcohol out of his liver, he'd like to take me out on a real date. "Somewhere nice, with linen tablecloths and a no-smoking section," he said.

The final message was from Dr. Street. "I've found a little information on that Wolf case," he said. "Give me a call at your convenience."

I dialed Street's office number, but got his service. I left a message saying that I had a plane to catch, but Dr. Street could fax whatever he had directly to Pop.

I saw Sarah Humphrey as soon as I pulled the rental car into the parking slot beside her mobile home. She was shaking the wrinkles out of a blue workshirt and pinning it to the umbrella-style clothesline in her side yard. She heard me walking toward her and turned to face me. There was no smile, just a vague look of resignation in her tired eyes.

At first glance, Sarah was like any other housewife surviving near the poverty line on a steady diet of carbohydrates and fats: bloated, even a bit obese, with the sallow look that can come from any number of evils (booze, cigarettes, stress, AIDS, a variety of cancers). But a closer look hinted at what had been there before, years earlier—softness, prettiness. She had probably been a beautiful child, a tempting teenager.

"I don't see how I can help you," she said, squinting against the brightness of the afternoon sun. "My brother and I aren't close. He sends money every now and then, but doesn't even enclose a note. He just wraps the cash in a plain piece of paper and sticks it in an envelope. He sent me five hundred dollars just a few weeks ago."

"From where?" I asked.

She looked puzzled. "I guess he was at home."

"Which is where?"

"I don't know. Somewhere in Vermont, I think. Like I said, we're not close."

Sarah went on to explain that Wolf owned a construction company.

When I asked to see a photo of her brother, Sarah told me that it was a family joke the way Paul was always just out of camera range at the few picture-taking occasions they ever had.

"But I do have one," she said.

"About the money he sends you—"

"I don't know why he does that," she said. Then, in an almost inaudible voice, she added, "Guilt, probably."

"Guilt?"

Her face reddened. "There were some incidents. When we were kids."

With a wave of her hand, as if she were shooing flies, she said, "It was nothing, really. Just the usual brother-sister stuff."

She continued pinning her laundry to the clothesline, not looking at me, working faster now than she had been when I arrived.

"Sarah," I began, "I need to know about the sexual relationship you and your brother shared."

She dropped the pair of jeans she had just pulled from the laundry basket and spun around to face me.

"Who told you that? Did *he* tell you that?"

"I've never met your brother," I said, realizing that probably wasn't true.

"Well, they're wrong—whoever said it. There was never any sex, ever. Just—"

I waited for her to continue.

"You know how boys are. They get curious, do things—"

She turned away from me again, but just stood there this time, not moving, not even pretending to care about her laundry. "What are you going to do with this? Are you going to write it down or something?"

"I'm just going to listen," I told her. "And remember."

"Let's go inside," she said, leading the way. "I need some coffee."

We sat down at her kitchen table with mugs of muddy brew before us. It looked like it had sat in the pot since dawn.

"My brother never had it easy," she said. "You have to understand that, because it explains a lot. My father was his stepfather, not his real dad, and he never accepted Paul. Not really."

"You were kind of stuck in the middle?"

"I always took my parents' side—you know, trying to defend them. But I know it wasn't right what they did, the way they treated Paul. My father would tell me how crazy Paul was, how worthless. But I know my father was a drunk, and he could be really cruel when he wanted to be. Like when he would send Paul down to the coal bin."

"What do you mean?"

"Now that my parents are dead, I probably shouldn't speak ill of them. I mean, they aren't here to defend themselves. But Dad really was awful to Paul. He'd make him go down in the cellar, then he'd lock him in the coal bin—sometimes for the whole night."

"As a punishment?"

She nodded. "I used to stand by the cellar door and listen to him crying. I could hear him talking—in a little child's voice, like he was someone else. Then he would go silent. Sometimes after my parents went to bed, I'd sneak out there and stand by the door. But there'd be nothing, no sound at all. I think the silence bothered me more than anything."

"What about your mom?"

"She was afraid of my father. Whenever Dad took a belt to Paul, Mom would go into her room and shut the door—to block out the noise. I never saw her take Paul's side in anything. Not once."

She looked down. "I was just a kid," she said quietly. "What could *I* do?"

When she looked up again, there were tears in her eyes.

"You know what happened that first Thanksgiving when Paul came home from college?" she said. "When he opened his bedroom door, he saw that all his furniture was missing. My parents had sold it, like he wasn't a member of the family anymore. The look on his face broke my heart, but Mom—she couldn't understand why he was so upset. Stuff like that is why I wanted to get away from my parents. I couldn't wait to get married. As soon as I did, I cut off all ties with them, just like Paul had done—although I did go to the funerals. Paul wouldn't even do that. After he was in college, there were long periods when he didn't come home at all. I'd hear that he'd been in town, but he didn't come out to the house. That hurt a little, you know?"

"It sounds like you loved your brother," I said.

"Yeah," she agreed. "But I hated him, too."

"Why?"

She looked down again, fidgeting with her fingers. After a long silence, she said, "He never forced himself on me or anything. I want to make that clear. I mean, he never touched me, okay?"

I nodded, but she wasn't looking at me.

"Once I woke up in the middle of the night and saw him standing at the foot of my bed. He was just standing there, in the moonlight, staring at me and playing with himself."

"What did you do?"

"Nothing. I waited till he was through, then I went back to sleep."

"What do you mean, 'through'?"

"He ejaculated all over my bed."

"He ejaculated and walked out, without either of you saying anything?"

She looked me in the eye. "Maybe you had to be there to

understand it. I was always a little afraid of Paul, never quite sure what might set him off. It's an understatement to say that he could be explosive."

"I know a little about the incident with the knife."

"That was a surprise. Paul had always ducked or cowered when my father came at him. I thought he was a wimp. Mom used to say that when he was a little kid, he wet the bed because he was too scared to get up in the dark and go to the bathroom. So I was really shocked when Paul pulled that knife. There was blood all over the place. I just froze."

I could see in her eyes that she was reliving the scene.

"I never would have thought that he'd have the nerve," she said. "After that, I never saw him act scared again. I think he was as shocked by the attack as I was. He was so insecure. He never knew how to get along with other people. When he was so interested in me, I think it was because he wanted a girlfriend—but he didn't know how to go about it. He was good looking, too."

"So when he jerked off on you, you thought it was safest to just keep quiet?"

"That, plus I knew that it was Paul's nature to watch. It wasn't unusual for me to catch him staring at me, and it wasn't unusual for him to handle his privates while he did it. Like when he used to sit outside the shower and watch me wash my hair. That was one of his favorite things for a while."

She seemed to be suddenly aware of me again. "You sure you aren't taping this?" she asked.

"No tape," I told her. "What I really need to know is if any of this activity between you and your brother ever led to violence. On his part, I mean."

"There was only one time when I thought it might," she said. "He was spying on me when I was with one of my boyfriends, making out. I didn't have any clothes on. He chased the boy away, then came toward me with a broken bottle in his hand. I knew what he was thinking."

When she saw the question in my eyes, she said, "He was gonna use it on me. Rape me with it. He didn't say so, but I knew it. For some reason, he changed his mind. That night is when I first realized that my brother was capable of terrible things."

"Do you think he's capable of murder?"

"Sure," she said—emotionlessly, as if I had asked her something benign. "Is that what he did? Murder someone?"

"We don't know."

"He was in Vietnam for a year. I think he spent the whole time in Saigon, not in combat. I don't think he killed anyone over there. He wrote to me a few times. He was a clerk or something—did the paperwork on the soldiers who died, the ones that were being shipped back here. I think he had to help with the bodies sometimes, too."

I wondered if that was where he fine-tuned his knowledge of physiology. He certainly knew his way around a carotid artery. According to the real Chadwick, Wolf had been a premed student.

"Did you know that he was listed as killed in action?" I asked.

"Why would they think he died?"

"It looks as if he wanted them to think that. He was drafted right about the same time he started using the name Paul Pease."

"I know he thought some man named Pease was his father, but I didn't know he used that name. I'd believe it, though. One time while he was in the service, I wrote to him, but the post office sent the letter back to me. I never understood that until right now."

"To get it into his military records, he had to get his name changed legally."

With a deep sigh, she said, "I guess I'll never know my brother."

"Is there anyone that Paul was close to?"

Sarah shook her head. "He was a loner. He loved to read, and he was real smart. I remember one book he must have read a hundred times—it was about mythology. Sometimes he told me the stories, but he changed them around. He said he was making them more interesting. I remember one story that he said was his favorite. It was about a guy who could fly. He never did tell me the real ending for that one."

"What else did he do with his time?"

"He was fascinated with birds," she said. "I mean, it wasn't like a hobby or anything. It was just something else he talked about a lot. Birds could fly way above everything and kind of see a whole place all at once—that was part of it. And he said he liked how secretive they are—living out their lives in the brush, migrating thousands of miles to different places every year."

Her face brightened, enlivened by a memory. "His big thing was ravens," she said. "Because they could make all these different sounds, imitate other birds. He loved how smart they are. They know when someone means them harm, but they can be sociable, too. They come right up to people when they know they aren't in any danger. I could go on a quiz show with all the stuff he told me."

Sarah looked down again. Her expression changed.

"There was a sad part, too. There was always a sad part with Paul. The birds they carried in cages into the coal mines to test for poisonous gases—if the birds lived, it was okay for the miners to go in. Paul hated that. He said he used to think about those birds late at night when he was locked in the coal bin—said he felt like Dad had sent him down there to see if there were any poisonous gases."

The cloud seemed to pass and Sarah brightened again.

"He always had to do things the same way. I thought it was funny, but he didn't like it when I joked about it. If he had a ten-page paper to write for class, he'd open his notebook and number the pages one to ten before he even started writing. I'd say, 'Paul, what if you can think of only nine pages to write?' He'd get all upset. Or when he had to do the dishes—he'd spend four or five minutes just lining them all up beside the sink before he started. Then he always did the glasses first, then the cups, then the saucers, then the dinner plates—or something like that."

Sarah Humphrey was lost in her thoughts, her memories. I reminded her that I wanted to see the picture of Paul that she had mentioned to me earlier.

She pulled a handful of loose snapshots out of a cabinet drawer and sorted through them until she found the right one.

It was a black-and-white photo of a young boy, snapped from behind, with his face turned away from the camera. He was outdoors, kneeling down in front of what looked like a miniature town.

"Paul built that, and he also tore it down—all those buildings that he spent so much time working on. He smashed the whole thing the same day he pulled the knife on my father. It was like he was trying to hurt himself."

She glanced away for a moment.

"I remember what he did to the animals," Sarah said. "It was so sick."

I prompted her. "What animals? What do you mean?"

"All the boys hunted. They'd put on their hunting clothes and their boots sometime in October and I swear they lived in them until after Thanksgiving. At least it smelled that way in school. Paul never owned a rifle. My father would never have let him have one. There wasn't any money anyway. But Paul hunted. He said all he needed were his hands, a knife, and a length of twine."

Sarah seemed to slip inside herself with her memories. She was trembling.

"I went up to his place on the hill one time. I wasn't very old. I was out playing, and I was curious. I knew that he spent most of his time up there. There was a path that led farther up the hill, beyond the clearing by the three old apple trees. So I followed it, going deeper and deeper into the woods. That's when I saw them. Red squirrels, chipmunks, a rabbit, some woodchucks—they were strung up with twine, hanging from the pine trees. They hadn't been shot or cut or anything. They were alive when he did that to them."

Tears rolled down Sarah's face, and I had to fight my own

reaction. Twine in a secluded forest. Yellow nylon rope in my closet. Animals swinging in the breeze. Sheila swaying when I touched her.

"I don't know why I kept going, but I did," Sarah said, "and I saw him. He was down in a ravine, crouching over something. At first I couldn't see. He was tearing at it with his knife. Maybe a twig snapped—I don't know—but he turned around. The knife and his hands were soaked with the blood of a small deer. At first I thought that he had blackened his face. The kids sometimes did that. But it wasn't face paint. It was more blood. It was even in his hair. He looked like a savage, like something primitive. When he stood, I could see that he was naked, and the blood was smeared all over his body. He didn't see me. I backed away and went down to the house. When Paul came in for supper, he was clean. His clothes were clean. He was my brother Paul again, not whoever he was up there on that hill."

She turned and looked at me. "Is that what he did? To people?"

I didn't respond.

She shook her head, shuddering. "I remember something else," she said. "That night on the mountain when I was naked and I thought he was going to do something? He cut himself on that broken bottle—kept digging at himself with it. It was as if he didn't even know that he was doing it."

Sarah's eyes met mine. "It was as if he couldn't feel any pain. His eyes were blank, like empty holes."

I handed the photograph back to her.

"Mom snapped that one," Sarah told me. "It's ironic, isn't it?"

"What?"

"Even then, Paul was a builder. But when he created that little city out of scraps, none of us had any idea what he would become."

BOOK THREE

Pop

I don't do well with people. Never have.

As I crossed from Massachusetts into Vermont on Interstate 91, I wondered if there were still more cows than people in the Green Mountain State. Probably not. Politicians were killing farms to make room for malls and parking lots. Last I heard, Vermont, with its half million people, was the last holdout against Wal-Mart in the lower forty-eight—if elected representatives with IQs about equal to their belt size hadn't given it up.

Maybe it was all symbolic anyway. McDonald's had run out of street corners and was turning up inside Wal-Marts. What would turn up inside McDonald's?

No, I guess I don't have the warmest feelings for people. Most of the years of fifty-minute hours weren't a problem. Therapy is a unique situation—an intense involvement between two people that defines its own structure. We share a direction, some goals, and we work together to get there.

It's the world without that structure—the way people pass time—that I don't tolerate well. People in the wild, with their passionate championing of one cause or another, the way they fling insults or lawsuits about, or tell us all to have a nice day. I don't get it, and it frightens me—keeps me awake nights.

Toward the end, even the office became a problem. I was burning out—scheduling two people for the same time slot, leaving at three when I'd scheduled a four o'clock. The symptoms were clear. There were days when I'd open my day book, see a name, and have no idea who the person was. It didn't have to be a new client; an old one would do.

I'd go office to office on the chance that one of my partners would know who Barry W. was. That usually got shrugs all round. It was either early dementia, or time to get out of the business altogether. I opted for the latter diagnosis, and walked away.

I was doing a lot of profiling work then. It was loner work—cerebral and visceral—and I had no idea the toll it was taking, the trap I was falling into (one which I had fashioned for myself). The techniques I had developed required that I extend myself into the worlds, the minds, of the most savage people we had created. I knew the intellectual fascination; I just didn't recognize the dangers to the soul.

Now there was a new danger—to Lane. Nothing else could have pried me from my own lair in Michigan, putting me on the road into the mountains of northern New England.

I exited the Interstate above Brattleboro and continued north on Route 5. Bullet holes in the road signs and the profusion of decorative lawn derrieres reassured me—I was in Vermont. I hadn't taken a wrong turn anywhere.

Hunters clad in Day-Glo orange jumpsuits, and black-and-red wool plaid outfits, emptied out of pickup trucks and ambled into the woods with deer rifles and six-packs. Someone would either get a trophy or become one.

The last time I was in Vermont was on our honeymoon. Before I met Savvy, I was the epitome of the confirmed bachelor, true to the stereotype in every way. Not only did I do my own cooking, cleaning, and laundry, I actually enjoyed it. When I proposed, Savvy said that I had her blessing if I wanted to keep on handling the domestic tasks. We compromised. We'd cook on alternate days, do our own laundry, and split the cleaning chores in half.

On our honeymoon, we stayed at the Woodstock Inn, where we played at being lovers and tourists, sipped cognac in front of the fireplace, and, without knowing it, began to drift apart. In those early days, we were inseparable, but both of us were elsewhere, too.

Savvy had her world of animals—caring and curing—and I had my world of murder.

I got my first police case by accident. We had a neighbor, Ray Bolton, who was a detective with the Boston police department. When he and his wife were at our place for dinner one night, Ray mentioned a homicide case that he was working on. He was stymied.

I plied him with questions, and all of us played a game of Clue involving an elderly woman who had met a gruesome stabbing death, apparently at the hands of a stranger in her fashionable Beacon Street home.

Finally I'd had enough. "It's elementary, my dear Bolton," I said, getting laughs all around.

"No, I mean it. It's common sense."

Ray bristled. "I've been working this case for ten months."

"Ray, it isn't a stranger. The woman opened her door to her killer—probably someone she knew well, maybe even a relative."

"How do you figure?"

Ray pushed his coffee away and helped himself to a beer.

"She had a heart condition," I said. "A serious one."

"Right."

"She wasn't supposed to climb stairs."

He nodded.

"And she was a good patient—took all her medications, kept all her appointments. But you found her in an empty room upstairs. There was no bruising on her body. Her half slippers were still on her feet. So no one dragged her up those steps. She walked. Why?"

"The perp showed her the knife," Ray said.

"And why didn't he use it downstairs?"

"He was looking for something. He needed her to go along."

"To a closed, unused, empty room?"

"The grandson," Ray said. "She'd go up there with the grandson. He's a strange guy. In his twenties, no real job, no real place to call home."

"She had a soft spot for him, didn't she?"

"Yeah," Ray said. "She'd take him in."

"And show him the room that was going to be his."

"Why'd he kill her?"

"Hey, I gave you who. You take it from there."

Two weeks later Ray showed up at the door with a case of Heineken—my first fee as a law enforcement consultant. We sat at the kitchen table.

"They're probably gonna cop an insanity plea with the grandson," he said. "The story he tells is they were in the room and she suddenly changes her mind, says he can't stay there after all. He loses it, and stabs her eighteen times."

"It's a sex crime," I said.

He opened a bottle of beer. "Educate me," Ray said.

"He's probably psychotic. Either he touched her in some sexual way, or he opened his pants or something. She says that's it, out, you're not staying here, and he goes into overkill mode."

I expected Ray to resist that line of thinking, but he didn't. "We've got this guy who does amazing things analyzing blood stains. He says her dress was raised up, then put back in place, after she was down."

"What do you know about the grandson?"

"Saw a shrink for about three years. We can't find out anything there. He was diddling around with a niece, a five-year-old. They handled it in the family. Set him up with an apartment and all he had to do was keep his appointments."

"The sexual curiosity of a child," I said. "And maybe the mind of one, too."

Savvy said she could see it coming then. Sometimes Bolton or someone else in his department called or came by, or a detective from another department would call on Ray's recommendation. I read the latest books on criminology and psychopathy, studied cases, and spent a lot of time thinking about them.

Savvy had her work at a nearby clinic, and we were both usually home by 6:30. We had dinner together, then spent the evening worlds apart, until we fell into bed. I remember the night she came into the room I used for a study.

"We've got a problem," she said.

I looked up from Jim Brussel's *Casebook of a Crime Psychiatrist*.

"I'm pregnant, and this marriage isn't working."

We talked until 3:00 A.M. I resolved to mend my ways—to keep all business at the office, and to adhere to normal working hours. No cops or autopsy photos at the kitchen table. No midnight runs to the latest strangling.

Savvy wanted to stop working when the baby came—just be a mother. I agreed. We didn't need both salaries—my practice was growing—and it would be best for the child.

Lane was five when Savvy went back to work at the same clinic, and seven when Savvy announced that she was going to Africa. She didn't want a divorce, she said, but would understand if I did.

I didn't. And I didn't want her to go. But I never did know how to hold her, either. So, for the next ten years, our marriage was a one-month-out-of-twelve affair.

It seemed to work. Savvy loved her life in Zaire. I immersed myself in my fascination with the horror people do to one another. And Lanie became a prepubescent jet-setter. She'd seen Africa and Europe before she was in her teens. When I took her to Disney World, she said, "Paris is better."

All of us loved the time we had together as a family—as limited as that was—and nothing ever interfered with it.

When Lane went off to college, Savvy's visits gradually became less frequent, and she didn't stay as long. Neither one of us talked much about it. When I closed the practice and headed for the woods of Michigan, I harbored a fantasy of Savvy's joining me there. I wrote to her and hinted at it. I received a ten-page letter in return. The first five pages described her fantasy of my dumping my forensic work twenty years before, and taking a job as a professor at some college in the Southwest. The last five pages explained how angry she was that it took me twenty years too long to get my head clear.

The deterioration of our relationship—the wearing away of my life—was a progression, something so gradual I never noticed. Savvy used to complain about that—the way I never noticed what was going on around me. I didn't pick things off the floor because I didn't see them. I lived out of my laundry basket because I never noticed the bureau. Then, when she pointed it out to me, I lived off the top of the bureau.

Only now do I remember and recognize the overwhelming need I had to go off alone, to withdraw, to live with my own thoughts. It was forever in competition with my need and love for Savvy. I won. And I lost.

As I drove toward Westminster, Vermont, I watched for the turn that would lead me into Saxtons River. Lane had faxed me copies of Robert Sinclair's notes, which included a crude map and directions to the house where Wolf had lived as a child.

The sky was slate gray with a few traces of white cloud stretched out across the horizon. The pickups parked at odd angles in fields and just off the sides of the road were the only remaining evidence of the hunters. They were in the woods stalking their prey, or sitting in a tree stand waiting for a buck to walk by. That method might work with deer, but never with human prey.

I found the road and continued north. After passing through the small village, I turned onto a dirt road that veered to the left. I drove slowly downhill, across a wooden bridge, then gradually upward again, until the old house came into view on the right.

I parked in front, switched off the ignition, and, as I got out of the car, I stared at the small, wood-frame building—the manse that had spawned its own twisted life-form. There was a rotting front porch and some boarded-over windows, but the basic structure of the place, at least from the outside, appeared stable.

This was the house that Sarah Humphrey had described to Lane. When I talked to Swartz and heard the details of Lane's conversation with Wolf's half-sister, I wasn't surprised. I had already accurately pictured Wolf's youth simply by studying the handiwork of his adult years.

I walked around the house, through the backyard, and up the hill to where I knew the apple trees would be. A doe stood under one of the trees taking bites from apples that lay on the ground. As I approached, her head came up, her ears cocked, but she didn't run—just watched as I approached, then moved off toward the bushes, stopping to look back occasionally at the rude intruder that I was. Even during hunting season, it wasn't easy to spook the prey—probably because she didn't know that's what she was.

There were bits of wood and old metal wire casing—the remnants of Wolf's town—still embedded in the sandy soil.

You constructed your world, lad, didn't you? You were an architect of sorts, a young man with design in his mind. There is no fear in this place. You were safe here. You slipped each piece lovingly into position. Safe. Ordered. Secure.

And you could move from here, up through that overgrown hillside, to go hunting with a knife, a club, a ball of twine. Your bare hands. God, what power.

A blue jay swooped low in silence, through the clearing

and into the brush on the uphill side. Only when it was invisible again did it pipe once.

And you flew above it, didn't you, lad? You learned how to split yourself away, to soar, to look back down at the earth and all you created. You discovered patterns you didn't know were here—relationships in space, the positions of objects. Angels always have a better view. There were no feelings here at all, were there? There was no fear. It was the only place and the only time where you had absolute control.

I sat on a rock near where the deer had been feeding. Only the roof of the house was visible from there.

The chimney—that's how you could tell when someone was home. Your mother or Corrigan would stoke the stove. Even if you had your back turned, you could smell the wood smoke, couldn't you? It registered somewhere inside, but it didn't require any attention. It was more information absorbed, tucked away somewhere in case it was needed.

And just what was it you were running from mate? Where was the fear?

I pushed myself up and walked slowly down the hill toward the house. The back porch hadn't fared as poorly as the front. I stepped up on it and peered through a window into what had been a kitchen.

The lock on the door was the type that required a skeleton key. Using the screwdriver blade on my pocket knife, I slid the bolt back, pushed the door open, and stepped inside.

James Brussel was the psychiatrist who, in the 1950s, told police what New York's "mad bomber" would be wearing when they caught him. A double-breasted suit, buttoned. He told them more, too, and most of it was right on the money, but the core of the legend was George Metesky opening his door to the detectives, wearing that conservatively cut, double-breasted suit—with all the buttons buttoned.

And it was Brussel who came to a Boston that was in disarray from "the stranglings" during the 1960s. The city had convened a distinguished panel of experts—medical doctors, psychologists, psychiatrists—to offer their advice to the investigators who were grappling with a case that had paralyzed the city. The good doctors were of the opinion that there were two stranglers—one for the early, elderly victims, another for the young women who were killed just before the murders stopped.

Brussel's was a solitary voice. There was one strangler, he said. And he described a bizarre course of sexual development he saw revealed in the killings. He also imagined a man who moved comfortably and anonymously through the city, his only remarkable characteristic a virtual mane that he loved to comb.

In time, the world learned that Albert DeSalvo had a full head of black hair, which he wore slicked back in place, and he was the only one responsible for the string of stranglings.

With characteristic humility, Brussel dismissed the mantle of seer. He stressed the need to be familiar with the facts of a case, but held out a special role for intuition.

In my work, I studied hypnosis and dissociation—everything from the natural hypnoid states (those momentary disorientations that we all experience) to the extremes of multiple personality. I concluded that what Brussel called intuition was an altered state of consciousness, a passive receptiveness to all that could be perceived. It was at once effortless, and intense.

Self-hypnosis became the key to my success as a criminal profiler, and I soon realized that a similar dissociation was the key to the success of many of the serial killers who claimed headlines.

In the dim light of Wolf's house I could see an old gas range pulled away from the wall, sitting near the center of the room. There was part of a kitchen chair, an empty picture frame, some old newspapers, rags and other debris from ages past, all in a heap on the floor. On the other side of the room there was an archway and, beyond that, what would have been the parlor.

I turned around and walked down a hall to the first

bedroom on the left. It was a small room with faded pink wallpaper still clinging to the walls. Sarah's room.

You were your mother's son. You were her only one. Nothing else was necessary. There didn't need to be any more people in your lives. When she was working at the diner, you did your schoolwork, took flight in your mind, and waited happily for her to come home. Until one time she came home with a man.

That was the first betrayal. Moving to this house was the second. Then Sarah. Three strikes and you're out.

You came to Sarah's room from the time she was an infant and you were just a child, really. You watched her sleep. You watched her breathe. Were you disciplined for that? If they caught you in her room, were you punished, lad?

And then later, of course, you wanted to touch her. But that wasn't enough. You wanted to cause her pain—ultimately to kill her. She had an innocent charm, then a seductive smile, perhaps, then a physical shape that inflamed you.

The second bedroom also was small—unpainted Sheetrock with holes in it. Seven holes, each one the size of a boy's fist. The holes were all about the same height from the floor, in a row. I wondered how many times Corrigan had replaced the Sheetrock—how many more holes there might have been.

When you learned how to fly—while you were learning how to split yourself away and cut off the rage—you felt no pain in your hands when you shattered the wall with a single thrust of your fist.

The largest bedroom—no doubt the parents' room—was at the end of the hall. The door had a sliding bolt on the inside. They were afraid of what might come through the door in the night.

When did they install the bolt? Not until later—not until after you had intruded, watched them, and been caught. You probably got the coal bin for that one, but then you grew. You were becoming more difficult for him to manage. So the bolt went on the door.

Outside their room, on the right, was another door. When I opened it, the smell of damp soil wafted up. The cellar. I walked down the aging stairs to the dirt, where I surveyed the floor joists suffering from damp rot.

It was a stone foundation, leaning dangerously into the cellar after years of freezing and thawing. The stones seemed laced together by cobwebs garnished with the sawdust residue from carpenter ants.

There was a disconnected furnace on a concrete slab and, beside it, the rusting hulk of a water tank. Large, gray barn spiders had discovered a perfect residence. And—judging from the remains—rodents in a variety of sizes had moved freely through the space, probably even while the house was still inhabited. On the left there was an archway, with an ell beyond.

I walked beneath the sagging beam of the arch, where I saw an oil tank lying on its side. Just past the tank, there was the coal bin—a wooden structure, still solid despite the dank passage of time. The door hung from a single hinge. Inside, on one wall, there were ancient scratches in the wood—deep gouges in a line, as if the marks had been used for counting.

Each night I am locked in here, I will make one mark. And someday, somebody will pay for each one.

When I saw no other marks inside the bin, I moved outside and walked around it. There were similar, but fewer, marks on the outer wall, and they weren't as old. One of them was fresh, carved there with a knife within the last week or so, I guessed. Wolf was so methodical, so rigid, he had to leave his mark, a sign that he'd been there. But he couldn't make himself go back inside the bin to do it.

So this is the place where you were caged. This is the place where fear lived, and continues to reside. And this is the place where thoughts of vengeance were born. If you were going to die, this is where it would happen, isn't it? Horror. The belief that you wouldn't make it through the night. The blackness—total, when Corrigan climbed the stairs and hit the switch up there.

But that life, that family, that house—it was all you had; you were trapped within it. You needed to find a way to survive there. So you flew—up and out of your cell, to other worlds. You split yourself away. Up and out of your soul—until sometimes you couldn't find the way back.

And you've been drawn back here, haven't you? Again and again. As you grew stronger, you had to test yourself. You had to return to your ghosts, confront your demons. Each time you took a life, you had a glimpse of power, a taste of invulnerability. But it was fleeting.

Within a few weeks—even days sometimes—you were restless, bored, vulnerable to the doubt that would start to creep in. So you would begin again, pick up a thread from your last one. Follow it. Build yourself up.

They had to be connected, one to another, like the strands of the spider's web, or the intricate weaving of the oriole's nest.

The times you came here were just after you killed. Why? To see if you could defeat this place? Or was it to become a child again, and rewrite the past?

I turned from the coal bin and walked out to the end of the ell. There was a small stream that flowed in under one side of the foundation, carved its way through the dirt floor, and disappeared. Corrigan had built a low stone wall to keep the water on its course when snow melt swelled the runoff in the spring.

Your sister Sarah told Lane how much you loved that book on mythology, especially the story about the man who could fly. Did you read about Icarus—about his wings of wax melting when he flew too near the sun? He fell into the Aegean Sea. Was this your sea, lad? This pissy little river?

I turned in the direction of a scratching noise, and watched a large water rat make his way along the sill of the house. Another set piece to amplify the horror. But no one could have designed this. Not even Stephen King. It was a natural.

I walked back through the cellar, up the stairs, and out into the light of the day. I hadn't passed any other houses on my way in, so I walked farther up the hill—perhaps 150 yards—until I found the nearest neighbor.

A young man wearing hunting garb and holding a hamburger in his hand answered my knock.

"I was looking at the house just down the hill there," I said.

"Corrigan's?"

"I guess. Do you know if it's for sale?"

He laughed. "Town took it for taxes years ago. Been for sale for as long as I can remember. The bulkhead isn't locked on it. You can get inside if you want. But what would you want with it anyway?"

"It's a nice piece of land," I said.

"Ledge. Oh, it's maybe ten acres, but it's mostly ledge. You'd live there?"

Now it was my turn to laugh. "Only after it had a little work done on it."

"Check with the town clerk." he said. "She's also the tax collector. I think they wanted thirty thousand for it, but that was a few years back."

"Do you know anything about what happened to the place?"

"She could tell you that, too. The Corrigans died, I know that. But they had grown kids. Maybe they just didn't want the place. I don't know."

I started to turn away, then thought of one last question. "Do you know if anyone else has looked at the place recently?"

He chewed his burger, thoughtful for a moment. "There was another guy. My brother seen him. I didn't. He said the guy went up there and looked around, came back out, and left. Maybe you'll have a bidding war on that old piece of shit."

I thanked him and made my way back to the car.

After a stop at the town hall—where I obtained an application to bid on the property, plus a rough copy of a surveyor's map of the land—I retraced the route to the interstate and continued north. I had no idea where Wolf would be, but it had to be within striking distance of the house. The marks on the outside of the coal bin told me that his business there wasn't finished.

I headed for White River Junction because it offered several motels, as well as highway access to a wide area of the Twin State Valley of Vermont and New Hampshire. The postmark on that package Sinclair received meant little. White River was a central office, serving dozens of towns and villages. But it was a place to begin.

Lane

When I got back from Florida, I went into hiding at Fuzzy's apartment. My place was a crime scene. Robert's wasn't safe. And, until I knew what Pop had going, I had no intention of dealing with Hanson.

Fuzzy had been out to Tranquil Acres and said that a minor miracle had taken place. "Even Bobby's paranoia is improving," he said. "He changed his mind about them having microphones in the walls."

I asked Fuzzy if I should tell Robert about Sheila.

"No way. Sobriety's a fragile thing."

It sounded funny hearing a word like "fragile" come out of Fuzzy's mouth.

"I heard that at an AA meeting once," he said. "He'd try to climb over Lymann to get out of that place. That'd be no help for you, and bad for him. I just finished chilling him out over a bunch of nightmares he was having."

I had heard all about those from Lymann. He called to tell me to stay out of Robert's dreams because I was getting killed in them.

"So the Wolf lives in the wilderness, huh?" Fuzzy asked.

"You ever been to Vermont, Fuzzy?"

"Farthest north I ever got was Yonkers."

I was comfortable—sitting with Fuzzy in his kitchen, drinking coffee and talking. I was also thinking about how my two years in the city had turned into four, and how keeping the peace had metamorphosed into coping with a serial killer.

On the flight back from Florida, I had watched a little girl in the seat next to me. She was struggling with one of those brain teaser games—the kind where you have to jump plastic pegs over each other and end up with a single peg in the middle. After about an hour of diligent work but no results, she leaned over and said, "My name is Shawna. Are you smart?"

"My name is Lane," I said. "Maybe if we work on that puzzle together, we can do it."

It's a simple concept, really, but one that you can see only when you step back from it. Each move must set up another, and all action must be toward the center. For a half hour, I had a great time and Shawna mastered the game. That was when I realized just how tired I was of having my life controlled by a madman.

Those sentiments echoed words I'd heard my mother say to my father many times. He would become obsessed with a murder, and Mom would ask him, *beg* him to leave it alone, set it aside for an hour, and come with her to the park, or the café on the corner, or even just the backyard.

He couldn't do it. And I had always sided with him, thinking that he was in touch with the true essence of life, the only work that really mattered. I had always believed that he was the one who was making a difference in the world, but what I failed to see was that Mom was making a different world. She was the one in control, taming her environment, staying sane—while Pop was drawn ever deeper into the twisted, labyrinthine workings of society's sickest minds. And I had followed him.

Mine was a love-hate relationship with Homicide. I hated the depravity of it, but loved the feeling of what Robert called "correcting God's mistakes"—getting the bad guys off the street.

Fuzzy was refilling my cup. "For about a day there, I thought I was going to put police work behind me and move on," I told him. "I was thinking I'd apply to grad school. Maybe go into medicine."

"Hey, Hanson had to suspend you," Fuzzy said.

"I know that."

My thoughts of becoming a doctor hadn't lasted very long. The bottom line for Pop had always been that the system wasn't equipped to deal with strangers killing strangers. That fact had always been more important to my father than the practice of his brand of medicine—psychiatry. It was for me, too.

"This guy has been dictating where I live, whether I can do my job, whether I get any sleep at night. I know what it feels like to be isolated, to be someone's target. When I made the switch to plainclothes, I already felt like I couldn't handle Homicide. The politics. Being young and a woman in the last citadel of the good ol' boys."

"Listen," Fuzzy said. "You know, I once did a stint in Investigations. That's what they called it back then."

"You were a detective?"

"Lasted two weeks. I had everything going for me. Talk about being a good ol' boy. Shit. The poker games, the booze. I had a patent on 'em. But I didn't have the smarts, Lane. And I didn't have the guts. The first scene I go to, the lead tells me we got four dead. I count three. 'Where's four?' I ask him. 'In there,' he says. I thought it was a doll stuffed down behind the radiator, this one tiny foot sticking up in the air. The kid was three years old. That's all the life she got to see."

Fuzzy shrugged. "I put the uniform back on. Homicide's a different world. You got the smarts, Lane. And you got the guts. You're gonna make a damn fine detective. But this may not be the case to cut your teeth on."

"I felt that way before, Fuzzy," I told him. "But this case doesn't seem so convoluted anymore. I can put a face on the madman. I can tell you most of his life history and a lot of the reasons he chose to become what he is. And I don't have any choice. If I don't get him, he gets me."

Pop

◆

The motel I found was a bit fancier than a fellow like me requires, but all the less expensive housing had been taken by hunters from down country. They didn't have the luxury of hunting camps, so they filled the motels just vacated by the foliage crowds.

What made the front page here wouldn't make it into any city newspaper I knew of. SCHOOL BOARD REFUSES TO CHANGE BUS ROUTE. CHURCH FUNDRAISER EXCEEDS GOAL. TRUCK FIRE ON INTERSTATE. Life in the slow lane.

The letters to the editor ran three to one in favor of the right to life and the right to own guns (not necessarily the right to take life away, I assumed, but couldn't be sure). There was a heated letter from a resident of Thetford defending Harry Truman's use of the atomic bomb. Takes a long time to get things settled in northern New England.

Maybe it was the contrast—the mountains and forests of that region versus the tenements and broken street lights of the cities to the south—but I found myself thinking about the Roxbury section of Boston, the place where I grew up. The building we lived in was a three-story walk-up. Although even then Roxbury was predominantly black, everyone was poor, and the overwhelming poverty seemed to transcend the issue of race.

I sat back in the motel chair, raised my bare feet to the table, and allowed my mind to drift. It's something I've done for years—this wandering in my own mind. Whether I'm relaxing, or seeking some avenue into a perplexing problem concerning the logistics of murder, the road always begins within myself.

I could see a young kid, years earlier. He was across a vacant lot from me, playing with a kite. I was about seven years old.

The kid with the kite took flight. The blue-and-black paper bat soared in an arc up over the vacant lot. My sister moved away toward the wall of wildflowers and weeds, clapping her hands. And the kid with the kite was running toward me—crazed, it seemed, trying to look up at the sky and run at the same time. So I picked up a rock.

We were the last white family on the street in Roxbury. I spent hours curled into a corner of the first-floor landing, watching the people pass up and down the stairs. It was a way to pass the time. It was a way to avoid the violence that went on inside our apartment on the third floor. One time a man went up the stairs and jumped off the roof.

Years later—in my teens, perhaps—I asked my mother if she remembered the man who killed himself.

"No," she said.

"Do you remember sirens?"

"No."

"Did I dream it?"

"What?"

"What I just said."

"No."

"Then, how do I know?"

"You shouldn't."

"But I do."

"Ask your father."

"Was he there?"

"No. He was watching Eddie Fisher."

I remember feeling a headache coming on.

"What about when I hit the kid with the rock?" I asked.

"That you dreamed," she said.

But I remember searching the world for my sister's eyes. She had turned away. There was no greater terror than not being able to find my sister's eyes. There was the kid with his bat kite running like a madman right at me.

I thought it was real. My mother said it was a dream. My sister doesn't remember. But the rock hit its mark and drew blood, and the whole world fell silent.

When I was in college, I used to dream that I was on a train going faster and faster, constantly accelerating on a set of straight tracks. Other times it was as if everything slowed down, like watching life in slow motion.

The man who jumped off the roof had a name: Cedric. I called him "the ash man" because the only times I ever saw him were when he was taking the ashes from his coal stove down to the barrel in the backyard.

"All he ever does is go up and down the stairs with his buckets of ashes," I told my mother.

"That's all you ever see him do," she said.

"What else does he do?"

"I don't know. I don't ever see him do anything."

I spoke to Cedric on the stairs one day—just to say hello, to try to get a conversation going.

"You the one hit the kid in the face with the rock," he said.

I couldn't escape my own violence.

A short time later, Cedric dove from the roof and landed on the jungle gym in the backyard.

Memory can be a loose commodity. It's sometimes difficult to know what's real and what isn't—what we're really remembering and what are only dreams. It's especially difficult when the others who were around are less than helpful, when they don't want to remember, or can't.

Something was wrong in the apartment. I knew it the moment I came to the door and couldn't hear the TV. The knob wouldn't turn, so I knocked. My sister opened the door and I looked into her eyes.

"You're late," she said.

"What's wrong?" I wanted to know.

"We're going to the zoo."

"I don't want to go to the zoo. I want to know what's wrong."

"Your father's sick."

She always called him "your father" because she had a different father.

"Again?" I asked.

"We have to go to the zoo," she said, continuing to hold the door in a way that didn't let me enter or even see inside.

"Where's Ma?"

"Sleeping. We can go look at the gorilla."

I thought about that.

"I want to see the gorilla," I said, "but I don't want to walk all the way to the zoo."

"Ma gave me money for the bus. I'll get my coat."

She closed the door and left me standing in the hall. In a few minutes she was back, and closed the door behind her, locking it. I watched her put the key in the pocket of her maroon coat, then pull on her black gloves.

She was five years older than I was, and I trusted her. For me, feeling safe was feeling warm, and my sister made me feel warm, even on the coldest winter nights.

"What's the matter with him this time?" I asked.

"Says it's his heart again. Ma says he'll be better later."

We walked down the stairs to the darkening street.

"Why does he hate me?" I asked.

"He hates everyone."

"Does he hate you?"

"He doesn't really know me," she said.

"My father knows me, and he hates me."

"I don't even know if he really is your father," she said. "There was another man before him, but I can't remember his name. Ma wants you to think of him as your father. Maybe he is. I don't know."

I considered that.

"If he isn't my father, I don't know if I could think of him like one."

"Maybe that's why he hates you."

"Does the whiskey hurt his heart?"

"I don't think it's his heart at all. I think it's just the whiskey. You haven't seen him go crazy."

"I can imagine that. I think that's worse—imagining something instead of knowing it. Maybe I should see it once. Did he hit Ma?"

"I don't think so. I think he just went to sleep after."

"Maybe he won't wake up," I said.

"Ma says maybe one of these times he'll wake up dead."

"She talks."

It was a short bus ride to Franklin Park. My sister bought me a bag of peanuts at the gate and we walked along the path eating them.

"You want to go to the elephant house first?" she asked.

"I just want to see the gorilla."

"Why do you like him so much?"

"I wish he wasn't in a cage. I wish they took him back to Africa and let him go. He makes me feel happy, though."

"I'm glad. You don't seem happy very often."

"I know," I said, and held tightly to her hand.

The African lowlands gorilla has fingers as big as bananas, and eats seeds. The one at Franklin Park lived in a small, hexagonal stone building with four barred windows. The enclosure was surrounded by an iron fence.

His cage was empty. The bars on the window were broken, twisted out of shape. I found out later that kids were throwing beer bottles at him, and that the last two had been filled with gasoline and stuffed with rags. The boys lit the rags, then threw the bottles into the cage where they exploded.

The gorilla went wild, broke free of the enclosure, and had to be shot by the police. They left the cage like that—the twisted bars, the blackened walls.

So many times I had wanted the gorilla to crash out of there, but not that way. Later I would dream about what happened to him. I would hear the wailing, the roaring. I would understand his terror, feel his horror. His rage lived inside me.

Our beasts can never be set totally free. They may have brief periods of freedom, but then must be restrained or put to death. The rage of beasts should not be led by the hand into vacant lots of kite-flying children—places where chaos and collision are all too likely to occur.

I opened my eyes. Through the sliding glass door in the motel room I could see the determined march of cows toward a distant barn. They were Holsteins mostly—a few Brown Swiss. The black-and-white slab sides of the Holsteins swayed as they walked. The brown heifers seemed not much larger than the white-tailed deer being hunted all over the state. Cows, too, have deep, sad eyes.

Everything in my life had been like that dream of the train that just kept going faster. There was never any way to stop it once it got going. It had a life of its own.

The rock had hit the kid square in the face. There were screams and blood. I knew if I ever yielded to my own terror, I would go crazy with rage. Yet I knew I had to tease it—feel it from time to time, reassure myself that it was still there. I had to reach inside and stroke the soft fur of the African lowlands gorilla within me.

Shortly before he died, my father scraped together enough money to move the family from Roxbury to the suburbs because he didn't want my sister dating black boys. Had he lived, he would have seen her marry a nice white boy. And he would have seen me select a wife from the race that frightened him so.

I worked my way through school as a cook in a Jewish delicatessen. I made the brisket and the pastrami, the salads and the deserts—and, occasionally, filled in for someone at the sandwich counter. I was making sandwiches that night when Savvy came in for a roast beef on rye.

I liked her sense of humor. She was bright, attractive, assertive, independent—but I think what I loved most about Savvy was her willing vulnerability, her belief in the goodness of others. I also envied that feeling she had of truly belonging in this world. But I, ever the outsider, remained the hardened cynic, trusting no one except her. She said she could change me, and, for a long while, I believed—perhaps even hoped—that she would.

I pushed myself up from my chair and retrieved the material that Street had faxed just before I left Michigan. It was a summary of a case presented as a problem in ethics. The issues raised by the case were later resolved in California's Tarasoff decision—that a therapist had a duty to inform when a client made an explicit threat against someone. At the time of the Paul Wolf case, the waters were still muddy.

Wolf, a ward of the state after assaulting his stepfather and mother with a knife, was seen in therapy by a licensed clinical social worker. The youth told his therapist that if he were returned to his family, "I'll probably kill them all."

In the course of treatment he stated his intention to kill other people—a teacher, the wife of a police officer, a neighbor. He went into considerable detail about how he would commit these murders.

One of the three women was found murdered in the precise manner that Wolf had told the therapist he would kill her. A mail carrier on her way to work described a young man she had seen leaving the victim's yard just before dawn. She picked Wolf out of a photo lineup, making him the prime suspect.

In the judgment of the therapist, the confidentiality

required by her profession, as well as that imposed by the state on matters related to minors in their custody, were sacrosanct. Besides, she argued, Wolf was in a residential school with twenty-four-hour supervision.

According to students at the school, however, the young man came and went pretty much as he pleased. Most of his forays away from the campus were at night, and he was never caught. Predictably, school officials insisted that any talk of his coming and going as he wished was fabrication. They didn't say it was impossible; just highly unlikely.

The police investigation produced nothing. The homicide remained on the books as unsolved.

Police theorized that the victim, Estelle Cummings, fifty-three, had been asleep in her bed when an intruder entered her home. The time of death was estimated as between 2:00 and 5:00 A.M. The presence of defensive wounds on the corpse suggested a struggle. The killer awakened her before he started plunging his knife into her. He stabbed her thirty-one times.

Wolf's second intended victim didn't die as he had promised she would. She committed suicide—hanged herself—six months after Cummings's murder. She left a note saying that she hadn't been able to sleep. She expected "him" to come in the night.

The third was married to a police officer, and it seemed as though Wolf had more sense than to try anything there.

I phoned the officer's department and learned that Captain Bruce Richards had been retired for a couple of years. He and his wife were living in Oakland Park, Florida. I got the number from information and called.

Bruce Richards was friendly enough, but understandably wary when I explained the reason for my call. I offered to provide him with law enforcement references before we talked, but the offer alone was enough to satisfy him.

"Paul didn't leave us alone," he said. "When I was out on calls, somebody was prowling around the house. A couple of times I found footprints. I also found jimmy marks on the back door. I went down to that school of his and had a private conversation with him. I told him if there was ever so much as another toe print outside my house that shouldn't be there—I didn't care if it was his or not—I was coming back to kill him. That was the end of the trouble. He knew I meant it."

"Did you ever talk to him after that? Your impressions of him would help me a great deal."

"I never talked to the bastard again. I saw him around town a few times. He was down in the city for a while, I guess, but he showed up back home now and then. Then the army took him. Why you digging all this up now?"

"I think Paul Wolf is still alive, and I believe he may be responsible for other murders."

Richards laughed. "I know he's alive. I saw him. That bullshit about his ashes—well, it wasn't my problem anymore. We were up visiting family and friends last summer. I've got a Winnebago and we drove that up—stayed in a campground near Quechee. I saw this guy getting into a pickup truck that had the name of some construction company on the door. I felt like I knew him—even walked over closer for a better look. He drove off, but I got the plate number. I forgot all about it until one day it just hit me. You know the way that works. I thought, 'That was Paul Wolf.' He looked his age—in his forties, I guess—but he was still in good shape. It was the eyes that gave him away. When I was working, I always called that kind 'nobody's home eyes.' "

"Did you ever check the plate?"

"Sure. Daedalus Construction. I checked on 'em. Legitimate outfit. Successful. They had kind of an absentee owner. Sometimes he was there, most of the time he wasn't. I figured maybe that was Paul—that he just wanted to start his life again, you know?—with a clean slate? Guess I was wrong."

Daedalus—the architect who designed a maze for the king

of Crete to imprison the Minotaur, a monster that was part bull and part man—was the father of Icarus. He designed the wings of wax for his son to use to escape from the maze and the beast, but Icarus flew too near the sun and his wings melted. He plunged into the sea.

I thanked Richards and got off the phone. Then I cracked open the yellow pages. Daedalus Construction.

Luck.

I hoisted my feet back onto the table and allowed my eyes to close.

For many years I supervised the training of young psychologists. Always, in the first session, I raised the question of power in the therapeutic relationship. I never had a trainee who was totally comfortable with that concept—that they have power and wield it, whether they realize it or not. Their clients give it to them, take it away, engage them in battles over it.

These young zealots always wanted to rush into the clinical world and start curing everyone in sight. They were well meaning, but blind. They were humanists. They were noble. They cared, and they knew how to communicate that. Graduate school had taught them all the necessary techniques.

The power to heal is the flip side of the power to destroy.

I always told them that. They grimaced. Some of them requested, and were granted, other supervisors. The ones who recognized the truth about power were the ones who went on to become superior therapists.

I started drifting again.

Luck.

The power to destroy.

The need to remember and to embrace our own horror.

I see myself hurling a rock into a child's face because I am frightened. My sister has gone away. I'm alone. He's careening toward me, totally out of control.

A man reminds me of what I have done, then dives to his death from the roof. Was I so evil?

I feel something stir inside me.

When abreaction occurs in the course of therapy, it is spontaneous. The client reexperiences a trauma, along with all the horrible feelings associated with it. It's as if it's happening right at that moment—there's that kind of immediacy, that level of intensity. But, because the environment is supportive and caring, the client won't be lost in the maelstrom. Healing can begin.

The power to heal is the flip side of the power to destroy.

There's an old Lenny Bruce bit in which a doctor sends a bill for services provided to a child rescued from a well. The public is outraged. The doctor withdraws his demand for payment—but the child will have to be returned to the well.

It stirs again.

I move farther down, more deeply inside myself—through time, faces rushing by—to a place with eight sides and four windows. My gorilla turns his head, slowly, and stares at me with obvious expectation. I tell him that it isn't quite time, but he continues to watch. We know each other well.

Sarah Sinclair, what can you tell me?

The child's black-and-white notebook lies there on the bed. Though it is Sarah's journal, it doesn't pulsate or call to me. I feel no urge to snap it up and devour its contents. But through all the years of reconstructing the choreography of murder, of drawing a psychological portrait of the killer, victims have told me far more than any other expert on the subject. I picked up the notebook and started to read.

> I tried to kill myself when I was 24. My husband had left me, my daughter was dead, and I couldn't see beyond the moment. I thought I would always hurt, always weep inside. And I thought that death would bring a welcome change, an end to all the pain. But the overdose failed, the emergency room doctors succeeded, and I didn't possess enough spirit to

try it again. I was too beaten down. Too tired. I'd also stopped believing that death could bring relief.

Since meeting John Wolf, my blood has started circulating again. I feel newly born, alive.

But I'm also confused. Robert's departure made me so sad, I wanted to die. Now, with John's arrival, death is still attractive—but for an opposite reason. Dying should occur at the height of happiness. A perfect moment frozen for eternity. If John were to place his hand on my throat—if I could feel the warmth of it, the pressure—I would want to tell him what a compliment it was that he would pick me from all the others. But I fear that he would think me crazy.

Sarah Sinclair had attempted suicide, and damn near succeeded. She wanted out. She was sure of it.

She also had a sense of the connectedness of things—the past, the present—the way we flash in and out of our wars with today. But there was nothing warlike about her Wolf.

I stared at the photograph of Sarah lying in a heap on her living room floor. The white dress, stained red. The blue-and-white feather, barely visible—just beyond her outstretched arm.

A wedding? No. *But her choice of that dress represented something, some kind of commitment. To what? Not to him. You were infatuated with the man, Sarah, but you barely knew him. You weren't a fool.*

Suicide—the most meaningful ceremony in anyone's life. Some might expect you to wear black to travel the long tunnels of night, but perhaps you chose white because it is so much like the light that guides you home.

The white dress—commitment—to death? to life? Did he simply kill you, Sarah? Or did he first need to bring you to life?

Why was he so drawn to you? So undeterred by the risks?

He took your freedom, but he set you free. Gave you wings.

Another stirring.

It's time.

Lane

It wasn't long before I heard from Pop. He had settled in at a rustic motel somewhere in the mountains of Vermont.

"We need to get this wrapped up," he said.

"We do," I agreed.

There were long pauses in the conversation—silences that told me Pop was somewhere else—that place he visits whenever he's clawing his way inside a killer's mind.

Actually, clawing is the wrong word. The way he describes it to me, it isn't something he does aggressively. If he were to *try*, he says, he'd fail. He has to just sit back and let it happen.

I guess it's also wrong to say that he gets inside a killer's mind. The reverse is closer to the truth: the mind of the killer enters Pop's head, allowing him to see the world through the psychopath's eyes. Judging from the change in Pop at such times, the view isn't very pretty.

When I was a little girl, I took those changes in Pop personally. I thought that he had stopped loving me; I barely recognized him. A terrible distance would come between us, affecting every aspect of my life—schoolwork, appetite, sleep patterns. Pop finally sat me down one day and explained what was happening.

"It's something I do to help the police," he said. "Something that has nothing to do with how I feel about you."

He went over to the window and opened it.

"A bird could fly in here," he told me, "because the window is up and there is nothing to stop it. It might be a beautiful bird, brightly colored—like a parrot. Or one that sings a lovely song in the morning. Or even an ugly bat looking for someone to bite."

I looked at the open window, waiting to see whether birds or bats would fly in.

"That's what happens to me, Lanie," he went on. "Sometimes an ugly bat flies in through the window of my mind. But it never stays. Soon, it flies away, and everything is fine again."

I'm sure that my father thought he was reassuring me with this story, but I was a literal child. I envisioned a whole family of bats hanging upside down inside his skull, and the image frightened me. I had nightmares, but it was always my mother, not my father, who rushed to my room to comfort me in the middle of the night. When I told her that my dreams were of birds and bats, she didn't understand, didn't see the reason for terror.

I knew the signs. John Wolf had already wandered into Pop's mind. That window is always open. He doesn't know how to close it.

"Look," I said. "Just tell me how to find the motel and I'll be on the road as soon as I can."

"I really don't want you here, Lane."

"I'm not giving you a choice on that one, Pop."

"I need a composite," he said, finally.

"Fine. Swartz will do that for us."

There's nobody better than Swartz with a pen and pad. He doesn't rely on just the overlays. Once he has the general features, he refines the drawing—makes it come alive.

"As soon as he's done," I said, "I'm on my way. I dragged you into this case, and I won't leave you alone with it. Besides, I couldn't let go of it now. I'm in too deep. I won't let this guy kill again."

"No," he said. "No more victims. No more sparring with evil. It's time for an ending."

I didn't like Pop's tone. It had the same drifting quality, but there was an edge to it.

He had gone silent again. "Hey," I said.

"Call me when you have the composite."

I'd barely hung up when Swartz called.

"Any news from your father?" he wanted to know.

"Just talked to him. He needs a favor."

"Name it."

"Pop has to know what Wolf looks like. He wants you to do a composite," I said. "Robert saw him when he was posing as Alan Carver. Let's see what he comes up with before I add Robbins to the mix."

On the ride out to Tranquil Acres, I told Swartz how much I appreciated his going out on a limb for me. He was risking his career just by talking to me and not turning me over to Hanson.

"Wolf is not one to toy with, Lane," he said. "If you come in, you'll be safe. I'll talk to Hanson with you. Show him what we've got. Get the feds up there with your father."

"There's no time," I told him. "I'm not sticking Pop with it while I go plead with Hanson. Wolf has to be stopped now."

"You're underestimating Wolf," Swartz said.

"Maybe in the beginning," I said. "Not now. What I *know* I was doing was underestimating me, but I got over that. Now don't you start."

Swartz looked at me. "I wouldn't do that."

We drove in silence for several minutes. Then Swartz said, "You know, your father and I worked together on a messy one about eight years ago. Guy's name was Orvis Hobson. He took a hatchet to a woman—left her in a Dumpster. And in the basement of a downtown hotel. And in a sewer over by the ball park. Your dad was able to tell us how the killer thought, how he lived—his personal habits, the kind of work he probably did, the type of vehicle he drove—the usual profiling stuff, only more detailed."

I looked over at Swartz.

"We got Hobson before he killed again," he said. "The profile helped us stay focused, even when a couple of leads pointed in other directions. He told us where we'd find the hatchet—wrapped in plastic and buried under some rosebushes. He said it was common sense."

"He's tried to tell me the same thing." I said.

"He got a confession out of Hobson. Your father walks into the interrogation room, sits opposite the guy, and doesn't say a thing for a long time. He just stares at Hobson's hands. Then your father makes some kind of gesture with his own hand. The guy's been real jittery, but he starts to relax. Your father says, 'I'm listening—whenever you choose to begin.' Hobson spills his guts."

I nodded. "Kinesthetic hypnosis. Pop says it's a distraction technique."

"That's not what Hanson called it," Swartz said, laughing. "He said it was voodoo."

When we arrived at Tranquil Acres, Swartz went in first, to make sure that the captain didn't have someone waiting there for me. After a few minutes, he came to the front door and waved me in.

Robert and Lymann were playing cards and listening to the radio in the solarium. Robert had already lost weight. His face was drawn, he hadn't shaved, and he looked as if he were in pain.

Swartz worked with Robert for over an hour, putting the composite together. When they finished, Robert asked if we could have a minute alone. We went down the hall to his room.

He dropped into one of the overstuffed chairs. I sat next to him, on the side of the bed. His eyes were dark, lifeless. I figured it was his medication.

"How's it going for you?" I asked.

Robert looked down at his hands—first the backs, then his palms. "It's scary. What about you? How are you doing?"

"I'm okay," I said.

He looked up then, and gazed off into a corner of the room. "The only way I ever coped with anything was booze. I don't know how well I'll do without my safety valve."

Robert was silent again, but when I put my hand over his, he looked at me and said, "You know, Lane, you've never seen me sober before. How will you get along with this guy?"

"I've been wondering the same thing," I told him. Then I leaned over and kissed his cheek.

From Tranquil Acres, Swartz and I drove back to the city to see Inez Flint, a plastic surgeon who had done work for us before. Swartz had put together a detailed composite. Now Inez scanned the image into her computer so we could see how it looked with a variety of changes and possible disguises: beard, mustache, different hair lengths, weight gain, weight loss.

When Swartz was satisfied with what he saw on the computer screen, he called me over. "Now, you tell me how this needs to be refined."

I looked at the monitor and saw Robbins's face—the

eyes—and felt a chill at the back of my neck. "No changes," I said. "That's him."

I called Pop to tell him that I had the composites and would bring them with me.

"I need something else. The thirty-two you pulled out of Robert Sinclair's desk drawer."

"I don't like the sound of that," I said.

There was a long pause.

"I'll reserve a room for you," he said.

"You've found him, haven't you?"

"Leave now. I need the composites first thing in the morning. I have an early appointment with him."

I looked at the clock. The late news hadn't even come on yet. I'd get there in plenty of time.

I was tired, but I like driving—especially at night. With a thermos of coffee and something decent on the radio, the trip wouldn't seem so long. I was packed and putting my things in the trunk of my car when the dark blue sedan pulled up behind me.

I saw Susan Walker coming toward me. Dexter Willoughby was right behind her.

"We need to talk about Alan Chadwick," Willoughby said. "Could we step inside, please?"

"I was just leaving."

"I'm afraid I have to insist," he said.

We went up to Fuzzy's apartment, but none of us sat down.

"As you know," Willoughby said, "the state police have been digging up Chadwick's land."

"Right."

"They've located eleven sets of bones. Our people are working on the IDs right now. But the ID that I'm trying to pin down is Chadwick's. He's not who he said he was."

I remembered my conversation with Walker—her

promise that she'd talk to Willoughby. "So you've finished with Purrington?"

"We're satisfied that he's responsible for the cases upstate," Walker said.

"So we work together on this?" I asked.

"Two of our agents were out to your father's place in Michigan," Willoughby said. "He's not there. He's working the Chadwick angle, isn't he?"

There wasn't going to be any "working together." This guy was going to crash into the case at the worst possible time—when Pop was about to get a look at the man he believed was John Wolf.

"Chadwick didn't die in that explosion, and we want to know where he is," Willoughby said. "We also need to know what name he's using now, and we think you and your father can tell us that."

"I don't know that I can help you," I said.

"Look, Detective Frank," Willoughby said, "You're on suspension, and I don't think Captain Hanson is going to be pleased when he finds out that you're still working this case. Let me make this clear. I'm not *asking* you to cooperate. I'm *ordering* you to."

I noticed Walker trying to make eye contact with Willoughby, probably to signal him to cool it. I think she sensed that I wouldn't respond well to his threats. But either he didn't catch it, or he chose to ignore it.

"If I have to charge you with obstruction of justice, I'll do it," he said.

Walker tried again to lower the heat a notch or two. "What he means is—"

"What I mean is," Willoughby said, "I won't hesitate to take you into custody. It's up to you."

I could see that he was serious. "I don't know what name Chadwick is using now," I said.

"You have the right to remain silent," Willoughby began.

"Okay, okay," I said. "Let me call my father."

I got Pop on the line and told him that my trip might be

delayed. I described the situation in as much detail as I could.

Pop said, "I don't have any secrets. Invite them to join us in Vermont."

So that's what I did. Our two-car caravan hit the highway shortly after midnight.

Pop

Waiting.

John Wolf had carved his way across the country, and I was convinced that we were sitting on his doorstep. But from the time the feds arrived with Lane, that was the assignment.

Wait.

They were checking with the local authorities, no doubt doing the kind of thorough job that would fit nicely onto a prepared report form. Date of contact. Time of contact. Officer interviewed. Location of interview. All easily keyed into a computer database.

When Quantico came into being, a computer was at the center of it. They could cross-check and recheck and search and match and generate all sorts of lists. Age of victim. Weapon used. Make of vehicle. Rural or urban setting.

Anything that couldn't be programmed into the computer was irrelevant to the task. Motive was in. Motivation was out. There on the cutting edge, they sowed the seeds of their own ineffectiveness. The computer, after all, was only as good as what went into it. And most of what went into it restricted inquiry.

Willoughby was a company man. He would go far. Walker was barely postadolescent—not quite home from the prom—but she was smart. Maybe she would be the one to break the lockstep procession toward ignorance. But at that moment, she was half of the team that was making me wait. I'd been told to postpone my appointment with the suspect for twenty-four hours while they checked him out. And, like the loyal American I was, I did precisely as my government requested. Changing the appointment hadn't created any problem for me. If anything, it added to the role I was playing—a busy investor constantly on the move and at the mercy of his cellular phone.

Lane spent the day wandering the hall between our rooms, while I sat and watched the light snow fall and blow around. Now she was pacing my room.

"There's a good pay-per-view movie," I said.

"When did you start watching TV?"

"Since it became a portable theater that I can enjoy without leaving my motel room. It's *Natural Born Killers*."

"You watched that?"

"It's a picture of what we have become. The old argument was about life creating art, or art influencing life. It's all the same now, from the cradle to the grave. Life is art."

"I can't believe you turned on a television," Lane said.

"It used to be a big deal to have a police scanner in the house. Now, when you hear the police call that A. C. Cowlings is driving O. J. Simpson in a white Bronco on the L.A. freeway, you turn on CNN. Pass the popcorn. I remember some media expert saying the only thing missing was a minicam in O. J.'s cell. Life and art have become indistinguishable."

"I thought the Oliver Stone thing was just an excuse to bloody the screen—another *Bonnie and Clyde*."

"Throngs leaving the theater in disgust," I said, remembering some of the reviews. "They couldn't see the message because they're living it. They *are* the message. Marshall McLuhan and all that."

"Who?"

"Jesus. Would you please go back to school somewhere and study something?"

I turned and looked at her. She was radiant—just sitting there, studying me so intently. I can raise my voice to my daughter only when my back is turned to her.

"Never mind," I said, returning to the snow. "Your friends should be back soon."

She laughed. "Right. My friends. And what will my friends have to say?"

When Lane was a child, and Savvy and I had friends coming to the house, Lane would say, "What will they talk about, Pop? What will they say?"

It was a game. I'd tell her—make some predictions about how the conversation would go—and at the end of the evening, or the next day, she'd say, "Right again, Pop."

"When I handed them Wrenville—" I began.

"Who?"

"Christopher Wrenville. He owns Daedalus Construction. He's our killer, but they'll say he's been here for years, a successful businessman well known in the area, highly respected—all that sort of thing. If they can find any record of prints on him, and I imagine they will, the prints won't match Chadwick's. They'll be diplomatic. They won't call me an old fool, but the charge will be there, hanging in the air."

"Then what?"

Another time I have trouble looking at Lane is when I'm lying to her.

"I don't know," I said.

A knock on the door cut off the conversation. Lane let the two agents in.

"This is a dead end," Willoughby announced.

The double-entry bookkeeper was blunt.

"It has to be him," Lane said.

"Wrenville has owned Daedalus Construction for ten years," Willoughby said, snapping open a narrow pad and scanning his notes. "It's pretty much a hobby for him. He's wealthy. Owns a condo on the waterfront in Fort Lauderdale. Has a sailboat docked there. Spends a lot of time on the ocean. From nineteen eighty-seven to nineteen ninety he was on the school board here. They were putting up a new building, and he played a substantial role in that. Even donated the land."

"That's just what we expected," Lane said. "Pop said he'd have a life like that to go back to."

Willoughby cleared his throat and straightened his tie. I knew he was about to drop his bomb.

"For purposes of his business, he had to be bonded," the agent said. "His prints were on file in the state capitol."

I finished it for him. "They don't match Chadwick's."

Willoughby looked at me. "Correct."

Walker was talking to Lane. "Our people feel he would create a new identity, leave the area completely. It's too hot for him here. They think one of the West Coast cities."

I shrugged. "Well, that takes care of that."

"Not quite," Willoughby said. "I have been asked to remind you, Dr. Frank, that you haven't been retained in this matter by any law enforcement agency."

I walked to the door and opened it. "Drive carefully," I said.

Lane and I had dinner at a restaurant in Hanover, New Hampshire, near the Dartmouth campus. The food was good, and the atmosphere decidedly collegiate.

We were both on edge by the time we returned to the motel. We said our good nights in the hall, and I headed for my room. I closed the door behind me and leaned back against it, staring at the red digital readout on the clock in the darkened room. Ten P.M.

I could see the shape of the package that Lane had

brought with her—composites and gun—on the bed. I touched it—felt the weapon—as I walked through the room, then opened the drapes and sat in front of the window.

Once more I picked up Sarah's journal, and read by the lights from the parking lot.

> In the house where I grew up, there was a fan-shaped window above the front door. One morning—I was young, no more than fourteen—as I was coming down the stairs from my bedroom, nearly to the bottom of the stairs, I noticed the way the sunlight was coming through the window, casting a rainbow on the floor. I stepped into that puddle of light, not realizing that I would remember it forever afterward as a magical moment. Although the rainbow never appeared again, I always looked for it whenever I came down those steps. I couldn't make myself quit hoping.
>
> Whatever love I've felt for Robert was like that rainbow—here and gone in an instant, never to return. One night, soon after we met, we were sitting on my sofa watching a movie when my cat jumped up on his lap. As I watched Robert's hand come to rest on the cat's back, I fell in love with the gesture, the gentleness of it. He was the hand, I was the cat—and so I married him, confident that he was the person I had assumed him to be in that snippet of time. For years, I waited for that man, that Robert, to reappear, but he never has. And never will. I'll see the rainbow long before I ever see that tender man again.
>
> It is good that Liza is still a baby, still unable to speak, unable to frame the question that may already be forming in her mind. I am afraid that someday she will ask me why I married her father. How can I explain to her about love that is born in an instant of misinterpretation or projection; how can I make her understand that much of my life has been spent

waiting for the return of someone who was never really here?

At least the rainbow was real.

She needed someone to bring her alive. John Wolf succeeded where Robert had failed.

All the pieces of the puzzle were falling into place. The elaborate preparations in Sarah's living room. The lack of defensive wounds. The incredible risks that Wolf had taken.

But now, I waited.

Quantico's limited understanding of people like Wrenville comes from the jailhouse interviews after they've been captured and convicted of some piece of their mayhem. The clerks march in with their questionnaires. The killers have their own agendas.

In the early years, I, too, followed them to their jail cells, until I realized that I already knew each one, and knew how they would answer my questions. Their signatures in the wild—carved into flesh, painted in blood on walls—told me volumes of truth. In their caverns of steel and stone, they reveled in their celebrity, quibbled over irrelevant details, and either justified or rationalized their actions.

There were exceptions, of course. Barry Lee Barnes was one.

"No one helped me to understand," he said. "No one listened to me. I clicked out. I went into a whole different world. I remember what I did. I know what I did was wrong. I can tell you every detail. It was me doing it, but it wasn't me, too."

Barnes didn't know it, but he was describing dissociation, that phenomenon that seems universal in the population of homicidal psychopaths. It's ironic. The strategy that allows victims of trauma to cope—the splitting away from the experience, becoming an observer instead of a participant—also allows the human predator to act on his violent fantasies.

"If they let me out of here today, I'd do it again," Barnes told me. "It was like a dream, like it wasn't really happening."

I asked Barnes a question that didn't appear on any of the forms. "Barry, if we were sitting over a couple of beers in a neighborhood bar right now, would you talk to me? Would you tell me any of this?"

"Hell, no," he said, and laughed. "I'm not gonna help you catch me and put me away. It didn't bother me—it wasn't a problem—until I got caught. Out there, it didn't scare me. It felt . . . okay."

I looked at the night outside, the flashing lights of the few cars up on the interstate. From this darkened room, to that darkened world—waiting—my eyes snapping back and forth from the backs of my hands to the edge of the forest.

I thought about Sarah. The purchase of the white dress. Her rapid infatuation with Wolf.

Sweet Sarah, you had been waiting for him, hadn't you?

Wolf was the worst of our plague of human predators. The world will be fascinated with his story—the book, the TV movie—and he was already fascinated with himself.

By making it personal, Wolf had forced the issue. When he targeted Lane, I no longer had a choice. If I didn't succeed, nothing stood between him and my daughter.

As I fell slowly into fitful sleep in the chair by the window, I know I looked out into the night for my sister's eyes. It was the habit of a lifetime—whenever I felt fear, and then rage, the stirring inside.

It was time.

Lane

I hate motels, hotels, any home away from home. This one made me feel caged at a time when every ounce of me wanted to take action.

I had packed my .22, and I knew what Wolf looked like, so I decided it was safe to take a short walk. I put on my blue wool jacket and went out.

There were no neon signs or street lights to brighten the midnight sky. There wasn't even any moonlight to reflect off the cover of light snow that had fallen. I felt as if I were wandering around in a sensory-deprivation tank, with only an occasional sound from the forest to keep me grounded in reality.

Words, other people's words, were running through my mind like an incessant soundtrack. I love poetry. Dickinson. Millay. Frost. Plath. Berryman. Stevens. For several minutes I walked, moving to the rhythm of random lines from their works.

As I headed back to my room, I counted off the windows on the west side of the building, locating Pop's room. His draperies were open—and I could see someone sitting there, staring out.

But at what?

It occurred to me once again how little I knew my father. Goethe said, "Whoever wishes to keep a secret must hide the fact that he possesses one." When I left him earlier, there had been no sign that he was intending to do anything but get a good night's sleep.

I went inside and walked down the hallway to Pop's room. I tapped lightly on the door. In a few seconds he was there, in T-shirt and jeans, his eyes heavy with the need for sleep. I'd never seen my father look quite so weary or so old.

"Just wanted to see if everything's okay," I said.

He looked at my jacket. "You're not going out, are you?"

"Nope," I said.

I didn't see any reason to tell him I'd already been out. "Why are you still up?"

"Just thinking. Go tuck yourself in, and be sure to lock up."

He watched as I returned to my room. I paused at the door and looked back at him. He gave me sort of a half wave, but continued to stand there. I knew what he was waiting for. The sound of my door, locking.

I was restless and had trouble sleeping. I kept waking up, looking around the darkened room, trying to figure out why I was so uneasy. Finally, it hit me. I got out of bed, walked to the window, and looked out at the graying of black night. It was almost dawn.

I had to see Wrenville. How long would it be before somebody told this guy that the feds had been asking questions about him? All that was necessary was that I see this guy from a distance. Certainly Pop would be willing to go along with that.

The shower had felt so good the night before, I decided to pay it another visit. I was getting ready to step in when I saw my reflection in the mirror—the furrows across my forehead. I looked tired. *Just like Pop,* I thought.

"Oh, God," I said, grabbing my clothes and pulling them back on.

I rang Pop's room, but there was no answer. I went down the hall and pounded on his door. Still no answer.

I returned to my room, called the front desk, and asked if Dr. Frank had left a message for me.

"No," the desk clerk told me. "He had some coffee here in the lobby, then left."

"Are you sure?"

"He didn't check out, miss. I believe he said he was going to breakfast."

"When?"

"Maybe a half hour ago."

Whoever wishes to keep a secret must hide the fact that he possesses one.

I knew, of course, that he had gone after Wolf. Carver. Chadwick. Pease. Wrenville.

Daedalus Construction. I pulled the phone book out of the drawer in my bedside table and found the listing in the yellow pages. A woman answered on the first ring.

"Daedalus Construction."

"Mr. Wrenville, please," I said.

I didn't know what I'd do if I reached him, but I didn't have to worry about it.

"Mr. Wrenville is out of the office at the moment," she said. "May I have him return your call?"

I hung up.

Pop said that he had rescheduled an early meeting with Wrenville because of the feds. But *where*?

All my life, I'd been watching Pop open that window in his mind—to let a killer fly in. Now I had to let Pop wander into my mind; only he could tell me where he was.

Pop knew that the man had a sustaining identity. A profession that served as a foundation for all his other identities. A source of support. The name—Christopher Wrenville—

was an adulteration of Christopher Wren, a great architect, but also a man whose namesake was a bird. Wrenville loved birds, especially ravens. He loved how they imitated other birds, moved about, avoided danger. But Wrenville, himself, was a homing pigeon. Hadn't Pop found him within twenty miles of the place where he was born?

Homing pigeon.

The place where he was born.

I knew where my father was. And I knew that Wrenville was with him.

Pop

Snow continued to fall, swirling in the light wind. Deer hunters loved this stuff. The white covering made tracking their quarry that much easier. The announcer on the local radio station chatted up the hunters' good fortune, and speculated about the probable increase in the deer kill.

Smoke from wood fires drifted up from chimneys along the sides of the state road as I drove west. Vermont was locking itself up for the winter months. The earth freezes, the wind cuts its way down from Canada, and it snows.

The roads were where my map said they would be. As I neared the end of an unnumbered road outside Brownsville, I saw the sign.

Daedalus Construction.

The previous night, after I had heard Lane turn her lock and drop the chain in place, I sat with the yellow pages until I found an ad for a hardware store that listed the owner's name. Then I turned to the white pages and found his home phone number. It required some gentle persuasion, and the promise of 250 dollars for eight bucks' worth of purchases, but he finally agreed to meet me at his shop.

I found what I needed, then drove again to the house in Saxtons River. I discovered what I expected to discover, made a few alterations, and returned to the motel.

The stage was set.

Wolf thought he was superior to every cop who ever wore a badge. He was probably right. None had ever posed a real threat to him, or a risk to his freedom. He never saw in any of them the power he attributed to the stepfather he was driven to destroy. But then, years later, he found the ultimate challenge, one that promised the highest of highs.

Let me tell you a story, lad.

Many years after my father's death, I dreamed about a white-haired old man. I was alone, walking through the alley to my apartment. He was there, sitting on the pavement, his legs stretched out in front of him, his back against the brick wall. I could see the white hair. I knew that he was drunk—passed out on the cinders, moaning. I grabbed him by his shirt, pulled him to his feet, and smashed his head against the wall, again and again, until he was dead.

I could see my breath in the cold, still night—puffs of air shaped like small ghosts.

When I awakened, I knew there was nothing of which I was incapable.

Somewhere along the line Wolf had made one final connection. In me he saw more than just the father of the lead investigator on the Sarah Sinclair case. He saw Dr. Lucas Frank. The one man left who was worth fearing, the one who might best him at his own game.

You want me dead, don't you? I'm worthy enough to inherit the mantle of the most powerful man in your universe. He died before you could get him, before you could slay your own ghosts. Once I'm out of the way, you won't ever have to return to the cellar.

It's your misfortune that I understand.

Wolf was so blinded by imagined omnipotence, he was

unable to envision his own demise. He *had* to play his game; he couldn't resist. And I was gambling that he wouldn't expect me to arrive until he was finished with Lane.

I turned onto the dirt drive and began climbing through a densely wooded area. After a mile and a half, there was an area of open fields, then a development—Birdland, the sign said—and a street directory. Blue Jay Way. Cardinal Lane. Blackbird Place. The main street was Raven Avenue.

Paul Wolf had built himself another town.

As crazy as his concept seemed, the man had designed and built a small and attractive settlement on the side of the hill. Each house was unique, and a careful attention to detail was evident. There was a sense of community about the place, yet each home had its privacy.

Beyond the self-contained village, the road climbed back through the woods to another clearing. There was a large red barn ahead with the Daedalus sign on the front. A pickup truck with the same business logo painted on its door sat nearby.

I parked next to the truck and walked toward a stairway on the side of the barn. Ahead of me, the mountain was engulfed by clouds and blowing snow. I climbed the stairs and stepped into a small waiting room.

You've left me no choice, lad. It's too bad you didn't handle the old man in your own dreams. Now I have to stop you.

I could hear his voice—he was talking on the phone—and I moved to the open door. His office took up the remainder of the long loft. There were bookcases and shelves carved from exotic woods as well as exquisite local oak and maple. The walls were crowded with framed photographs of birds—no doubt specimens he had stalked and captured on film. He waved me in.

Christopher Wrenville was about six feet tall, 185 pounds, well built, with graying hair, a mustache, and a ruddy, outdoor complexion. As I walked toward him, I continued my inventory of the room.

A large stereo system dominated the wall behind his desk, but was silent. There was a computer screen filled with swans swimming back and forth on a pond. The bookcases held leather-bound collectors' editions of classics, including several editions of Peterson's *Field Guild to the Birds*, Bulfinch's *Mythology*, books on building design and site preparation, and a single, worn copy of John Fowles's *The Collector*.

"Impressive," I said, as he hung up the phone.

"I've had the time, and, fortunately, the resources to indulge myself a bit."

We shook hands and he gestured toward the leather chair in front of his desk. I sat, and continued to survey the room.

"I have a castle," I said, still looking away from him.

"A castle."

"In Stratford, England."

I turned toward the desk and looked into his blue eyes.

"I want it moved—stone by numbered stone—possibly to this piece of land here in Vermont."

I spread the crude copy of the surveyor's map in front of him.

"I want to hire someone who will give his complete attention to each detail—someone to oversee the entire project, beginning with the site assessment."

"There's a building on here now," he said.

"Remove it. I have no interest in that. It's the water that runs under the structure that I'd like you to look at this morning. I'm flying to London tonight, and I want to be able to close the deal on the land before I leave. Obviously I'll leave a retainer with you as well."

I watched as he studied the map.

"There's no indication of a stream on here," he said. "If there's something running underground, it wouldn't be shown on this map. Where is the place?"

"A small village south of Bellows Falls. It's called Saxtons River."

"I know where it is," he said, never looking up from the map.

We agreed that I would lead the way in my rental car, with him following in his truck. When we stepped out of the loft, it was snowing heavily, nearly obscuring the mountain.

"Early for this," he said. "A dusting, maybe, but not this."

I led the way back down the hill, toward the interstate. He had his headlights on because of the weather, so I could see him driving right behind me.

The best psychopath will beat the best shrink nearly every time. He knows how to create doubt. His normal state is barely a degree above lethargic. Calm, laid back, unconcerned. Wrenville was one of the best. His mask of sanity was intact.

The man never even batted an eye when I said Saxtons River. If it hadn't been for the walls of birds, the books, his town of Birdland, I would have doubted myself.

But Wrenville was Wolf. I was sure of it.

I opened the envelope beside me on the passenger seat. The .32 slipped comfortably into my jacket pocket. I sifted through the composite drawings until I came to the one I wanted—right down to the mustache and the expressionless eyes. It was Wrenville. It was Wolf.

Twenty years earlier I had worked a case on Boston's south shore. Three young men, all hitchhikers, had—in separate incidents—been sexually assaulted, stabbed to death, then dumped in wooded areas off main roads. The police had developed a suspect, a twenty-eight-year-old man who lived with his mother and sister.

Investigators questioned Oscar Ray twice, but got nowhere. His alibi was flimsy. The route he traveled on his way home from a job in a bowling alley took him right by the three locations where the bodies had been found—and, in one case, the timing was perfect. Both he and his car fit descriptions provided by witnesses. And Oscar had a prior: the sexual assault of a fifteen-year-old when Oscar was nineteen.

Oscar Ray was a religious man, a Roman Catholic who had attended Mass twice a week until the murders started. After the first of the killings, he avoided the church—no confessions, no Masses. Something was bothering him.

"We need a priest," one of the cops said.

With that as the inspiration, and with the cooperation of one of Oscar's neighbors, two weeks later I arrived at the house next door to Oscar's, to spend ten days visiting my "cousin." In priestly garb, with a microphone taped to my chest, I spent hours rocking in a chair on the porch, reading, sipping iced tea. Two officers were parked a block away in a telephone repair van.

On his fifth visit to the front porch, I listened to Oscar Ray's confession. So did the cops in the repair truck.

Others in my profession raised questions about my ethical behavior. A small—but powerful—group of insufferable, self-righteous twits went after my license. They almost succeeded. At my hearing I asked how each of them would feel if their children were corn-holed and gutted by Oscar Ray. They weren't fond of my language, but they backed off.

The law played out its own game—was it a case of entrapment? Ultimately the court said no. It could just as easily have gone the other way. All the myths and madnesses of the people become the law, and then the law is bent and twisted to suit whatever circumstances happen to be given the greatest weight.

We don't seem to have gotten the message yet: predators don't play by any rules but their own. We can be fools and victims, or we can terminate their stay with us—by whatever means necessary.

My cop friend, Bolton, and I used to argue the death penalty. He was for it. I wasn't. The state can't run itself. How can we allow it to engage in the business of homicide?

"What if it was Lane?" Bolton asked me one time.

"I'd wait outside the courthouse and kill him myself," I said.

The power to heal is the flip side of the power to destroy.

I pulled in to the driveway with Wolf right behind me.

You're on alert, aren't you? A stranger arrives, talks of castles, and takes you to the one place you fear—the one place that could be the death of you. You don't believe in coincidence, do you? Connections are necessary, and they are made by men. All things are connected. Events never spin out of the wild universe by themselves.

Wolf walked up to the car. "Why this piece of land?" he asked.

"The isolation, the view of the hills. We used to visit this area when I was a kid. My father liked to ski Stratton. I never got into skiing, but I always loved it here."

"Do you believe in coincidence?" he asked, studying my face.

"No," I said, and started walking toward the house.

"This land is pretty much ledge. That shouldn't be too much of a problem for what you have in mind. You've got ten acres or so to play around with."

"Let me show you this water," I said.

Wolf moved ahead of me, stepping through the back doorway into the house. Then he waited for me to direct him. When I indicated the cellar door, he charged ahead down the stairs.

Lane

I knew I had to drive south on I-91 to the Westminster exit, and from there to Saxtons River. Allowing for the snow, I figured about an hour. One lane of the interstate was clear, and there wasn't much traffic, so I pushed it up to 50.

Pop's remark on the phone came back to me. I hadn't understood it then, but I did now. *No more sparring with evil. It's time for an ending.*

I remembered reading some old newspaper articles about my father, from when the medical board tried to strip him of his license to practice. His techniques were "unorthodox," one board member said. Dr. Frank had provoked serious ethical questions, and probably was in violation of board policies. "Arrogant," another of his peers had said. The reporter quoted Pop as saying that the country was faced with a new public health menace—the psychopath who kills for pleasure—that we damn well better recognize his presence among us, and that we don't treat cancer with aspirin. We annihilate it. Cut it out.

Time for an ending.

I was hitting 60 when I crossed the Williams River near Bellows Falls. An eighteen-wheeler came up fast behind me, then thundered by in the snow-covered passing lane, sending up billows of white powder that blocked my view of the road. Minutes later, when I slowed for the Westminster exit, I peered through the falling snow and saw another of those big rigs on its side in the median. The state police had set out flares.

When I came down the highway off-ramp and drove west, I knew that I was looking for a left turn onto a dirt road. Bridge Road was somewhere in or very near the village. Then I saw it—just beyond the general store. I made the turn, and five minutes later I saw Pop's rental car parked beside a pickup truck. Daedalus Construction, the truck's emblem read.

The house was smaller but every bit as decrepit as what I had imagined. Two sets of footprints led away from the vehicles toward the rear of the property. I followed them, stepped up onto the back porch, and pushed open the door.

Pop

You're perfection, aren't you, lad? Who's afraid of the big bad wolf? Not you.

I called to him, told him where the water was—through the archway. Then I walked slowly down the rotting cellar stairs.

Wolf moved at an angle across the dirt floor and stopped under the arch. My hands were in my jacket pockets—one of them wrapped around the .32.

With his back turned to me, he extended his arms up and fastened his hands onto the cross beam.

You're staring at the new hinges and hasp assembly on the coal bin door, aren't you?

Without turning his body, he looked back over his shoulder. His eyes were gray, lifeless. Like mine.

We're the same now. What you see, lad, is what you are.

"Does *your* castle have a dungeon?" he asked.

Once the animal inside stirs, there is no quieting him. When fire laps at his fur, he grabs the bars between us, wrenching them away. He holds the throne once held by reason. All is dictated by a focused, intense rage, laserlike and precise. Calm, deliberate.

"It would appear I've underestimated you. Let me guess," he said. "A weapon in the pocket?"

I pulled back the hammer on the .32. He heard the click.

"You're playing a very dangerous game."

"Sarah Sinclair," I said, almost not recognizing my own voice.

"By any chance, did a blue jay fly in through her window?"

You've made your choice, lad. You're going all the way. You have a design in mind.

"Step into the coal bin," I said.

What do your dreams tell you? You've lived this scene, this nightmare, so many times before. How do you disarm your own dreams? How do you defeat them? Do you kill them?

When he hesitated, I squeezed the trigger on the .32. The bullet tore through my jacket, slamming into the support beam six inches to Wolf's right. He flinched.

"Sarah," I said. "Your sister. Your imperfect lover. Sarah Corrigan. And Sarah Sinclair. Your perfect victim."

"Look, old man—"

I squeezed off a second shot, grazing his right hand. Again, his body jerked, but he kept his grasp on the cross beam.

Lad, the boundaries of your cage have been drawn for you. For an effervescent twenty years, you included the world in your dream. Now this cellar is your world. The coal bin is your cage. The dream is mine.

I heard the back door click shut upstairs. He heard it, too. I listened to the soft padding of footsteps across the floor. They stopped at the top of the steps.

Have you fled your body, lad? Are you flying somewhere up above us now, gazing lazily down, watching that blood as it trickles from your hand, down your arm, into your sleeve?

"One of us won't leave here alive," he said.

It was an acknowledgment of sorts, a realization. It wasn't a threat.

I heard a tentative creaking at the top of the stairs.

"Maybe two of us," Wolf said. "I can smell that one. A woman. Hotel soap. No cloying perfume. I like them that way."

My third shot hit him in the upper right shoulder, knocking his right hand loose from the beam. He continued to suspend himself, apelike, by his left hand.

"Lane, don't come down here," I said.

"Pop? Is that you?"

Wolf looked back over his shoulder again.

"Pop," he said. "The little girl, protected by her father, watches the boy receive his punishment in the cellar. Can you do it, Pop?"

When I look into the face of my own beast, lad, I know him. I love him. It's so seldom he gets to be free. He lusts for his freedom. Has a taste for blood. Loves to kill. I'd never try to send him away, lad. To do that would be to deny who I am.

"Tell me about Sarah Sinclair," I said.

I was aware of Lane coming down the stairs, but I didn't turn. I looked at Wolf's eyes.

"Lane," he said, "did you like your feather tree?"

When Lane didn't answer, Wolf said, "Sarah Sinclair was just one more."

"You had to have her," I said.

"I had to have them all."

"You took risks with her."

"She was a victim before I ever got to her," he said. "She wanted to die. She was waiting for me or someone else. When I had the knife in my hand, and she knew—"

"She reached out for you," I said.

"She practically asked me to cut her throat."

It was as if his voice were coming toward me from a distant land—a topography I knew well.

"That never happened before, did it? None of your other victims were so ready, so willing," I said.

"Never. It was in her eyes the first day I saw her. I killed two men who had seen me in her shop. I destroyed Chadwick—my cover for six years."

"So you could accommodate her."

"That's it," he said.

I heard Lane call out to me. She was at the bottom of the stairs now, maybe ten feet to my right. I ignored her.

"You kept a record," I told Wolf. "Where is it?"

"Find it," he said.

I had noticed the PC in his loft. "It's in the computer. Someone can figure out the password, and I'm sure the connections are there."

He laughed. "For more than twenty years, no one even *saw* the connections."

"What about your trophies?"

"Most of them were less than memorable," he said.

"Maxine Harris and Sarah Sinclair—the connection was the bookstore. The trophy was that volume of Rimbaud's poems you sent to Robert Sinclair. Educate me."

"You seem to know everything already."

"The woman found dead in the horse barn."

He sighed. "Someone from the past. A loose end."

"Why the burial ground on your land?"

"They were the throwaways—the garbage. There was nothing noteworthy in the artistry."

I expected Wolf to make a move—something. This man was not about to go quietly. But I didn't expect him to move as fast as he did.

Lane

◆

Wolf swung away from the arch. He seemed to bounce off the support beam and careen in Pop's direction, a long knife in his hand. It was fast—a blur. I had no time to get the .22 out of my jacket pocket.

Pop fired a round and hit Wolf, but the killer didn't slow down. He slammed my father against the stone foundation, and thrust the blade up toward his throat.

My first kick caught him in the side. As he fell to one knee, I aimed my second kick at his head. Wolf had the reflexes and conditioning of an athlete. He rolled under my leg, knocking me off balance. Before I could react, he was on his feet behind me, grabbing me under the chin with his forearm and pressing the knife against my throat. The tip broke my skin, drawing blood. I could feel it trickle down my neck.

Pop glanced up at the arch, at the narrow ledge that ran the length of the carrying beam.

"It's too late," Wolf said.

Then he laughed. "Once you've resigned yourself to your

own death, everything becomes possible. We're all going to die, old man. Some of us very soon. Put the gun down."

Pop raised his arm and aimed the revolver in our direction.

"You won't kill your daughter. Or has prowling around in the world of murder made you a bit like us? If I were in your shoes, I'd just start firing away."

Pop pulled back the hammer.

"Pop," I said.

Wolf laughed again, then tightened his grip, drawing blood a second time. "Maybe you do have it in you."

Pop's eyes were locked on Wolf's. "Since we're all going to die, what difference does it make?"

"I'd really enjoy discussing the philosophy of all this, but time *is* slipping away. You've had your moment of bravado. Put down the gun."

Pop brought his left hand up, parallel to his gun hand, then moved it slowly in an arc away from his body. Wolf's eyes must have shifted to the right, following Pop's hand.

"Now," Pop said.

My elbow hammered Wolf's sternum, then shot up into his face. Blood sprayed from his mouth and nose as he fell back against the stone foundation and went down. The knife clattered off the old furnace.

I whipped the .22 out of my pocket and flipped off the safety. Nothing was going to stop me from emptying the nine-shot clip into his face.

Pop

◆

"Lane, get up the stairs and out of the house. Go now. Get as far away from here as you can."

She had her gun aimed at Wolf's head. It was as if she hadn't heard me.

"Lane, get out of here," I said.

"What—?"

"*Get out,*" I shouted.

She moved—slowly at first—backing away toward the stairwell and then disappeared up the stairs. I heard the back door slam as she ran outside.

I dropped into a catcher's crouch beside Wolf. "You wired the house, just like you did in Hasty Hills. You used a timer switch that you installed up on the cross beam."

"You don't have much time," he said.

In the years of my childhood, only my sister knew that it wasn't possible to fool me. No one played sly tricks on me and walked away laughing.

"I want you in the coal bin," I said. "If I have to shoot you again to get you there, I will."

"You don't get it, do you? This place is going up any second. You're going to die."

"Then grant me a final wish, Wolf. Get into the coal bin."

I grabbed him by the shirt, the gun pressed against his neck, and half dragged, half threw him into the enclosure.

"How can I be afraid of this place when I know I'm about to die?"

Fear loves this place . . .

I looked into Wolf's eyes. "You're sprawled on top of your own bomb. I moved it all here. I also changed the timer."

The power to heal is the flip side of the power to destroy.

I stood up, moved back from the stall, and slammed the door. I wedged a large wooden peg down through the hasp.

"Any final words, lad?" I asked.

After a moment, he spoke—but the voice was that of a young boy. "I'm sorry," the boy said.

"Damn right you are," I said.

I walked across the cellar, up the stairs, and out into the backyard. I saw Lane standing up on the side of the hill and walked in her direction.

"Have you been up by the apple trees?" I asked, taking her arm and leading her toward the weathered remains of Wolf's miniature town—the world he had built as a child.

"I feel like you almost killed me."

"Up the hill," I said, adding pressure to my grip on her arm.

"Is he dead?" she asked.

"No. He needs some time to think."

She looked at me in disbelief.

"Why did you chase me out of there?"

Then the earth shook as the house blew apart and pieces of a murderer's life flew a hundred feet into the air. Lane crouched low to the ground, covering her ears. I could feel the blast of hot air wrap itself around me, then blow right on by.

"Pop, what the hell did you do?"

"Clean this," I said, handing her the gun. "Replace the cartridges, then return it to the PD—put it back where you got it. Have the state police seal Wolf's loft until you can get the feds back up here. Everything they'll want is in there."

"They're going to know that you shot him, Pop."

"There'll be less of him left than there was of that maintenance man in the Hasty Hills explosion," I said. "I'll fax them a statement."

I turned and started back down the hill. Flames danced in the debris and plumes of smoke blew up into the air. Snowflakes and ashes met and merged.

"You killed a man, Pop. It doesn't work like that."

I stopped walking and stared at Wolf's pyre.

"So how does it work, Lanie?" I asked. "For a time in there, *you* were going to kill him."

I looked back at my daughter, but she didn't respond.

"Is there another way you would have preferred that this be handled?"

She looked at the fire, then at me.

"How did he get so twisted?" she asked.

"Same way we all do, I guess," I said, and walked away.

Lane

◆

My father didn't want any part of the aftermath. By the time Willoughby finished debriefing me, Pop had already slipped out of Vermont. He knew what lay ahead. The circus. The hype.

Susan Walker worked behind the scenes to ensure that I would be invited to the press conference. Louis Freeh, Director of the FBI, took center stage, with Walker, Willoughby, and a few of the Bureau's clones off to the side. Hanson placed me behind the group, but, because I'm so tall, I stood out. In any case, reporters from the tabloids gathered around, taping my remarks for broadcast that night. By the time the story made it onto the TV screen, there was no mention of Pop. It was as if he had never been in Vermont, and I knew that he'd want it that way.

But suddenly I was the one who had tracked down and destroyed Wolf. That's what the media wanted. A woman who had gone face-to-face with a serial killer, and not only lived through it, but brought him down.

On my neck there were two cuts made by a madman, but

I didn't cover them with gauze and tape. I wanted to see them, to be constantly reminded that life is full of risks, some of them mandatory.

Robert returned to work—sober and eager to help mop up in the aftermath of the Wolf case. I thought it would be good therapy for him, a way of putting Sarah's death behind him. I gave him the job of sorting out the victims, determining which were Wolf's. He did some follow-up interviews with Purrington, and determined that the man truly did kill the prostitutes in Albany and Troy. But he had nothing to do with the Maxine Harris case. He was just feeling so guilty about what he *had* done, he was willing to confess to everything, including what he *hadn't* done. "He would have taken responsibility for the crucifixion, if I had let him," Robert said.

Before it was over, Robert had established a potential link between Wolf and forty-two homicides. His trail covered a lot of states, a lot of years, with deaths wherever he went. We were sure that many went down as naturals when they were anything but. Wolf was that good.

Robert made it his mission to identify the connection between Wolf and his victims. All we knew for sure was that every victim was in some way connected to the one who preceded her (as Sarah was to Maxine), and to the one who succeeded her (as Sheila was to Sarah, and I would have been to Sheila). There was a logic behind his every move.

Robert also dealt with the aliases. He found twenty-three possible IDs used by Wolf over the years, with the most enduring and elaborate being Chadwick and Wrenville. For the most part, Wolf's aliases were selected with the same warped logic that his victims were. The name he used in Colorado was the same as the name of a guy he worked with in California. Chadwick, as we knew, was the boyfriend of the young woman Wolf had thrown off a roof in Cambridge. And so it went, name after name, year after year, victim after victim. It was another example of the rigidity that Pop had talked about.

Wolf established the Wrenville ID, along with Daedalus Construction, after "dying" in Vietnam and returning home. Robert worked with military intelligence to identify the soldier with whom Wolf had switched dog tags. When it came time to notify the dead soldier's next of kin, Robert handed that whole aspect of the case over to the army and moved on.

It was exactly sixteen days after his discharge from Tranquil Acres when Robert pulled the tab on his first of many cans of Old Milwaukee. It was a slip, he said, part of the disease. He stuck a note in my box at the office. "Three days of familiar solace," he wrote. "I loved it going down, and I remembered the bliss of being blitzed. I can't say it won't happen again. One day at a time, and all that. I know it drives you farther away, but that's for the best right now."

I knew then that I was putting a lot more than the Wolf case behind me. It wasn't that I didn't care. Robert was a great cop, and an even greater friend, but he had become like a brother to me, not a lover.

Once the feds had taken control of the offices of Daedalus Construction, searching for evidence, I couldn't get my foot in the door. I'm sure it was Susan Walker who copied all the files from the construction company's computer and sent me the disks. The package arrived in the mail, with no return address.

Most of the files were of little interest to me. Ordinary business correspondence. But, in a six-year-old memo to Mort Westphal (Wolf's right hand man at Daedalus Construction; the person he trusted to run the place whenever he was away), Wolf gave instructions for filling out the necessary forms for the firm to obtain bonded status. He told Mort to take care of everything—and not to "muddy the waters" by explaining that he wasn't Wrenville when he took the paperwork to Montpelier. "Just go ahead and let them print you," Wolf said. "Otherwise it will take months for me to get there, and customers are insisting that we be bonded."

I felt that I was getting to know him better every day. His manipulation of Westphal was masterful. I read through years of memos, watching how skillfully he persuaded the man to do his bidding. There was one memo of recent vintage telling Westphal he'd be away for a while, and asking him to mail a package to Robert Sinclair in his absence. The book of poetry. If Wolf hadn't been in Vermont at that time, where was he? Playing the part of Robbins, and watching me?

The most chilling files were those that could be opened only with a directory password—"design"—a subdirectory password—"chaos"—and an additional password for each file. Sarah Sinclair's was "Rimbaud." The entry was brief:

> To the prettiest of my prettiest feathers:
>
> With you, I have put into motion the process of consuming myself. But I have no regrets. The danger is what drew me to you, the curiosity is what clipped my wings. Some of us mate for life. Some of us mate for death. You and I are the latter.

I printed out this file and tried to fax it to Pop, but his machine wasn't on. Several days passed before my attempts at transmission were successful. Then there was another long wait for him to respond. Nearly two weeks. It was in the middle of the night when I finally heard my fax machine switch on and begin its familiar, gentle purr.

I was in bed, but I wasn't asleep. I was replaying the whole story of John Wolf in my mind. It wasn't terror that haunted me; it was the questions. Pop had helped me see what drove Wolf, but what had driven me? I had asked myself that question a hundred times, and each time my hand had drifted up—to touch the rough, parallel scars on my throat. I was within a split second of killing the man, and I understood my rage. If he had to die so that we could live, so be it.

I also knew now why I would continue to work Homicide—why I couldn't stop, even if it threatened my life again. The quality of life is seldom the same for the victims of other crimes, but they go on living. Sarah Sinclair and forty-one others wouldn't have that option.

But I didn't understand Pop. He hadn't simply reacted to a desperate situation. He had planned to kill Wolf. When he stood in the motel hallway that night and waited for me to lock my door, he knew exactly what he was going to do.

I switched on my reading light and lifted the flimsy sheets of paper from the fax machine.

TO: Lane
FROM: Pop

Sorry to shut you off. Haven't been sleeping well, and I'm off my feed. Also too much porter. It takes a while to cleanse an aging mind. Haven't even started on the soul (although I did buy a new CD: Clapton, *From the Cradle*, but haven't played it yet).

It's funny—I don't know where to begin, but I do know where this will end. I would have preferred to tell you all this over dinner, then take in a movie (a musical? a comedy? do they make those anymore?).

When I got back to the lake, I picked up Max the cat from the friend who was caring for him (not that he requires much). We crossed the water at night, by boat—something he and I have done a dozen times. Max usually wants to sit in the stern with me, but that night he curled up on top of the rope at the bow, glaring at me with hateful eyes. A spiteful cat angry at a neglectful owner (if, in fact, a cat *can* be owned)? Or a talented predator who picks up the scent of another in the same confined space?

After we were home, he avoided me for two days. Only time he would come out to eat was when I wasn't around.

When I did sleep, the dreams came. Explosions. Blood. The stench of death (how many bodies did they end up finding in Wolf's cellar?). And the worst part of all: looking into a mirror and not recognizing the man who looks back at me. I tell you all this for one reason. Never again. Not even for you. I don't think I've ever feared death. Haven't really thought a whole lot about it. But what I *do* fear is going out there one time too many, and one inch too far. I'm afraid that I'll lose myself, that I'll go irretrievably mad. A single, final thread will snap, leaving me sitting in a puddle of my own waste.

So, please. No more. There is so little that separates us from them.

A man like Wolf feels nothing. He is moved only by vengeance. The destruction he brings to the world is payment for the injustice he has suffered. He believes that only he has endured pain. To be in his mind is to be in a primal black hole of sensory disregard. He is a walking impulse, a bundle of short bursts of static, surges regulated only by his obsession with control and design. We matter to him only as objects, pieces of his community in need of rearrangement. Murder is his way of imposing order on his world. When you are the reaper, you do not fear the reaper.

No doubt the feds are still celebrating their victory—and you, by now, are enshrined as the patron saint of tall, tan, feminist sleuths. But I think you will be as sobered as I was by what follows. It arrived here shortly after I did.

Dear Dr. Frank:

I have so little time to say all that needs to be said. If you are as good as your reputation, you will be arriving soon.

But don't flatter yourself. You've had a willing coconspirator.

Near the end in Hasty Hills, I experienced something I never had before. I believed, for several minutes at least, that I couldn't continue, that it would be best if

I just stood in place and allowed the inevitable to happen. Obviously, that passed.

I expose myself to death because I refuse to be locked away. And what do you get? A confession? Gladly. I would enjoy talking about my exploits.

If you're reading this, you beat me. And there's only one way you could have done that. Was it so grand a conquest? Are you sleeping well? Dreams, Doctor? I don't share your liability of conscience, or your need to pull back from the edge. This is what gives me my strength. It is also what causes my bouts of weariness.

In Sarah, I found a woman who wanted to die, one who participated in her own death, and in her eyes I saw myself. Think carefully about what you saw in mine, Dr. Frank—and don't push your luck.

Wolf

ABOUT THE AUTHORS

JOHN PHILPIN is a nationally renowned forensic psychologist. His advice and opinions on violence and its aftermath have been sought by police, newspaper writers, TV producers, mental health professionals, private investigators, attorneys, and polygraph experts throughout the country. He is the author of *Beyond Murder*, the story of the Gainesville student killings, which was published by NAL/Dutton in 1994. His forthcoming true crime book, *Stalemate*, which tells the story of a series of child abductions, sexual assaults, and murders in the San Francisco Bay Area, will be published in August 1997 by Bantam Books. He lives in Reading, Vermont, with his wife and son.

PATRICIA SIERRA is an award-winning writer whose short fiction and poetry have been published in several small literary magazines. She has written three young adult novels as well, all of which were published by Avon Books. Her interest in crime and law enforcement led to a brief career as a private investigator. An avid lifelong fan of true crime books and mysteries, Sierra lives in Toledo, Ohio.